Baqca

Copyright © 1993 by the author.
Cover design by Andrew B. Crow.

Published by G.A. Publishing, Inc., P.O. Box 742705,
Dallas, TX 75374-2705

Printed in the United States of America.

Visit The Golden Wyvern website at:
www.goldenwyvern.com

Library of Congress Cataloging in Publication Data

Stewart, Alan Breck.
    Baqca / Alan Breck Stewart.
        p. cm. — (The golden wyvern ; bk. 1)
    ISBN 0-9753946-0-6 (pbk.)
    1. Church history—Primitive and early church,
    ca. 30-600 —Fiction.
    2. Shamans—Fiction. I. Title.

PS3619.T4934B37 2004
813'.6--dc22
                                            2004021190

THE GOLDEN
WYVERN

by

Alan Breck Stewart

Book One

Baqca

G.A. Publishing

This book is dedicated to the memory of MM.
Even though it's been over thirty years,
we … I … haven't forgotten.
And yes, the song of the Master was learned.

But, just as importantly, this book is also dedicated
to Pouie who, if I had ever forgotten, would never
have given me a moments peace.

If an owl taps lightly at your window,
listen.
If she tries to enter,
act quickly.
If a feather falls,
wear it.
And if a wolf stares at you without blinking,
you must, at all costs, remember.

-- Master of Moonlight
          Owl Steppe
          March, 1993

CONTENTS

The other books of The Golden Wyvern

Book Two: THE OWL AND THE WOLF
- Master of Moonlight
- Omnis Moriar
- Friday the Thirteenth

Book Three: DEATHWALKER
- Alex
- The Fool's Apprentice
- The Fool
- Wyvern
- Epilogue

PROLOGUE

Present day -- August, 2004: The Year of the Wreath

Colin Campbell was once again beside himself. He leaned forward in his chair, placed his elbows on his desk so that they straddled the open manuscript, and buried his face in his hands. "One more manuscript about this goddamned Holy Blood crap," he muttered to himself, "or this godforsaken Priory of Sion conspiracy bullshit and I'll *personally* publish the *Dossier Secrets* myself if for no other reason than to put an end to this absurdity and expose it all as the 1950's genealogical con that it is!"

Letting his right hand fall to his desk in a sign of abject resignation, and then running his left hand through his fiery red mane of hair, Colin continued muttering, "Templars in the woodshed, Rosicrucians under every rock ... there's *got* to be more interesting things to write about in this world ..."

"Red," Crackled the voice over the intercom, interrupting the editor's ravings, "There's someone here I *really* think you should see."

Colin sniffled and then straightened up a bit upon hearing his nickname. Since he was seven years old, he had always been called 'The Red Fox' -- a nickname acquired, no doubt, because his red hair looked somewhat like the tail of a fox -- but only since he became an adult was it shortened to just 'Red'. Undoubtedly because there was a bit less mane now than back then. It wouldn't be too much longer before 'Red' became 'Gray', mused Colin ...

Placing his finger on the intercom button, he replied, "What's this in reference to, Sharon?"

No response ...

Again, "Sharon, who is this person you think I should see?"

No response ...

This just isn't my day, thought Colin. I don't know why I put up with her.

However, Colin did know why he put up with Sharon. She was the best assistant he ever had in his nineteen years in the publishing business, and the best he would ever hope to have -- just that she could be a bit eccentric at times....

"SHARRRON!" Colin screamed hoping his voice would carry better through the closed door than through the intercom.

"Shush, Red," Sharon gasped as she flung open Colin's office door and stepped in without closing it, "we have a potential client in the outer office and she doesn't need to be hearing one of your temper tantrums."

"Ok, ok … I'm just tired of all these conspiracy manuscripts that keep getting sent here from all over …"

"You shouldn't be," interrupted Sharon, "after all, we *do* specialize in publishing controversial books …"

"Yeah, yeah, whatever. Who is the agent, and what does …" Colin peered past Sharon and caught a glimpse of the person sitting in the outer office "… *she* want?"

"Well, she's not an agent exactly."

"Um, Sharon. We only accept manuscripts from agents."

"Well, she *is* an agent of sorts."

"Sorts?" Colin asked while leaning forward, raising his right eyebrow, and clasping his hands over his desk while, once again, resting his elbows on either side of the open manuscript.

"Yes, sorts. When I told her we only accept manuscripts from agents, she said she was a special agent for her brother -- who, by the way, is the author …

"What exactly is a *special* agent?" interrupted Colin a bit impatiently.

"Well," started Sharon a little sheepishly, "she, her name is Kailie Talbot by the way. Well, 'special' is my word. She used 'secret' …"

"Are you telling me she is a 'secret agent' for her brother? Is that what you're telling me?"

"It kinda sounds that way, doesn't it? Ms. Talbot is a bit more convincing when *she* explains it."

"Who is the author? What has he published before?"

"Well, boss ..."

Uh oh, thought Colin. When Sharon calls me boss, there's a *true* conspiracy afoot -- she's already made up her mind about these yokels and their manuscript.

"... His name is Alan Stewart and he's never published anything before. Apparently he's somewhat of an eccentric character and lives mostly as a hermit up in the High Country of Wyoming."

"Mostly?" Colin queried.

"Um, yeah, apparently ..."

As Sharon spoke, Colin noticed the woman in the outer office rise from her seat and walk toward Sharon's desk. For a brief moment, the open doorway and Sharon's position offered him a clear view of this allegedly mysterious woman. She was tall, fair-haired, and strikingly beautiful in a somewhat odd way ... a way that was difficult to describe, but it captivated Colin nonetheless. Her looks, the way she moved, even her instincts became obvious to Colin and they all seemed to weave together to capture something of an animal nature....

Just as she was about to pass behind Sharon so as to be blocked from Colin's view, Kailie looked up and intentionally peered deeply into Colin's eyes, and for the briefest of moments, a fire passed between the two ... She smiled an odd smile, softly laid a bundle she was carrying on Sharon's desk, turned, and walked out the door into the hallway, never looking back....

Did she have yellow eyes? thought Colin. I swear they must be, but I can't be certain ...

"Red, are you listening to me?" asked Sharon in a slightly raised voice.

"Um, yes ... apparently. You said apparently."

"And I said more after that, too. As I was saying, he apparently travels a bit and spends a lot of time in various deserts around the world. Apparently he just returned from ..."

"Uh, look, Sharon," Colin interrupted, "it seems your mystery woman left something on your desk and walked out."

"What!" exclaimed Sharon as she quickly turned and began racing toward the outer office.

That's odd, thought Colin. She seems awfully wrapped up in this. Something else must be going on. Colin got up and walked toward the outer office, too.

When he got to Sharon's desk, she was already opening the bundle which was, oddly, wrapped in a newspaper and tied with a string.

"Whew," sighed Sharon, "she *did* leave the manuscript."

Colin looked down at what must be at least one thousand pages ... and the condition of the top pages, dog-eared and yellowed, betrayed that the manuscript must have seen better days ... years ago!

"Sharon, when was this thing written? Do you know?"

"That's what I was starting to tell you when you zoned out on me ... Ahem, according to Ms. Talbot, her brother wrote the manuscript almost twelve years ago and then laid it in the corner of his cabin never looking at it again nor ever trying to submit it to publishers."

"Cabin?" queried Colin while flipping through the yellowed pages noticing they were obviously written on a typewriter -- an old one at that -- and not on a computer. "Don't tell me, no electricity, right?"

"I don't know, boss, I just know what Kailie told me and she said her brother wouldn't let the book be published until the Year of the Wreath."

"Year of the what?"

"Wreath."

"What does *that* mean?"

"I have no idea, Red. Just that ..."

"Look, Sharon," Colin interrupted, "this is getting *way* too strange … and talk about lack of professionalism … hey, we don't need this. Bundle up that mess and send it on back to Hicksville or wherever it came from …"

"No boss!" Sharon almost screamed.

Colin was quite taken aback by Sharon's outburst, which caused him to sputter out his last words, blink in surprise, and to bend slightly backwards in his stance.

"… I think we really should seriously look at this manuscript," she finished.

"Why, Sharon? Why are you so intent about this? What else is going on?"

"Do you promise not to laugh?" But before Colin had a chance to answer, Sharon continued. "Because last night I dreamt about Kailie Talbot. She came to me so vividly in the dream and asked for my help and I said I would help her."

"So, in effect, you're saying we're … no, *I'm* being bound into a contractual agreement made in one of *your* dreams?"

"Well, it can't be any stranger than those Holy Bloodline conspiracy books and novels that seem to flock in here all the time."

"You might have a point there," added Colin somewhat resignedly.

"And look, we even have a photograph of the author we can use."

"Why is that important?" asked Colin puzzledly. "I'm sure we'll have plenty of opportunity to gather all the photos we need if we decide to publish this thing."

"Um, apparently not," added Sharon, "according to his sister, the author isn't too keen about publicity …"

"Oh, great," quipped Colin, "this is all we need." Looking at the out of focus photograph of a man with long hair sitting atop a horse, he added, "The picture isn't even in focus. Do you have any idea where it was taken … at least?"

"The back of the photo says 'near Owl Steppe'." Sharon

replied.

"And, Owl Steppe is where?"

"I don't know. Maybe it says in the manuscript."

"I can't believe I'm falling for this," added Colin. "I should've known that the moment you called me boss, I was done for … Well, I might as well take a look at it." Colin said as he picked up the bundle of papers off Sharon's desk. "Kinda big …"

"It's a trilogy," Sharon chimed in, "It's to be published in three parts …"

"Assuming it will be published at all," Colin said finishing Sharon's words. But he couldn't help notice a sly smile of satisfaction on her lips as he turned to head back into his office. There's gotta be something more going on here, Colin thought as he closed his door.

Sitting at his desk, The Red Fox looked at the title page … *The Golden Wyvern* by Alan Breck Stewart, Book One, Baqca. What the hell is a Baqca, thought Colin? Something tells me this guy is going to be the death of me….

Sighing, Colin turned the page to the Prologue and began to read:

In the latter quarter of the fourteenth century, the wyvern began to appear upon the coat of arms of certain families. It was depicted as a chimerical animal seen as a winged dragon. But unlike the dragon, it had two feet, not four, and they were like those of an eagle. It also had a serpent like barbed tail.

Depending upon who you were, the wyvern was either feared as an evil and wicked creature that was a bane to humankind. Or, it was a kind saviour of our race which should only be feared by evil and wicked men. Certainly, this point was debated from Chaucer to Browning.

Geoffrey Chaucer, in 'Troilus and Criseyde', had referred to that creature as being wicked. That was in the year 1370. That was before the truth was known. That was before certain events occurred which would make that truth obvious to certain individuals. However, in

1394 when Chaucer wrote, 'A Treatise on the Astrolabe', he corrected his ignorance. Admittedly, that correction was a bit veiled -- but then, a secret of truth is well worth seeking.

Incidentally, the wyvern's favourite food was the goat. Unfortunately, as some would argue, there were too few wyverns to have any lasting effect. This is their story ...

SISTERS

1

Kirghiz Steppes, Sixth Century B.C.E.

The old woman had never married. She had never made love nor could she ever remember a time when strong, calloused hands caressed her young and sensuous body. She remembered her youth and those playful days with her friends as they talked and giggled about the young men who would one day take them as their mates. They anticipated with a mixture of fear and excitement the moment when hardness and softness would touch for the first time. But, the old woman thought, those are the memories of others. They are not mine.

She looked down at her nakedness, at her sagging breasts and wrinkled skin and remembered the pre-dawn darkness of the morning when she left the warmth of her yurt wearing only the feather of an owl in her hair and the necklace of wolves' teeth around her neck. She recalled the two hour trek to the village and the crispness of air which had caused her to shiver. If it had been any other day, she would have been *a fool* to attempt such a journey appearing as she did, but this wasn't any other day. This was today and it mattered little if the cold air sapped the warmth of her life or not. In truth, the only thing that mattered was her tribe. Her only worry was in the knowing that such an early chill in the air meant a very hard winter -- and she would not be there to comfort, soothe, and heal. Today she would die.

She remembered the expressions of shock on the faces of the three children as they watched her approach the village. She recalled, with an air of sadness, their shouts of warning of her arrival and the looks of concern from the adults as they glanced in her direction to see what alarmed and disrupted the children's play. I am so tired, she thought, so tired of these long, hard years of life.

She thought about the chieftain's distress when she told him that today she returned to the sky and would travel the woven fibres to the heights of the Great World Tree. "What are we to do?", he had asked with the dismay of worry in his voice. "There is no one to guide the dead, to protect them during their final journey ... or to speak to the spirits and to keep them happy."

But she did what she went there to do. She had blessed them. She had *assured* them that another would soon come. She had explained to them that in spite of their fears, the tradition of the sons of the eagle would not die with her on this day.

The *sons* of the eagle, she thought silently to herself. How ironic it is that there had only been daughters. From where would the sons come? I am the first and as far as I know, the last of my kind. But as the fire roared, her attention turned to the warmth she now felt, the last she would *ever* feel. Savour this moment, she told herself, for soon my journey will take me to the land of the dead and only spirits will I ever know again.

While she prepared the grey, powdery ash made from the bark of the sacred ash tree, the old woman allowed herself one last memory of her people. An eerie green mist began to envelope her spirit and awakened her recollection of that warm afternoon ninety years before when she was in her fourteenth summer of life. Thoughts of her newly found sexuality haunted her memories and she remembered taking off her clothes as she lay beneath the very same tree under which she now sat. She remembered her first and only orgasm. It did not occur when she touched herself, oddly enough, but rather after she fell asleep and dreamt. It happened during the vision. So vivid and real. It *was* real! The eagle had mounted her, made love to her, and more than satisfied her curiosity. But had it really been an eagle, or was it a man? He, or it, shifted shape back and forth so rapidly it was hard to tell. Only after the ecstasy of the moment was completed could she see the figure clearly. Indeed, he was an eagle, but had the *head* of a man!

The words he said as he stood before her were so clear that they seemed to have just been spoken. Still lingering in the air ninety years later. Still reverberating against the earth and sky weaving a harmony never before felt. He said that he was Tengere Kaira Khan, the father of the clan of the eagle of which she would be the first mother. "To you will be born my daughters, the owl and the wolf. You are to name them Pouie and Kaltak. And to you, my wife, you are to be given a gift of the gods. I have been tasked to give man the gift of shamaning, and you are the first shamaness." He then disappeared, never to be seen in reality or dream world again for such an eternally long, long time.

But, somehow she knew the truth. Was the knowledge acquired during one of her many spirit walks? Or was it dreamt? It didn't matter. All that mattered was that a man, a powerful shaman would someday appear. She had hoped to one day see him. But by now she guessed that sight would be denied to her. She resigned herself to knowing she would never see his face.

As the fire blazed and as she placed more bark into the flames, she allowed herself to continue in her memories as there were still a few moments before she was needed. She remembered keeping her vision to herself having been ashamed of what had happened. But days turned to weeks and then to months. It became blatantly apparent she was with child. Her family, her tribe, shunned her as she had no husband and she became an outcast. But what made it worse was that no one believed her when she finally recounted her vision. A tear ran down her cheek as she recalled everyone thinking she had been lying to protect the identity of the father. No one believed her story when she explained that the gods of the West were gifting man a shaman to counter disease and death brought forth by the gods of the East. She now wept openly for the life of the young man who had shown her one act of kindness during that time. That act, now long forgotten, was witnessed by another and he paid the price, as her father had said, for rape.

His death was so very cruel for the crime -- not of rape, but of sympathy.

As she extinguished the flames with the dirt taken from beneath the roots of the tree, she shuddered. Was it because of the cold which struck her body? Or was it the memory of her first realisation of the coldness of people's hearts? It no longer mattered, she thought. I wish I could believe that, but I know it *does* matter. It is the *evil* that will be our undoing.

"It is almost time." She realised she had spoken those words out loud -- but, to whom? The wind which will carry my words to all corners of the earth? And then she smiled -- smiled at the distraction thoughts can cause and allowed herself to embrace one last memory -- the memory of the birth of her children. The midwife delivered twins. Two beautiful totemic girls. One with green eyes and dark hair, and the other with fair hair and eyes of the most penetrating gaze she had ever seen. Try as she might, she could not remember their colour -- but she thought they may have been yellow.

She remembered the look of fear on the midwife's face when she, as a young girl, no, now a young woman, pronounced their names. "Pouie, my daughter the owl. Kaltak, my daughter the wolf," said out loud for the wind one last time. "Go to your father." When uttered, the bodies of the infants became engulfed in a silverish blue light and disappeared. She never saw them again but her love for them never died. Most of all, her people finally knew that she spoke Truth.

The old woman touched herself between her legs but did not allow herself to remember. Rather, she made the sacred marks upon her body from the ash of the fire and began to chant her last song.

2

The man stood before the ashes of a dead fire now as cold as the bitter chill in the air. He reached down and gathered the ash and placed it into his leather pouch. He picked up the feather of the owl lying upon the ground and braided it into his long hair. He took the necklace of wolves' teeth which was hanging upon a low branch of the ash tree and placed it over his head so that it hung around his neck. Somehow, he knew that the night before an old woman had been there singing songs of the spirit world as she journeyed into the realm of the dead. How he knew this, he was not certain. But know it, he did. It was then when he realised he had no other human memories of his own before this moment. Anyway, it did not matter. His life before this day was of no concern.

He looked upon the ground and found what he was looking for -- five small stones which he picked up and swallowed. He felt their burning intensity as they sang their way into his soul. Once done, he set out for the village that was so very familiar to him but which he had never before visited. He never really considered how he knew about the village, its people, or the old woman because he already knew everything that truly mattered. His memories, or lack of them, were not important. He was a *Deathwalker* and his people needed his protection.

For centuries, his people sang his story, *their* story, during rituals and initiatic ceremonies. They sung of that day when a deathwalker came into their midst and announced that his father was an eagle and his mother was of their clan. They also sang the song that he sung of his two sisters.

NICAEA

1

Alexandria -- 320 C.E.

Arius could *not* believe what he had just witnessed! He could not even *remotely* comprehend that it was *he* who was the centre of the most *absurd* controversy the Christian world had ever seen! Perhaps, would *ever* see. I'm in shock, he thought. I must compose myself. I must be prepared to fight this evil that so deceitfully infiltrates the Truth of our Faith.

Arius walked with seeming resolve and purpose through the winding streets of Alexandria. He paid no heed to the cries of baksheesh or to the wail of beggars whom he so frequently comforted and, on occasion, had even given a few coins. He did not stop to haggle over the price of bread or to look with feigned interest at the trinkets in the bazaar as he often did. He passed by many people who knew him, who knew of his kindness, and who knew of his fame. They watched him quizzically, unaccustomed to his odd behaviour that day. They had not yet heard of his condemnation. They had no way of knowing that such an important and powerful man, a man of God, was at that very moment feeling the agonising terror of spiritual turmoil.

Outside the door Arius paused, suddenly realising he had forgotten to relieve himself. But he knew that would have to wait because what had to be said, could not. God will forgive me, he thought, if I soil these robes. His predicament suddenly struck him as being funny and for the first time since this whole affair began, he allowed himself to chuckle. It was enough to ease the tension he felt, if not his bladder. He opened the door without knocking.

"Ah Arius," Didymus said. "What is it that you find so amusing this fine afternoon?"

Arius never ceased to be amazed at the perceptive ability of his good friend and companion, Didymus the Blind. Indeed, he was blind. But his soul perceived truth that was so imperceptible to those who had eyes to see. Didymus was a true friend even though he was nearly forty years his junior. At age thirty, Didymus had just been appointed head of the Catechetical School of Alexandria. An exclusive school already in existence for over one hundred and fifty years and dedicated to the propagation of the Christian faith to the cultural classes. Arius truly respected this man. After all, a blind man at the age of thirty being placed at the head of such a prestigious school, one which had produced such greats as Clement and Origen, was no small achievement. This man was truly bound for greatness.

"Didymus, I cannot tell you how good it is to see you," Arius responded.

"I am unaccustomed to being greeted with a chuckle, especially from such a serious man as yourself. Tell me, have I failed to properly dress myself this day?"

"Oh, no brother Didymus, you are dressed impeccably as always. I had just remembered as I was opening the door that I had forgotten to relieve myself and I was hoping God would forgive me if I were to soil my robe."

"If that were to happen my dear brother, I am certain that God would pay no notice. I would think that He would have other, more pressing matters on His mind ... I feel the breeze of this afternoon so I know the shutters are open. Feel free to relieve yourself out the window if you like."

"I think I can wait, those on the street below ..."

"Brother Arius," Didymus interrupted with a serious note, "you are troubled and I think it not because of your bladder. What is it?"

Arius contemplated the man sitting before him and felt a wave of love and relief. I am old, he thought. But I am eternally grateful for the compassion, friendship, understanding, and support that this friend will undoubtedly offer me. Not so much to myself as a man, but for my representing the truth of God.

Perhaps if Arius was a little younger, or a bit less troubled, he would have noticed a strange look in the eyes of the blind man. A look that even blindness could not conceal.

"Didymus," Arius continued. "You are well known for your adamant support of Origenism. The knowledge of the truth of the pre-existence of souls ..."

Didymus interrupted, perhaps too quickly, "I do not see the relevance of such common knowledge ..." but stopped short before finishing his words.

Arius missed his friend's defensive irritation and continued, ignoring the interruption as if it never happened, "but what if a faction within our Faith were formed and for reasons known only to them, attempted to pervert the truth by claiming that the pre-existence of souls was not only an impossibility, but that the entire concept is and *always* has been contrary to the Christian faith?"

"Don't be *absurd,* Arius! To say, or even to *think* such a notion is ridiculous! Everyone knows the truth. Even the illiterate beggars living in filth on the streets. Do you truly think that even if such a faction were to be formed that they could gain any credence? My God, they would be *laughed* out of existence."

"No brother, listen to my age. Listen to my wisdom. The true teachings *are* being changed. Perhaps the pre-existence of souls is not now an issue, but nevertheless, the Light of God within is being subverted. They are being twisted into evil by a faction who call themselves orthodox. They have motives other than faith. They bend truth to their whims. They change the words of the Apostles to conform to their own political ambitions and greed. If this is to happen, if we *allow* this to happen, what will become of our souls? God could take no other course of action but to abandon us -- to destroy us. I am disturbed, for if truth means so little, what could possibly mean more?"

A long silence ensued and neither brother dared to interrupt the mystifying power of that moment. Didymus prepared himself for what he knew would occur next. It was extremely important that he be prepared to react properly at the appropriate instant. Too late or too soon would reveal all to this astute and pure man.

"Arius," Didymus responded at long last. "What is it? What happened today?"

"Today, dear friend and brother, the Council condemned and excommunicated me. I am to be banished."

"My God, *why?* What have you been unjustly accused of doing?" Didymus hoped he had feigned proper surprise and that the slight hint of cynicism in his voice remained undetected.

"I was accused of telling the truth. Or I should say, to be more exact, that I was accused of refusing to agree with the orthodox faction's perception of their own deceitful lies. I am stunned to think that those men who profess to be priests have gathered so much power that they can sway the opinions of others and indeed to influence the Council. I fear for our future."

"What was said Arius?"

"They claimed that my contentions, the truth, was heresy and that I was on a campaign to subvert the Church by denying the true divinity of Christ. They had twisted my words to mean something other than what was intended. They have branded myself and my supporters as Arians."

"Yes, I could imagine that if someone perceived you as a threat that they might, in the heat of passion, make wild accusations. But to be excommunicated for heresy? Did you say something in your own passion that justified such an accusation?"

"No Didymus, I did not. I simply pointed out the truth which everyone knows. But what *they're* claiming is that not only was Jesus a Son of God, but that he was the *only* Son! Furthermore, they're also claiming he is identical *with* the Father and therefore *is* God! Can you *imagine* what they are attempting to do? And they're *even* trying to argue that Jesus was also the Christ. They're attempting to merge the identities of two men into one so as to *erase* any knowledge of the *Sons* of God!"

"They sound like those fanatical Desert Fathers who have been touched in the head by the heat of the sun," Didymus responded attempting to feign sympathy. "I cannot believe their words will carry any weight."

"They *have* carried weight my brother and I fear that unless we Christians unite and dissolve our petty differences, this faction who call themselves orthodox will rewrite history to their own advantage and for their own ends -- undoubtedly for ill. It is obvious to anyone capable of thinking that history is written from the historian's perspective, and we all know with certainty that only those historians who are favoured by the ruling class will ever have their words recorded for posterity. If we allow deceit to replace truth, how many generations will it take before our faith is forgotten? How long before our solid foundations crumble and we are accused of being, and accepted to be, superstitious fools believing in a myth of fantasy? Our very *core* is at stake. All of this is too *incredible* to believe!"

"I agree Arius, this is indeed too incredible to believe. What is *your* truth?" He bit his lip as he unintentionally uttered those last words.

Arius was shocked at that last question. In fact, he thought he detected an aggressiveness in his friend that he never knew existed. But, he shrugged it off and figured it was because Didymus was just as shocked by this nonsensical nest of lies.

"Didymus, my truth is the truth of common knowledge. It is the truth of the obvious. Could you imagine what *Christ* would think if He were alive today to hear that He was being proclaimed to be God? His anger directed at the money lenders would be *nothing* in comparison to His reaction to what was said today. I even said as much to the Council. I pointed out that no one would believe that even Christ, let alone, Jesus, died on the cross for our sins. Christ didn't die on the cross. He died over fifty years later of *old* age! And Jesus didn't die on the cross either. He was stoned and hung!

This is *outrageous!* They cite passages about the resurrection that were taken *entirely* out of context. They stood there, Didymus, and had the *gall* to attribute to the one known as Jesus acts that were performed by the Essene Teacher of Righteousness and Apollonius of Tyana. Do you know what they said?"

"No, what did they say?"

"They said that no one would believe Josephus Flavius because he was a Jew and that it wouldn't take long to discredit those anti-Christian writers by claiming that they, not we, but *they* were trying to subvert the true faith by attributing to that pagan Apollonius those miracles which were 'really' performed by Jesus. My head *still* swims in confusion at this outrage to intelligence and common sense ..."

"Arius, ... I ..."

"Don't interrupt Didymus. If I were not a man of God and if I had not sworn myself to a life of peace, I myself would do as Jesus had done and take up arms against the Roman oppressors. Only these oppressors are not Roman, but rather, orthodox asses that ..."

"*Silence* Arius! I now see why you were banished. You stood before the Council and threw a tantrum. This has *nothing* to do with truth or lies and everything to do with your heated passions. Settle down. I know, as does the Council, that you speak the truth. When everyone calms down I'm *certain* your excommunication will be rescinded. I'll wager they're doing it right this instant."

Arius suddenly felt the urge to urinate. "Perhaps you speak the truth Didymus. Maybe I did overreact. Those orthodox fanatics will never be believed nor permitted to carry on as they are."

"Good. You are regaining your senses. I'll speak to the Council myself tomorrow. But it is wise not to underestimate your enemies. Let us plan to expose the *true* heresy. Do you still keep a copious diary?"

"Of course."

"And is not Eusebius of Nicomedia still a close friend and ally of yours?"

"Why yes. Of course, Bishop Eusebius. He has great respect and influence. He would *never* allow a compromise of truth. If anyone, he could stop ..."

Didymus interrupted, perhaps a bit too impatiently, "Then I propose we do this: this night, bring me your diary and anything else you may have written about this affair because tomorrow a visiting student to this school is leaving for Rome. I will redirect his journey home so that he first stops in Nicomedia and personally delivers your diary to Eusebius."

"But why would I want to give him my diary? What importance could it possibly have?"

"My brother, you are not thinking clearly. You have been, rightly or wrongly, excommunicated. Even though I'm certain the time will be brief, nevertheless, do not underestimate your enemies. If they can lie so blatantly and still have the ability to sway the Council with lies, they may also be able to twist your true words as spoken and convince a *different* Council that it was *you* who lied. Indeed, your diary is important for it may be the only evidence of your innocence in the remote possibility that it may become necessary to defend you from malicious and unjust accusations."

"You speak with wisdom and foresight Didymus. I am grateful that you are my friend and not my enemy. But who is this courier? Can he be trusted?"

"His name is Damasus. Even though he is only a boy of fifteen years, he can be trusted. His father is a good friend of mine and indebted to me."

"But do you think it wise to involve so innocent a lad. If he reads the diary, would it not unduly influence him?"

"He is illiterate," Didymus lied. "He will not know the nature of his task. Go home and recount the events of the day in your diary and bring them to me by messenger at midnight. I will dictate a letter to Eusebius on your behalf and I will use a trusted scribe. Do not worry, I will see to it that all will be well."

"Agreed brother Didymus. I am truly blessed by your friendship and integrity."

Didymus thought to himself as he heard Arius leave, truly is Arius a danger to our cause. He is so short-sighted. He could never understand that we *must* do what we are doing. After all, in the long run, it *is* for the ultimate good of our faith and Church! He then thought of Damasus. So young and already so arrogant and greedy. He will indeed do us well when I place him on the throne of St. Peter one day.

As Arius discreetly relieved himself in the alley at long last, he thought to himself that Didymus was taking far too much upon himself. I, too, must defend our cause. While Didymus works in one arena, I, too, will not be idle. I will strengthen our support here in Alexandria.

With resolve, Arius smiled. It was important to him that Didymus know that he, too, fought for truth and did not lay idly by while others took the cause. Even though he wants me to keep silent until the storm abates, thought Arius, he *must* know that even though I am old, I can *still* fight effectively. Perhaps in later years, he will speak highly of me as he sits on the throne of St. Peter.

2

"What is so urgent Master Didymus?" Damasus said as he burst into his teacher's room.

Didymus told him.

"But you want me to go to Nicomedia and deliver Arius' diary to Eusebius?"

"No, that is only what I told that fool Arius. If asked -- no, *tell* people that you are delaying your return home to Rome because I had asked you to go to Nicomedia on business of grave importance. Be prideful of the trust placed in you when you tell others this story. I want your words to get back to Arius. Your *real* journey will be to Byzantium where you will deliver that damned diary to Bishop Ossius of Cordoba. Then you may go home. If you do this simple task well, we assure you, young man, that your life from now on will be to your liking."

"Deliver, too, this letter which I will dictate."

With that, Damasus took out the quill and ink and on the parchment, he wrote as Didymus spoke:

Alexandria, the year of our Lord, 320

My Dear Brother, Ossius,

Enclosed is that cursed diary of Arius. Today, we managed to have him excommunicated and banished. But for how long, I cannot say. He does have powerful allies and no doubt they will exert influence to have him recalled. Therefore, we must move quickly.

With his diary safely in your hands, you must destroy it along with this letter. I fear the consequences if you do not and both fall into the wrong hands. We must effectively destroy this Arian heresy. Although all their claims are truth, they cannot understand the importance of our acts and their need to firmly establish the One True Faith. It will take time, but it is imperative that it be done if we are to control all peoples of this earth. It is, after all, for their own good.

Arius will appeal to the sense of honour and integrity. He will cite passages of truth and will speak of the Essene Teacher of Righteousness. He will deny the virgin birth of our God and will point out the grave of Joseph and Yeshu Pandera. He will speak too much and might be heard.

You are the Ecclesiastical Advisor to Emperor Constantine. Use your influence to gain his favour in this issue. The Emperor is not Christian and probably cares little about our theological arguments. But he may side with truth if what we say is revealed to him that way. He understands very little Greek, so ensure that his interpreters explain to him what you want him to hear. But at all costs, get him on our side. It is the only way that we can win.

In Faith,

Didymus the Blind

The next day Damasus began his journey and carried the diary of Arius and the letter of Didymus. Many of Damasus' friends spread the word that he was on a secret mission of importance to Nicomedia. This infuriated Arius when he heard what was said and he cursed himself for allowing such a young boy to be trusted with so important a task. But he was comforted by his thoughts of his trusted friend Didymus.

Didymus, too, had second thoughts. It wasn't really necessary to send that letter to Ossius. He knew what to do, after all, this was all *his* idea to begin with ... But what if the letter fell into the wrong hands? No, Ossius wouldn't be so stupid. He would destroy it. But until then Didymus knew he was most certainly in a position of vulnerability. He shrugged and turned his attention to other matters.

3

Rome -- 325 C.E.

Silvester the First didn't know what frightened him the most. All he knew and cared about was that he indeed was truly frightened. Was it because he held that damned diary which made his palms sweat and his hands shake uncontrollably? Or was it because of those two priests now standing before him and telling him that they would be his delegates? Telling *him*, the Pope, what *he* was going to do!

He hadn't the nerve to look them in the eye and pretended to be occupied by flipping through the pages of the diary. But he was acutely conscious of their presence and suddenly wished that he had never been elected to this Holy Office.

"Most Glorious," said the first priest.

At least they call me by my proper title, Silvester thought as he pretended not to hear. I don't even know their names and I haven't even heard of this alleged Nicene Brotherhood they say they represent....

"Most Glorious!," the priest shouted. "You need do no more than simply *see* the diary. You are *not* to read it!"

Silvester responded promptly to that last demand by almost dropping the diary. He meekly looked up but his gaze could go no higher than the shoulders of the greenish brown of their robes.

"Give us the diary, Most Glorious. We will take excellent care of it."

Silvester wondered, why did they show it to me to begin with? I have no say in this matter. And as he handed them the diary, he noticed that his hands still shook uncontrollably.

The first priest sneered at the Pope as he took it.

Trying to maintain his dignity and the authority of his office, Silvester made an attempt to take control of the situation, "You are to ..." He stopped mid sentence. He could only manage a high pitched squeak. He did not attempt to speak again.

"Now listen carefully, Most Glorious."

Silvester nodded.

"You will refuse the invitation of Emperor Constantine to attend the Ecumenical Council at Nicaea and claim that old age prohibits you from travelling so far. You will send us in your stead by so signing this document."

The priest handed him the document and watched as Silvester signed.

He continued, "You will also sign this document affixed with your seal. It is *your* creed, the Nicene Creed which states that the Son is one in being with the Father. It also condemns the teachings of Arius which proclaim that Christ was a creature who was inferior to the Father."

At this point, Silvester would have signed a document stating that Jesus was a pagan. He signed.

"Now, this last document," the priest continued, "is a letter that *you* dictated. It is written to Bishop Ossius of Cordoba and you are commissioning him to preside as president of the Council of Nicaea that is being held next month and which *you* had summoned."

He signed and the Priests left.

Silvester sighed with relief as the two men left his chambers. He thought to himself that they were mad. That this whole predicament was madness personified. Everyone knew that the Emperor himself had summoned the Council. If he ever got wind that I was claiming to have summoned it ... He didn't allow himself to finish the thought but changed to another.

This is indeed very dangerous. History is being changed even before it happens. What else have they done in my name? Somehow I must survive. I suffered terribly during the persecution of Diocletian, but I survived. I have absolutely no intention of *ever* becoming a martyr....

During a moment of bravery, Silvester chose a course of action. He decided that he would have this Nicene Brotherhood investigated. Perhaps he wisely thought better of it. Or perhaps he simply forgot in the heat of passion that night as he taught his servant boy the facts of life.

4

Ossius wrote in *his* diary on the eve of the Council of Nicaea:

... the spurious documents from the Pope were delivered to me today. Timing is critical. I feel the power to change the course of history even before it is written. Athanasius was brilliant to conceive of a renewed manifestation of an old brotherhood masked with a Christian flavour to ensure the establishment and continued power and control over the Church. A brotherhood that will exist parallel

*with the Church and which can introduce whatever documents that
are necessary at any point in time is truly ingenious. And many are
not even forged ...*

5

Nicaea -- 325 C.E.

Ossius of Cordoba stood victoriously before the two hundred
and fifty assembled Bishops. He smiled triumphantly at the
obvious absence of those who represented the Arianizing Party
and he gloated in his success. Everything turned out even better
than was expected.

He glanced over to where the Emperor sat and noticed the bored
look on his face. For twelve weeks, thought Ossius, Constantine
sat there pretending to show interest in the proceedings. He doesn't
even speak Greek and our interpreters weren't exactly clear in their
choice of words. Still, he thought, it would be a politically good
idea to acknowledge his presence. Ossius spoke in Latin:

"I, Ossius, Bishop of Cordoba, ecclesiastical advisor to Emperor
Constantine ..."

It's obvious the bastard takes me for a fool, thought
Constantine.

"... and president of this Council of Nicaea congratulate the
integrity of all assembled Bishops, priests, and dignitaries for
their strength of conviction and love for Jesus Christ, our Lord
and Saviour. I congratulate each and every one of you on behalf
of our Church for your dedication and conviction in ridding this
world of the Arian heresy."

"But," Ossius continued, "before we close this ecumenical
council, I have a very important and opportune announcement
from the Most Glorious, Pope Silvester I. I should first point out
the fact that this announcement was made by the Most Glorious
nearly four months ago when, because of old age, he made his
apologies for not being able to attend this historic meeting. He

asked, in his infinite wisdom, that I not make this announcement until the conclusion of these proceedings. He did not want, in all fairness, to unduly influence the arguments and opinions of those here assembled because of his glorious office. He did not want it to be said by the heretics that this council was unfair and therefore requested that the reading of this statement be deferred."

"I shall now quote from his letter: *Ossius, it is important, no, crucial to the very existence of our Church, our faith, that Arius and his Arianizing Party be exposed as being the heretics and pagans that they truly are. There has been a grand conspiracy to subvert the Truth, to make claims about incidents that have never occurred. Our enemies attempt to write their own history, and we, the servants of our Lord Saviour, have as our only recourse to fight these lies and deceits, the glorious truth. Truth will prevail! Our Lord Jesus Christ is one in being with our Father and not, as Arius claims, an inferior creature whose divinity should be denied ... My dear Ossius, your heart is pure and I, the Most Glorious, commission you to preside at the Council of Nicaea ...*"

At this point the assembled Bishops roared with applause, shouts, and stomping feet. The interruption is timely, Ossius thought. I wondered how I could appropriately conclude the letter without reading the part about that contemptuous glorious ass having called this Council.

He handed the letter to the two sombre looking priests from the Nicene Brotherhood who had delivered it. Perhaps they snatched it from his hands. Ossius didn't remember. He only recalled later that he was fortunate that no one asked to see the letter.

He raised his hands, looked heavenward, and spoke. But it was a full fifteen minutes later before order was restored and his words could be heard.

"As it was proclaimed at the Council of Alexandria just five years ago, it is now reconfirmed that Arius is banished and excommunicated. I, as president of the Council of Nicaea, will be the first to sign this historic document."

He thus signed. The two sombre delegates from the Pope, the Nicene Brothers who never said a word during the twelve week session, signed next.

6

It took almost three hours for the document to be signed by all those in attendance. Ossius stayed for the duration and watched as each elated face took quill in hand. Hysteria, Ossius thought, our work is *truly* remarkable!

At long last he, too, could leave. Strutting, although somewhat wearily, through the corridors, Ossius couldn't stop smiling. When he arrived at the predetermined location, he opened the door and walked through. He closed, latched it, and turned to look at the two occupants in the room.

As expected, he saw Athanasius. Thirty years his junior, of small physical stature, but a spiritual giant. A genius. A man to be respected. Standing next to him was Nicholas of Myra. He was an obese man, had a white beard, and was obsessed with wearing the colour red. Ossius did not see the expected presence of the two Nicene Brothers, but knew enough *not* to ask about their absence.

Athanasius was the first to speak. "Well done brother Ossius. Well done."

"If I say so myself, I did not expect it to be so easy. I dare say that it is now over."

"Do not be so quick to think it over and done and never, never underestimate your enemies."

"But we have won at every turn," Ossius replied a bit indignantly. "Ever since I went to Alexandria and returned to report to Constantine of the Arian heresy, every planned event has gone our way. We have made no mistakes. We managed to get Silvester's blessing. I have been Constantine's spiritual advisor for twelve years ..."

"Yes you have," Athanasius interrupted. "Twelve years and he has yet to become a Christian. There is no dispute that he has supported us thus far, but as his advisor can you truly say that you have been effective? I will agree to your effectiveness only when you have baptised him."

"Your words are harsh … and unfair, Athanasius, you know good and well that it is a secular custom to wait until the deathbed to receive conversion into our faith …"

"Ossius, Ossius. My dear Ossius. How naive you truly are. Arius has lost two battles, but the war is far from over. Listen. The Arianizing Party is far from weak. Arius has not been silenced nor has Eusebius of Nicomedia who is now the leader of that Party. Yes, they are both banished and we have time to breathe. But that is all. You know as well as I that those who one day are exiled are the next recalled as frequently as the wind changes direction. Never for a moment forget that the Emperor, although at present our champion, is not yet controlled by us. He is not like that imbecile we have as Pope. He can as easily become the champion of the Arian heresy as he can decide to have all Christians persecuted, tortured, and martyred."

Nicholas of Myra spoke for the first time. "Constantine will never support Arius. He has only seen him once and will never see him again. In that the Emperor is not a Christian can also work in our favour. After all, he understands little, if any of our doctrine and I doubt if he really cares. To him, it is all political. And Arius, ha! He was so astounded when he stood up to speak and I socked him on the nose and flattened him …"

"Yes," Ossius interrupted hardly able to contain his merriment as he recalled the event, "he was *surely* a sight! You flattened him all right. He flew two feet into the air and landed upside down with his robe over his head. He was so scared, he thought he was being killed. He pissed all over himself and the way people scrambled, I bet he pissed on a few others as well. What a sight! From now on, whenever he is remembered, he will be remembered as the fool who pissed instead of spoke at the Council of Nicaea. To be fair, he will also be remembered as the biggest and most well hung Priest ..."

It was Nicholas' turn to interrupt with laughter, "What a sight indeed! He was so flustered that he never did compose himself. His face was redder than the blood pouring from his nose. He was an orator's nightmare. He couldn't get two words out without stammering or forgetting what he was speaking about. He never even realised until Eusebius came up and straightened his robe, that everyone behind him could see his bare arse. He certainly made a fool of himself, no one will *ever* take him seriously again."

Athanasius made no attempt to suppress his anger, *"Fools! You God damned fools!"*

Nicholas and Ossius were shocked into stunned silence at the power of the voice of this small man shouting at them.

"Not everyone laughed at that incident. Did either of you perchance take your eyes from that fool Arius and look at Constantine?"

Both shook their heads back and forth.

"Well, you should have. There was no laughter on his face. He simply stared showing no emotion. I fear what he thinks but not half as much as I fear what he might do."

"But he supported the Nicene Faith *after* that happened," interjected Ossius.

"Surely, if he was concerned he would not have given his support to our cause," defended Nicholas.

Athanasius ignored the stupid remarks and continued, "for now, all is well. But Arianism is not our only enemy. For the time being, I will occupy my time with two things. First, I will attack Apollinarianism as its doctrine is consistent with the Arian heresy. And, second, I will form, let us say, a public arm of the Nicene Brotherhood and we will call it the Nicene Party."

"But won't that call attention to the existence of the secret brotherhood?" Ossius asked.

"No. In fact the opposite. No one will suspect a secret if it is disguised and made public."

The genius and cunning of this man, thought Ossius.

"Oh yes, one more thing," Athanasius continued, "we must plan to ensure that Origen is banished and Origenism is also declared heretical."

Ossius immediately saw the wisdom in that statement and said so. Then he said, "we must tell Didymus. He is a devout Origenist and he must begin to develop doubts."

"No," Athanasius responded. "Didymus must not know of this. For now he is useful. Let him go his merry way. But never is he to be trusted. If he can betray Arius, what does that tell us?"

"That he has sided with us," Ossius replied feigning confidence to mask his growing fear.

"Oh, really? A betrayer is a betrayer. They have no conscience. If he betrayed once, he will do so again. We are to make guarantees that it is not us that Didymus betrays next!"

"But he knows too much. He will talk if he so much as even *thinks* that his life is in danger or suspects of what we speak. How can we ensure ..."

"... his silence?" Athanasius interrupted. "Poison is not unheard of, blind men can't see where they walk, and beggars do have knives ..." He noticed the look of horrified shock on the face of Ossius and that of stupid indifference on Nicholas'. He knew that these two would be essentially *useless* when it came time for the final objective ... "but don't worry Ossius, I jest."

Ossius wondered and shuddered.

"It will take at least two hundred years to complete our plan. We will all be in the Kingdom of God by then. Didymus will never know of the fate of Origenism. But at all costs, we must completely annihilate our enemies so that even the memories of their heresy no longer exist. As I said, for now we can breathe but we cannot let our defences slacken. Ossius, you are the ecclesiastical advisor to Constantine. At all costs you are to remain as such. You are to convert him immediately. You are to ensure his loyalty to the Nicene Faith. Do you understand?"

Ossius nodded.

At this point, Nicholas seemed to wake up. "What do I do?" he asked.

"Nicholas, I fear you may have endangered our cause because of your hands. I suggest that you return to Myra and remain silent. If you ever see an Arian again, keep your fists to yourself. Better yet, grab and play with your privates as I am told you so frequently do."

Ossius watched Nicholas' face turn redder than his coat and knew the truth of Athanasius' words. How could he possibly know so much, he thought. What does he know that he hasn't yet said? It was at that moment that Ossius realised the severity of the scheme in which he was involved. He knew that no longer would he be allowed the freedom of choice. Suddenly, he shivered. He saw a vision of a *darkened maggot* and he felt as if a presence from the past was watching their every move, hearing every word, and knowing their every thought. He felt sick.

7

It was two months after the Council of Nicaea when Constantine had the dream. No, not a dream exactly, a *vision!* Its' eerie reality caused his life to change and affected the course of history.

He recalled the vision in acute detail as he waited alone in his chambers for Eusebius of Nicomedia to arrive. As a result of his vision, he had recalled Eusebius from exile, and now, a month later, the bishop was due to arrive at long last. As Constantine waited, he recalled his vision for the millionth time, it seemed. He just couldn't get it off his mind....

It all started when Constantine saw an old woman entering backwards into his bed chamber. She was nude except for a feather hanging from her hair and a necklace made of some type of animal teeth hanging around her neck. After entering, she turned around. She was holding some sort of rattle and had lines of some type of grey, powdery substance intricately woven on her body. The woman let her eyes look deeply into his and he saw that they glowed eerily. Mysteriously, mystically they glowed. He was drawn into them. They became his eyes and he saw himself. He saw himself and then she saw himself. He couldn't tell who was doing the seeing. It was so dizzyingly strange, switching back and forth so quickly that they merged into a oneness. It was if he could think and act as two separate entities and yet he knew that only one was present.

The old woman began to chant in a language that was so foreign to hear. She shook her rattle and began to move rhythmically. Slowly, ever so slowly. He saw himself. He saw himself standing naked. He saw the old woman but could only feel her gaze because he dared not look into those soul piercing eyes. Rather, he became fascinated with the swaying of her breasts. They were old and sagged a little, but at the same time, they were still erotically beautiful. He felt himself becoming aroused and became embarrassed.

Once again, he saw himself as *she* would see him. He saw, or perhaps she saw, as her hand reached out and touched his hardness. Immediately, her caressing touch caused a pleasing orgasmic explosion of lights and colours and he began to fall -- to endlessly fall into forever.

He lay upon silvery strands woven into the web of a spider. He lay helpless and unable to move. He watched more in fascination than with horror as unseen hands took pieces of his body away, only to return and reassemble his parts at the end of eternity. He lay motionless and felt the reticent flowing of the fibres beneath his spirit and knew that they were truly named. He gently moved as they moved until all motion dissipated causing him to once again fall. Swiftly and silently he fell.

Suddenly, he appeared at a strange place lit by dim shadow. Constantine found himself near a small lake in a clearing nestled comfortably deep in an ancient forest. It was a hauntingly quiet place and the motion of wind was uncannily absent. The shadow of dimness appeared as a kind of ethereal twilight, or so it seemed, and as he lay upon the bluish green grass, he felt its soothing coolness seduce his body. And then, there was a noise -- a playful sound of splashing water. He sat up to locate its source and what he saw was astounding! There, playing in the water were *two* nymphs. Their naked beauty was sensually arousing. Their breasts were firm, but still moved in seductive rhythm with their play. He remembered wondering if they were innocently playing or if he had inadvertently caught them in the act of making love. He desperately wanted to know.

Silently, he rose and hid behind a rock conscious of the fact that he, too, was naked. Almost painfully, his erection seemed ready to once again explode into ecstasy at the slightest touch. Nevertheless, he continued with his unworldly obsession and secret vigil confident that he remained unseen. Soon, the two nymph-women tired of the water and waded to shore. He was too far away to hear their words, but close enough that he could see their every move and feel the exhilaration of their profound beauty.

As they stood upon the grass, he was shocked to see them embrace. He watched as their caresses became heated -- their kisses, impassioned -- and their touches excitingly intimate. Suddenly, he had the urge, the longing, to join them and would have done so had it not been for his conscience. He began to think of himself as an intruder. It was obvious that the two women were discreet and that they walked a very long way into the deep forest for their privacy. It was wrong for him to spy. He felt ashamed. Ashamed that he had seen as much as he had. Ashamed that he did so naked. And ashamed that his hardness betrayed his desires. He turned silently to sneak away.

Startled, he felt a slight touch on his shoulder that caused him to turn abruptly. He was surprised to find that both women were so close that he couldn't help but brush against the woman with long, straight black hair. She had the deepest green eyes he had ever seen, but it was the woman with fair hair that reached down and seductively held and played with his hardness as she spoke. Her touch was oddly soothing but strangely wasn't erotic or sexual. They seemed to be beyond such human desires. He noticed that her eyes were very strange but he couldn't remember their colour. They were yellow he thought ... but he wasn't certain.

The fair haired woman spoke and proclaimed that he had passed a crucial test. Then the dark haired woman spoke in a whispery voice to say that they had sought him out in the dream world and found him to be a man who would one day understand honesty and integrity. She then said an incomprehensible thing -- his *fibres* were rewoven so he could withstand what was soon to occur. Your sensations, she said, are only understood by you as erotic and sexual pleasure but they are truly much more beautiful and satisfying. We had to test your fibres to ensure they would hold together and be strands of great strength and flexibility. We assure you that they are.

Constantine remembered that he was about to speak but the dark haired woman put a finger to his lips and whispered that he should lie down and let her and her spirit sister teach him of blissful elation. As he allowed himself to be gently laid down upon the grass, she kissed him. Their tongues met and as the kiss became deeper, so did their shared intensity. Simultaneously, he felt as the other spirit mounted him. He felt the damp soothing warmth and pleasing softness as she slowly slid down causing him to enter the depth of forever. She moved with seductive eroticism and with such rhythmic harmony, that it reminded him of the bewitching dance of the old woman.

He closed his eyes as the dark haired woman left his lips and slowly, with her tongue, moved down his body. He felt the momentary touch of cool air as her sister moved away only to be replaced with the warmth of her mouth and the fondling of her tongue. At that moment, he climaxed. But, he remembered, they were right. The orgasm was not sexual. It was more. He felt a strange oneness. He knew all that was needed to be known. He saw clearly and most *certainly* he knew that the alleged Arian heresy was indeed the truth. He was suddenly disgusted by the idiot Ossius.

He opened his eyes to tell the two sisters of his realisation only to find that he was at a different place. His body felt different. His memories were not his, but rather, of another. He still lay upon his back and felt the softness of lips completing his climax. But he saw that this new world was bright. It was hilly. It reminded him of the land of Gaul that he travelled through years before after his Coronation at York and on his way to the East. He looked to his right and saw a pile of clothing which appeared to be strewn about and tangled together. He saw a sword of a uniquely different design from those to which he was accustomed. He reached up and felt his hair and pulled it in front of his eyes. It was dark, thick, and long hanging well past his shoulders. He looked down and saw a familiar face. The dark haired woman with green eyes looked up at him and let his softening penis slide from her lips. She smiled and *as* she smiled he noticed that his body was one of youth. He lay back and looked at the clear, blue sky and saw the graceful and silent flight of an eagle high above. He closed his eyes.

Suddenly, he heard a deafening noise and he opened his eyes with a start. He still lay on his back, but the ground was wet. The heat was intense. The trees were of a type he had never seen before. And then the pain set in ... Excruciating. Intense. The air was filled with the smoke of fire. And the smell. Such a smell never before came to his senses and probably would never do so again. But he would never, *ever* forget. He heard a dull, thudding sound like chop, chop, chop. Almost like a very fast chopping of wood. And then he saw its source. His eyes widened and he thought that he must be in hell, because in the air he saw the strangest and largest bird hovering high above him. It had a large red cross on a white field on its -- *beak?,* and a square hole in its side. And inside the bird's belly were people. People who were alive and moving. One person, whom he recognised to be wearing a helmet, although the likes of which he never saw before, was behind a large stick which was fastened to the bird in such a way so that it could rotate. It was making a tat, tat, tat, sound and was spewing forth flashes of flame. And then he saw a streak of smoke and the bird became a ball of fire. Greek fire, he thought, and bodies that dripped fire fell from the sky.

He looked at himself and saw that he wore strange garments. They were different shades of green, black, and brown. And in his hand he held a strange stick that also made tat, tat, tat sounds vibrating while it did. He saw that his hands were of a strange greenish colour, not unlike his clothes. He then looked up and saw several men wearing strange conical shaped hats. They, too, carried those sticks. He watched three of them fall before him, but there were so many more. He kept hearing or feeling, he didn't know which, thudding sensations jar his body. Then he thought, I have been betrayed. They did this on purpose. Darkness overcame him.

8

Constantine recalled thinking that he woke from his dream because he was once again in his bedroom. His surroundings were familiar as he lay in his bed. As he looked up in the semi-darkness, he thought he saw threads of faint silver light form as they had done in his dream. And then, a bluish flash and before him stood a strange man. Tall, well formed, and with long black hair. He wore only a feather braided into his hair, a necklace of teeth, and strange marks. He remembered thinking at the time that he was still dreaming. But now he knew differently ...

The man had spoken to him and said that he was a baqca. That he had travelled the net of the universe to reach him and that he had caused his vision. He told him that he saw the future and was shown these things so that he could teach him the consequences of what had transpired over the course of the last several years. He told him that it would take sixteen centuries to correct the wrongs committed. Even then there would be no certainty that they *could* be corrected.

No, the man who had arrived in that mysterious fashion was not a dream. He was real. He stayed for three days. Select others in his court remembered him and had *known* him as a visiting Magi from a land far to the East. And then he left -- *they* left. Because with him left a woman he had *learned* to respect during those three days and to whom he became more and more deeply attached. A woman, he knew, who, like the mysterious man, was destined for greatness.

As Constantine awaited the arrival of Eusebius, his resolve was final, clear, and certain. No longer would he embrace the Nicene faith. No longer would that ass Ossius be his spiritual advisor. I could teach him many lessons he thought, but my motive now is not spiritual. It is political. The politics of truth! He would appoint Eusebius as his new advisor and support his cause to fight the Nicene Party. He would even allow Eusebius to baptise him on his death bed. Not to be converted to Christianity -- that would be silly. But, rather, for purposes of making a clear statement. Constantine had already begun to teach his son of the truth and merits of Arius.

At long last the knock came at his door. Eusebius had arrived. He never told him about his dream except that it was a dream of an owl and of a wolf which made him see clearly and to change his mind.

9

Ossius thought it odd that Athanasius was strangely subdued and obviously not in control of the situation. It was apparent that the bearded man in the greenish brown robe, the robe that

Ossius identified as the habit of the Nicene Brotherhood, not only controlled this meeting, but also the soul of Athanasius.

Why am I here at this meeting? Thought Ossius. He had travelled by donkey for three days to get here. Led by a guide who never once spoke. Not even to acknowledge the many questions that were thrown at him. For three gruelling, hot days they had plodded along hearing only the sounds made by their donkey's hooves as they padded across the rocks. Their occasional snorts. The sounds of flies and birds. The only human voice was that of mine, he thought with embarrassment. He remembered he had stopped attempting to communicate late in the afternoon of the first day when he realised the whining quality in his voice.

He remembered early that first morning when the guide appeared at his door with a letter and two donkeys. The letter stated simply that his Church needed him, that he was to go immediately with his guide, and was not to tell anyone that he was leaving. I would have ignored such a mysterious request except that it was signed by Athanasius, Ossius thought. Perhaps I should have.

Ossius had arrived at this sombre looking place about an hour before. He was only a few yards away from the complex of mud brick buildings before he even saw them. So extremely well hidden were they. He was then brought straight to this room, winding his way through a maze of corridors to get here. He had stood here for an hour and nobody had, as yet, so much as acknowledged his presence.

Athanasius was present as was the bearded man and two others who wore the same coloured robes. He had not seen them before. For an hour the others had spoken with muted voices. Ossius could only make out occasional words and phrases. He did not hear enough to know thoroughly the topic that was being discussed. Only that there was a problem. A problem indeed! Ever since the Council of Nicaea, it was feared that Constantine might abandon the Nicene faith and ally with Eusebius. Ossius knew that sooner or later the problem would appear. It looked as if it finally had.

Ossius' thoughts were interrupted when he heard Athanasius shout. He began to listen. "... It will be that damned fool Ossius," Athanasius shouted, "it will be *his* fault ..."

The bearded man interrupted in an intimidating voice of deathly calm, "he is not a brother, Athanasius. You are. He did not break a vow. You did."

Athanasius shook. Perhaps with anger, but most likely fear, Ossius noticed. I can feel the fear swell within myself.

For the first time Ossius was noticed. The bearded man motioned for him to come over to him. Ossius did.

"Tell me," said the bearded man in that same tone of voice, "whose fault will it be when Constantine renounces the Nicene faith?"

Ossius carefully considered his words before responding, "Your Excellency," a sign of respect certainly would not hurt, "as of three days ago there has been no indication that such will occur. In fact, I have defeated him in a major debate. But, if such *were* to occur, it is obvious it would not be the fault of Constantine. He is ignorant of our faith and yet he still has done much on our behalf. The Edict of Milan guarantees freedom to all religions, and not just ours. It could, therefore, only be the fault of Bishop Eusebius of Nicomedia. He perpetuates the Arian heresy knowing full well his deeds and in spite of the rulings of two ecumenical councils. Eusebius has somehow managed to reach the Emperor through lies and deceit. Only he can rightfully be held responsible."

"Were you not tasked to *ensure* that you remain as his advisor?"

"Yes, but may I point out that the Emperor has not converted to Christianity in spite of my attempts and, even if Eusebius' ultimately wins favour with the Emperor, it is doubtful that he will convert. That is not the fault of any one individual. It is the failing of the Church. The Church simply does not have the power to influence the entire secular world as it should."

"You are both fools," said the bearded man. "But you are also right, Ossius, when you say that the Church does not have the power. But I guarantee you that situation will soon change."

The bearded man looked deeply into both of their eyes and was silent for a moment as if carefully choosing *his* words and *their* fates. Finally, and at long last he continued, breaking the tension: "The one who is at fault for *all* of our inconveniences is the Master of Moonlight."

Ossius having never heard that name before, considered that he probably never wanted to hear that name again.

"Athanasius," the bearded man continued, "these are your orders. You know what will happen if you fail. We will remember that if you do fail, it will be for the second time. You are to go to Alexandria, the centre of this heresy, and within five years you are to become Bishop. You are, henceforth, to be the Arianizing Party's most vocal antagonist. As well, you are to ensure that our preliminary work regarding Apollinarianism and Origenism is not effectively countered. How you do it is your business. But do it you will! Now go prepare yourself for this night's activities."

Athanasius left and Ossius noted that he was much relieved. But for the life of him, he wondered, how will he ever manage to become a bishop?

"Ossius, we have two things in mind for you. First, we need to use your -- albeit somewhat questionable -- influence with Constantine to get him to sign a document. However, he is not to know what he is signing."

That would be unnecessarily dangerous, thought Ossius, I will simply forge his signature and no one, not even this brotherhood, will ever be the wiser. It won't be the first time I did that. Speaking aloud Ossius then asked, "May I know the nature of this document?"

"It is a gift," was the response, "it will be known in history as the Donation of Constantine. The Emperor will bestow upon Pope Silvester I and his successors to the Throne of St. Peter, primacy over Antioch, Byzantium, Alexandria, and Jerusalem. The Pope will also be gifted temporal dominion over Rome, Italy, and all Western States. The Pope will be the supreme judge over all of the clergy. Constantine will even offer Pope Silvester the Imperial Crown, but Silvester, being a modest man, will decline."

"B ... b ... but," Ossius tried to speak.

"Don't worry," the bearded man interrupted, "that, and other documents will not appear until the Emperor is dead, having been converted by Silvester himself, and the Arian heresy is well under control."

"And what is this second request?," asked Ossius.

"After careful consideration, Ossius, you have been nominated to become a brother of the Nicene Brotherhood. You should know that only a brother may leave our abode."

Ossius understood all too clearly. "I would be honoured, your Excellency. However, I know very little of your brotherhood."

"There is little you need to know. Only that our existence is to remain carefully veiled in secrecy as it has been for the past one hundred and fifty years; that any betrayal will result in a most uncomfortable existence at best, but most likely death. We exist solely to make the Church powerful. Indeed, our faith is the *only* true faith. To assure our supremacy, we will accomplish our 'altruistic' objectives at all costs."

Ossius knew he had no choice. He agreed.

"Good, your initiation commences at midnight. Prepare yourself."

Ossius was left alone until the appointed time. For the first time since he was a child, he wept. He wept many times after that night. He did not cry because of the pain, but rather for his soul.

10

Ossius had been home for three years before he even contemplated writing an account of that night's initiation in his journal. It was another two years before he finally did. Perhaps he did so in an attempt to atone for his sins. Or perhaps it was done with the feeble hope of easing his burning conscience. He wrote, in the year 330:

I have not slept with a clear conscience for five years. It is not because I had forged the Emperor's signature to that document nor because of what we do in the name of the Church. Each act was and is now necessary. I have not slept because I know my soul is damned and there can be no way to escape the horrors that await me. I live them even now, every breathing moment of my life is filled with the fires of hell.

Two years ago I learned that Athanasius, my brother in hell, indeed became bishop of Alexandria. I am bound to him and even though we will never hear from nor see each other again, we are bonded. He is my master, and I, his slave. I am comforted to know that with his success, I am safe -- but only in this world. I hope God understands our motives, but I fear not.

My brother and I left that cursed place at dawn after my initiation. We never spoke during the three day journey home. What he thought, I do not know. I tried to busy myself with my plan to forge the Emperor's name to his alleged donation to Silvester rather than jeopardising myself by tricking him into signing it himself. If ever the brotherhood discovers that I did forge it, my descent into hell will be much sooner than expected.

I must write of that initiation. Perhaps to do so will ease my conscience.

I was made a brother of the Nicene Brotherhood although that is not its true name. I dare not even write that name here or pronounce it out loud. After our meeting, I was taken to a chamber so small that I could only squat in the most awkward of positions as I could neither stand, sit, nor lay down. There I waited until the appointed hour of midnight when two men appeared and opened the door to my cell. They each wore violet robes -- so deep a violet they were that they almost appeared black. Their faces were hidden in the shadows cast by their cowls. Each carried an oil lamp. One gave me a cup and told me to drink. I did. Shortly thereafter as they watched, I became dizzy and felt very strange indeed. Oh how I wish that the potion I drank caused me to forget all that happened next. But, I fear, I'm cursed to forever recall with vivid lucidity.

I was blindfolded and my hands were tied tightly together behind my back. We walked for a long time until I could faintly hear the droning sound of chanting. It became louder and louder until we arrived at a door. We stopped and when I heard the door open, the chanting stopped. We entered and I was immediately told to stand where I was. I was told many things which I dare not write, and then I was asked if I agreed to be a brother and then made to take many vows -- again, of them I dare not write.

When this part was completed, I was told I would consummate my vows and would be required to do a number of things without hesitation. Indeed, I was told that any hint of hesitation would result in my immediate torture and death. First, a knife cut my clothes from me until I stood naked. Then, I was hit behind my knees so that my legs buckled and I knelt upon the floor. My blindfold was removed and I saw that I knelt near the point of a pentagram facing outward. A circle of men was made around the pentagram. But most shocking was that a mere inch from my lips was the erect penis of the man speaking and at the base of his shaft was the scar of a goat's head made by branding. He told me to suck it until his seed came into my mouth and was swallowed. I did this horrendous act to four other people. The last being none other than Athanasius. I was then told that Athanasius was my master and I, his slave.

I was told to turn around and I saw that I was at the bottom of the pentagram and that at the top, between its two legs and on the wall was a painting of a goat's head. But in the centre, I could see for the first time, an altar also in the shape of a pentagram. Upon the altar was tied a young woman. Perhaps she was thirteen or fourteen years of age. She appeared to be so innocent, so beautiful. She was naked and her body glistened and smelled of oils and perfumes. My bonds were cut and I was given a knife and told that I was to mount her and at the moment of my orgasm, to slit her throat. I obeyed, but still, I am tormented by the look of fear, terror, and acceptance of her fate in her eyes. She never made a sound. I cried, my God I cried as I slit her throat. I cried as I, and then the others drank her blood. I cried as they replaced her with myself on the altar and I lay there, unfeeling, as I was raped by everyone in the room. I lost consciousness on the altar and when I awoke, I lay nude on a bed in a cell. At first, it felt numb, but as I looked down at my groin, I saw to my horror, the brand of a goat's head just above my penis. I screamed in agony as excruciating pain set in.

I am a brother of the Nicene Brotherhood. A brotherhood of the Beast who is our god. We will take control of the Church and bend it to our will. Perverting it, committing sins of deceit for it. To kill for it. I knew of evil, but I never truly understood it until I became it. God, our Holy Father, I would pray for your forgiveness except that I renounce your existence.

Three days later, Ossius thought better of having written what he did and chided himself for his lack of discretion of even secretly writing of his initiation. He went to retrieve his diary from its hiding place and to his horror, found that it was gone. He never kept a diary again.

11

336 to 381 C.E.

In the year 336, Constantine recalled Arius to Constantinople as it was obvious that under the leadership of Eusebius of Nicomedia, the Arianizing Party had acquired prominence. But neither the Emperor nor Eusebius ever saw him. Arius had died suddenly in the streets of Constantinople on the very day that he arrived. Everyone thought it was a result of his old age coupled with the exhaustion of his long journey. No one had seen the beggar who had the brand of the head of a goat below his belly, scratch him with a poison knife as he walked by.

The following year, the Emperor Constantine died but not before Eusebius baptised him into the Christian Faith. That year also saw Constantius II become Emperor and by his acts, Arianism became binding upon the entire Christian Church. The new Emperor was determined to depose Bishop Athanasius of Alexandria and forced him into exile several times. The last time, Athanasius was forced to live as a hermit in the desert.

Ossius never faltered from his support of Athanasius and consistently fought what he considered to be the Arian heresy until his death in 352. He was banished as a heretic in 355. Three years after his death.

The Arian Party thrived until the year 361 when Constantius II died and the Arians lost their last vestige of support. After Eusebius died nineteen years earlier, no strong leader of their party emerged and it began to divide into factions. Some thought because of infiltration, but it could never be proven.

In the year 366, rumours flourished of a document that had appeared in Rome which was called the *Donation of Constantine.* The new Pope, it was understood, fully endorsed the authenticity of the document. Athanasius was recalled from exile and he built a new and more powerful Nicene Party.

Even though Athanasius died in the year 372, his Nicene Party thrived. In the year 380, the Edict of Thessalonia prohibited Arianism in the East and Athanasianism became the State Religion. The following year, 381, the First Council of Constantinople was called and the Nicene Party proclaimed its final victory over Arianism.

12

The Deceit of History

The year 325 marked the end of Christianity and ushered in the beginning of Christian hegemony supported by lies, intrigues, persecutions, and massacres. All, allegedly in the name of God. But as the Brotherhood will attest, in reality, it was in the name of the Beast.

On the 12th of May, in the year of our Lord, 330, Ossius had enough foresight to realise that since Constantine, on the previous day, had changed the name of his capital from Byzantium to Constantinople, the forged document had to be changed as well. He had the document recalled. But instead of redoing the entire document, he simply smudged out one word and replaced it with another. No one seemed to notice.

Damasus became Pope in the year 366 and used the document known as the *Donation of Constantine* to the advantage of the institution known as the Church. No one questioned the smudge marks near the word 'Constantinople' and subsequently the document served its purpose. Even in the 16th century when the document was proven to be false, its falsity had little if any effect on a sixteen hundred year old manifestation of power.

At the Council of Alexandria in the year 400, Origenism was condemned. Pope Anastasius I and bishops in Palestine and Syria adhered to its condemnation. At the second Council of Constantinople in 553, the final condemnation of Origen's teachings occurred. Of lesser importance but significant nonetheless, Didymus the Blind was also condemned as an Origenist.

In the fifth century, a rumour was circulated that Pope Silvester I was the individual who had actually converted Constantine and performed his baptism. Also, at the same time it was said that he had cured his leprosy. With such rumours abounding throughout the Christian world, no one was surprised when the Church began to assert, later in that century, that Pope Silvester I was responsible for summoning the Council of Nicaea and that he had commissioned Ossius as its president. After all, the Church produced the documents to prove their claim.

The Arian heresy was truly dead. It did manage to remain alive in the Teutonic tribes. At least until the conversion of the Franks in the year 496, but shortly thereafter, their beliefs disappeared from Christian theology.

As for Athanasius and Nicholas of Myra, they were canonised after the tenth century.

And, finally, the Nicene Brotherhood felt a true sense of accomplishment and continued to secretly recruit adherents throughout the centuries so as to ensure the perpetuation of the 'True Faith.'

Although it was never proven, it was unequivocally suspected that certain individuals were recruited into the Brotherhood for a particular purpose. For certainly, in the year 374, Valens initiated a massive sorcery persecution that spread throughout the entire Christian world. That event, in itself, was not remarkable. What was remarkable was the fact that suspected magicians and their like, and *even* their employers, were prosecuted, not for witchcraft, but rather, for high treason against the state. This meant that *anyone* so accused was not entitled to a trial. Their possessions and their lives became automatically and irrevocably forfeit. Interestingly, the first accusations were made *against* those *in* the Imperial Court!

The libraries in Antioch and elsewhere were burned on the assumption they contained magical texts. Apparently, someone did not want them to be readily available. However, it was rumoured that such books were removed *prior* to the burning. In short, any pagan idea or *any* form of magical practice became controlled. Not suppressed, but controlled! If one even *argued* against dogma, they ran the risk of being accused -- that is, unless they wore greenish brown robes.

Incidentally, Valens became Emperor one year later in 375.

LADDER OF KNIVES

1

Kirghiz Steppes 315 C.E.

"Celestial spirits, sister Märküt,
Ye with the mighty copper talons,
    keeper of the tiger's claw!
Copper talon is the moon's making,
And the moon's beak is of ice and wind;
    Rear your head and spread thy mighty wings,
Like a thread is thy long serpent tail,
    Hide the moon with wing of west,
And the sun with wing of east,
    Thou, the mother of the nine eagles,
Who strayest not, flying through the Yaik,
    Come to me and sing your song!
Come, allow me the sight in my right eye,
Take me by my right shoulder!"

    The old baqca Mampüi listened as the young man sang the words that he had taught him. He listened very carefully because his student, of necessity, had not only to be able to distinguish between the subtle tonal variances of the words, he had to also be able to *exactly* duplicate the sounds with his voice. The slightest variation would have *disastrous* results.

    Mampüi thought to himself as his student was about to complete his song, he is good, very good. He has learned well. He took one last look around the crowded yurt where they sat and noticed that the space had begun to fill with a smoky mist. Even though it was bitterly cold outside and the wind was making a shrill whistling sound, inside was very warm.

    Suddenly, it was quiet, except for the wind. His student had finished the song and he looked at his master who returned his gaze. Their eyes met and the student knew that he had done well for he saw, in the eyes of the old man, approval. The old man, in turn, saw in his student's eyes a wisdom and a capability of their ancient past. It is odd, he thought, that this young man has deep blue eyes. He must truly be descended from Pouie, the owl, and born from the age of air.

"It shall not be long," Mampüi said breaking the silence. "Soon he will come and take us to the House of Bai Ülgän."

His student nodded in response.

Suddenly, the wind stilled and both the young and old man felt the familiar tugging sensation in the solar plexus. The flap of the yurt opened and both saw the huge figure of an eagle with a man's head. Tengere Kaira Khan reached out with his right coppery talon and grasped the young man's right shoulder. With his other talon, he grasped the old man's right shoulder. Upon his touch, both men saw the yurt disappear as all three soared. The man eagle's wings were so vast that the two men could neither see the sun nor the moon. The earth nor the sky. They knew only that they ascended.

Suddenly, they were alone. They each stood on a world they had been to before on many occasions. But it was the first time that they stood here as a result of the young man's singing.

"Look around you and remember this place," said Mampüi breaking the silence, "this shall be your home for a long, long time."

The young man looked around. He stood in a strange world. The earth was black, slick, and hard as rock. It was clearly made of obsidian. The sky was an emerald green which occasionally flashed with the palest of yellowish lights that swirled and danced creating pleasing patterns. It was always twilight in this world. Perhaps a bit darker, appearing even darker still because of the black and green combination of earth and sky. There was no moon, but this world had, prophetically, two suns. Suns seen as mere specks in the sky because of their extreme distance.

He knew where he was, of course. He had been here several times, but only for short durations. Perhaps for only a few brief moments at a time. From his home, so far away, he would look up into the sky and see the hunter and his dog as they chased the seven sisters. This world, he knew, was hidden in the belt of that great star system. From here, however, the other stars in the sky took strange and unrecognisable forms. They had different stories and songs. He must learn them all.

He turned to look behind where he stood and saw a small hut made out of that same black earth rock. This was new. It hadn't been here before. He looked at himself, naked but for the marks of ash -- ash made from the sacred fir he had prepared and placed upon himself back at that other world he knew as the earth. Back in the old man's yurt. His long black hair hung well past his shoulders and a few strands of it were braided so as to hold an owl's feather on the left side. He also wore the necklace of wolves' teeth that the old man had taken off himself and placed over his head for the first time only moments before. When he did, it sent chills up and down his spine. He looked at Mampüi, his teacher, and he saw an old man. Tired, but still filled with the life that wisdom brings. They both entered the hut and sat down.

2

"Your young life," Mampüi began, "has seen twenty summers. The last nine summers you have lived and been taught by myself the ways of our ancient forebears. When you were very young, your mother and father gave you over to me so that you might become a baqca. Do you remember your parents?"

The young man nodded because he knew he would not be allowed to speak. But, he thought to himself, I can barely remember them and try as I might, I cannot recall the name by which they called me.

"Listen carefully, my student, for you must remember this last story very precisely."

The old man dropped five small stones that he had been holding onto the ground in front of where he sat. He continued:

"The words of the song that you sang to summon the tutelary spirit that brought us to this world also tells you the story of your heritage. You sang the song of the first shamaness, the young girl who lay beneath a sacred ash, the Great World Tree, and there copulated with Tengere Kaira Khan."

The student recalled the story that every child was taught by the tribal elders.

"You know that she bore two daughters," Mampüi continued, "but only select baqcas know that she also bore nine sons. Nine eagles. You are the ninth and last son in that lineage."

The young man hadn't heard this before and began to listen more attentively.

"Each son lives for one hundred and four summers, so it was over nine hundred summers ago that our clan, the clan of the eagle began. Your eighth brother will die five summers hence."

His student nodded in understanding.

"The gods of the West gave man the gift of shamaning so that we could combat the evil of the gods of the East. So that we could heal the sick brought to us by their diseases. So that we could retrieve the souls of the dead that were tied and taken to the underworld. We were taught how to untie those putrid knots which bound those unfortunate souls of the dead to evil. We were taught the attributes of goodness so that we could combat the forces of evil ...

"... Shamaning was taught to many people and soon many clans were formed. The clans of the wolf, the bear, the egret, and many more. Within two hundred summers, shamanism had spread to all of our lands. Even across the frozen North and into new lands far to the East. Truly, our people came to us for help. They came to us for our wisdom."

The young man knew this well. He had been taught well.

Mampüi then said, "But many baqcas soon began to swell with the pride of their achievements. They became arrogant and kept themselves apart from the people they served. They began to teach their gifts without prudence by accepting into their numbers those with unqualified hearts. They accepted into their midst the sons and daughters of fathers who held positions of importance. It wasn't long before the arts of healing were lost to the art of politics and only those of influence could ever hope to become a baqca. Those of power then began to assert that power over the people. The people then began to believe, not what was in their hearts, but what they were told to believe. Truly, the evil gods of the East learned and manifested that deceit in the world of man."

The young baqca nodded with understanding. He also knew in his heart that this did not happen to the clan of the eagle. We had remained pure.

"The fifth son of the eagle was indeed a very wise and very proficient baqca. He was capable of travelling the fibres of the net of the universe, not only through space, but also through time. He travelled forward through the fabric of time the distance of twenty two hundred summers and there saw many wondrous yet dangerous things."

The young man had not heard this before and vowed to himself that he would remember and savour every word.

"He conceived a plan to counter the evil gods and subsequently marked his vision on sacred stones. Twenty two stones there are and each stone tells the story and identifies the objective that we are to achieve over the space of one hundred summers. Twenty two hundred passings around the sun in all. It will take that long to counter the deceit of the evil gods."

Mampüi then pointed to the corner of the hut and said, "there, in the pouch are those stones. They have been safe here for nearly four hundred summers."

His student looked to where his teacher pointed, and he saw.

"Your task is to see and to learn of those visions and to ensure that our objectives are achieved. When you leave this place five summers hence, you are to form a secret society of nine qualified baqcas who will perpetuate our plan throughout the centuries. Always will the number of baqcas in this society be nine. They will be replaced as others die. They will represent the nine sons of the eagle Tengere Kaira Khan, our father."

"You, my student, are the ninth son of the eagle whose wife is your mother. Your sisters are Pouie the owl and Kaltak the wolf."

The young man nodded in understanding. His heart pounded as he heard his teacher's words.

"I have taught you all that I can," said Mampüi. "There is still much more that you must learn, but it must come from within your heart. You will either succeed or fail. To fail is to die. To die is to allow the evil gods of the East to take possession of our souls. Listen very carefully of what you are to do."

His student listened.

"For five summers you are to remain in this hut in this secluded world. You may never venture outside nor may you ever utter a sound. You must remain in the silence. You are to learn of the visions of the sacred stones so that you may teach of their importance to those of your society that you form. You must also, on your own, learn to see the true fabric of the universe. To know where each fibre leads and to learn how to travel upon them. If you fail to learn this, you will die here."

The young man nodded in understanding.

"You must also learn the final song of your training which will take you to Bai Ülgän. If he accepts you as the son of his son, he will give you a name by which you will be known. Only when you sing the song may a sound leave your lips. Do you understand?"

He nodded.

"I shall then make you a deathwalker. Lie upon your back."

He did.

Mampüi then picked up the five deathwalking stones lying on

the ground in front of him and placed one on the forehead of his student, one on each palm, and one on each leg. He then started to sing. His words were soothing. They had a hypnotic effect on the young man which helped to ease the pain as the stones burned their way into his body.

The young man wanted to scream as the searing heat of the stones coursed through his body as if they were his blood. But he didn't. After what seemed to be agonising hours, his teacher spoke:

"For forty days you may not eat. Instead, you are to place one drop from the liquid in this goat skin onto your tongue each day after you awake. Then for forty days you are to also eat what your sisters bring you. You will never see them as they will bring your sustenance while you sleep. When the goat skin is dry, five summers will have passed. Pray that you have learned."

With that, Mampüi left.

The young man lay upon the black floor in a solitude that would be unbearable to anyone other than a deathwalker.

3

Orion's Belt -- 320 C.E.

By the time he had half finished the goat skin, the young man had seen the fibres that made up the fabric of the universe. They were thin silvery threads that looked like the silk of a spider web. Except that they were about the thickness of his little finger. He learned that he could make them appear, or rather, learn to see them at will. He could see the entire weave of the shimmering strands as he looked past the door into the heavens. Or, at will he could make one appear that connected two different places or two different times. The fabric of the universe was like a net cast out over the sky and which collected all the stars into its space.

The twenty two sacred stones also had their own unique weave. He had learned to understand them and marvelled at the abilities of his brother.

But now, he had other concerns. The goat skin had been dry for nine sleeps and he had no idea of what he was to do next. Then suddenly, he began to sing. He heard his voice for the first time in a long while. He listened as if someone else sang the song:

"Lord Mergen, to whom the ladder leads,
Bai Ülgän with the three flocks that is one,
    Blue sky has appeared,
Blue sky that is seen!
    Blue cloud, has flown away,
Blue sky cannot be reached,
    White sky is far beyond,
Watering place too far away!
    Bai Ülgän, thrice exalted, once perceived,
Whom the moon's knife blade spares,
    Who uses the horse's hoof!
    Thou didst create all men, Ülgän,
All that make a noise around us.
All cattle do not forsake, Ülgän!
    Spare us from great misfortune.
Let us withstand the Evil One!
    Allow not körmös the darkened maggot,
send us not into his lair!
    Thou who the starry heaven's veil
Hast shimmered a thousand times,
Condemn not my sins!"

As he finished his song, an owl appeared outside his door. He picked up the twenty two stones and walked outside. Before him appeared a bluish thread, a bridge to another state, and he jumped upon it thereby travelling to a new world. He knew that this thread, this bridge, was indeed one of the eighty one branches of the Great World Tree. He had solved the puzzle.

At the end of the bridge was a world of no substance. Only a mist of bluish haze. He floated in that ether and heard the thunder of the voice of his grandfather:

"You," boomed the voice of Bai Ülgän, "deathwalker, ninth son of the wife of the eagle, are a baqca. You are of the sky and as such are to be named Tengri."

His name was uttered. It was heard. Tengri then made the fibre that would take him to his home. As it appeared, he jumped upon the shimmering thread and was suddenly standing outside the yurt of his teacher.

4

Kirghiz Steppes -- 320 C.E.

It was winter when Tengri returned home. It was bitterly cold and he shivered in his nakedness.

He hurriedly opened the flap and stepped through. What he saw did not surprise him. Upon his death bed lay his old teacher Mampüi tended by a young woman who Tengri had known five summers before when she was a child of eleven. His teacher had begun her training and now he knew that she would be his first student.

Mampüi looked into Tengri's eyes and pronounced his name. After which, his eyes closed and Tengri watched as the spirit of his teacher soared in its journey to the land of the dead. It had been freed of all knots. Oddly, at that same moment, Tengri also felt another death. He felt the infusion of the essence, the wisdom, and the experiences of his eight brothers. The sons of the eagle.

Tengri's student and first recruit into the new secret society wrapped a blanket around her teacher and began to weave him clothing of the wool of a camel stitched into the hide of a wolf. The next morning they performed the funeral rites for Mampüi but did not mourn his passing.

Several moons later when summer arrived and along with it

the sweltering heat and hordes of flies, Tengri began the ritual of descent and had to break through seven pudaks to find what he sought. With revulsion at the abyssimal depths of evil, the fifth sacred stone revealed to him what had been seen by his fifth brother. Tengri sang:

> "Foul creatures be not here,
>   Writhing creatures slither not here,
> You darkened maggot of chaos,
>   Where did you come from?"

Tengri did not travel the fibres because the net he wove connected two times and not two places. He could not *physically* walk this type of dream. He could only simply observe a future discussion between three strangely dressed men in a strange yurt. Although he did not speak their tongue, he understood their motives, their deceit, and their conspiracy. He learned the names of Athanasius, Ossius of Cordoba, and Nicholas of Myra. He retched in revulsion and knew that he must later meet and talk to this man they referred to as Constantine.

Tengri saw the man known as Ossius shiver and knew the man had felt his presence. It is strange, he thought, the fibres that connect the realities of the past with the future create a third reality that becomes the present. We experience it as if it were truly happening. I have learned the secret of prophecy. In the weave of the universe, past and future are only one event.

5

It had taken Tengri two summers and twelve moves with his people to find an additional seven baqcas whose abilities were real and whose hearts were pure. It had required the assistance of his two sisters to help make the necessary choices. It had taken an additional summer and one winter to teach and train them in the ways of the new art. Now, the secret cell was complete. Now, the initiations were over.

Yesterday, each member of their cell had parted company. They had said their goodbyes and travelled home to be with their respective peoples. Each was tasked with a specific objective, and Tengri knew each would succeed. His choices were good.

Only he and his student remained together for he still had much to teach her. They sat together in his yurt and both were quiet. Perhaps they both thought the same thoughts. That only on the rarest of occasions would all nine of them ever be together on this plane again. And only then to select a new member of their cell as the result of a death. That meant that one of their number would never be seen again in this world by the others. There was sadness in that thought because they all had become the closest of friends. A friendship that would endure the conflicts of their tribes.

But, it was decided, all nine would meet on the eve of each new season. They would travel the fibres, the silvery threads to that remote world in the hunter's belt and there discuss their purpose and share their wisdom so that each could become stronger. That strange world was chosen as their meeting place because they could never take the chance of being seen together in this world. In fact, during the past months, their meetings had been in secret. No one knew of their association with each other. After all, it wasn't strange that a baqca would disappear for long periods of time. He had been absent from his people for five summers and no one thought it out of the ordinary. His people, their people, accepted the strange ways of his kind without question. After all, a sacred spirit journey did take time.

Yes, Tengri thought, we have done well. Each member had varying abilities and talents. But only three, including himself, were able to travel the woven threads of the universe without difficulty. But fortunately, everyone had learned to travel the weave to Tengri's spirit home without getting hopelessly lost. That is the problem with the net, thought Tengri, one must be careful to understand the flow of the fibre. Without proper understanding, without the proper feel, it is easy to become lost and trapped in the web.

His eyes turned to look at his student. She had grown to become a beautiful woman now nineteen summers old. She was presently occupied with cleaning the goose Tengri had hunted that morning and which would soon be their meal. She had chosen to remain with Tengri for a few extra days before returning to her own yurt on the outskirts of her people's wintering place. She had constantly chided Tengri about his self imposed seclusion. After all, their people were the same people. She had asked him on many occasions why he would not move closer to them. She was concerned that one day their people would move to a new place without his knowledge and he would not be able to find them. If that happens, Tengri remembered saying, then it will happen.

Tengri admired her beauty; her long flowing black hair; her eyes, which, like his, were extremely rare in colour and shape when compared to the peoples of their own and surrounding tribes; but unlike his, they were an emerald green. Most likely, thought Tengri as he watched his student work, she is a descendant of the Old Ones -- the tall, light skinned, fair haired, and round eyed people who had come from the West with their strange arts of pattern weaving, smithing, healing through the use of herbs and tattooing needles, and who had primarily settled, lived, flourished, and died far to the South in the deserts of the Takla Makan. That was so long ago that many of the scarcest and most fragmented of songs about their life had been long forgotten even to the memories of the memories of the oldest of story tellers. But, those memories still persist, thought Tengri, to those desert travellers who know how to listen to the stories the ghosts of the Old Ones still sing to the winds when traversing the lands where they once lived ...

But even more striking than long forgotten remembrances, when Tengri looked at his student's face he mostly saw the world of his spirit home. He could clearly see the colours and the depths of intensity. Her body was strong but not muscular. Rather, it was thin and wiry. It reminded him of a doe. Her spirit was free, her body, quick and although she was thin, her hips were rounded which would make child bearing less difficult. And, although her breasts were full, they were not large. He could see her breasts clearly, now that she had taken her shirt off to work, and noticed their firmness. Tengri knew that firmness would hold well into her old age.

As he watched he wondered why she had never married. Most women her age already had four or five children and had lost two or three to the harshness of their existence. Indeed, she was a shamaness which meant that people had a tendency to fear rather than accept. But not all the young men were like that. Tengri wondered if she would stay unmarried and, as she aged, be referred to as an old hag like most shaman women.

No, I think not, thought Tengri. She may never marry but she will never be thought of as an old hag. She is too beautiful and too well loved by her people. At nineteen summers, she is an accomplished healer. Better than myself. Even better than Mampüi.

He noticed her nipples beginning to harden and he suddenly realised that he had been staring at them while he contemplated. He looked up at her eyes and saw she was looking into his own. She had noticed his stare and she blushed.

"What is it that you think about that causes you to watch my breasts?" she asked.

Tengri, not knowing whether to be embarrassed or not replied, "your ability to heal." That should change the subject, he figured.

"I did not know one could heal with the bosom," she said matter-of-factly. "Is there some secret that you have yet to teach me? Is there some magical power that my breasts hold that cause your notice?"

She realised as she finished her sentence that she may have betrayed her innermost protected secret. The secret which hid the reason why she never married or paid attention to the wooing of the young men. The secret that would reveal her deep love for this man who looked at her ...

"Within your bosom, your heart, is a rare existence," he said interrupting her innermost thoughts, "which holds the secret of your art. It is called love ..."

He *knows!* She panicked as she continued with her thoughts. She blushed more deeply and felt her nipples harden even more.

"... a deep, eternal spiritual love which transcends all worlds. That is the secret of your art. That is what makes you a remarkable healer."

She sighed quietly to herself. Perhaps he didn't make the connection. She changed the subject, "Tell me, Tengri, tell me again how you chose my name."

Tengri noted that she asked this question often. Wanting to hear the same story over and over as if each time it was told something new would be revealed. She is indeed perceptive, he thought, and he began to speak as she requested:

"When the mother of the nine sons of the eagle died, she never knew that she had nine sons. She never knew that their spirits were born at that same time as her two daughters. At that time their spirits did not take human form and thusly weren't seen by her. Rather, the spirits infused their essences into the sacred tree under which she dreamt of her husband."

"Did her sons know that they were alive?" she asked.

"Not as we know life. I am the ninth son and I did not know of life until my spirit was released by the tree and entered into the body of an infant. Rather, our life before birth was a spiral of ever moving force captured so as not to be prematurely born into the wrong bodies. We were destined to wait for the proper moment to manifest.

"My oldest brother," Tengri continued, "was not born into an infant's body. Rather, a wanderer passed by the tree at dawn after our mother died. The tree spoke to him and asked if he would allow his own spirit to be released so that my brother could enter.

Since the man wandered in loneliness at the loss of his family and saw no joy in his life, he asked if he were to do so, could he know peace. It was agreed and my brother came into life with no memory but that of shamaning.

"He then burned the body of his mother and rubbed her ashes onto the blade of his knife. He then carved a spiral groove into the tree thereby mixing her essence with that of ours. For the first time we knew of our mother and she knew of us. It was truly an act of kindness and of love for our brother to do that. The groove made into the tree is called 'Tapti' and that is the source of your name. It represents the second act of ascension."

Tapti was always moved to tears as she heard this story and now her eyes were moist. Somehow, she thought, I do not know why, but there is a depth of beauty in these words that I do not fully understand.

She leaned forward so that her face was close to his. So that she could see clearly into the depths of his eyes. So that she could peer into his soul, and she whispered ever so quietly so as to be certain that only he could hear and so her words would never ride upon the wind. "What is it that you have failed to tell me, Tengri? What is that secret locked deeply in the depths of your soul? Why have you chosen as my name, Tapti? How do I relate to that act?"

Tengri then said something he never thought he would ever tell her, "Because, Tapti, to me you are the manifestation of that love. In you I see that love. To you, I give my love."

Tapti understood what he felt. Again, she whispered, "there is Truth in names and I feel the magical power of their sounds. My name flows through my being. My name is me and I, my name. I can feel your love and I return ... no, I *have* returned that love to you many times over. I have no choice but to share my life with you."

Tapti and Tengri spoke of many things well into the night. They never ate the goose she was preparing for their supper. She never put her shirt back on while they talked. It felt appropriate that they remain as they were. It was almost dawn before they tired and their thoughts turned to sleep. But it was almost midday before sleep took them. As she stood to ready her bed, Tengri rose and took her face into his hands. He kissed her ... and removed her remaining clothing. They shared the same bed and he had taken her as his wife.

The following winter, Tapti bore their first child.

6

Kirghiz Steppes -- 325 C.E.
Even though Tengri and Tapti had married, very little had changed with their lifestyle. Tengri remained secluded for the most part and had refused to move closer to his people. Tapti, on the other hand, had duties to perform and on occasion lived in her yurt with their daughter. But those occasions were rare and were generally timed to coincide with her husband's sometimes lengthy spirit journeys.

She had just returned home from a month's absence and saw Tengri sitting outside their yurt. It was early summer and pleasantly cool that day. She rushed to greet him.

After their kiss, she said, "You seem troubled, share with me your concerns."

"I have just returned from my spirit home. I felt that it was necessary to leave the sacred stones there where they could be safe."

Tapti had intuited that the stones were not present and said, "do you foresee danger?"

"I have done little else but to contemplate the weave of those stones for the past two summers. We now live in the era of the fifth stone and its foretold event has started today."

"Does that event coincide with your descent through seven pudaks of five summers ago?" she asked.

"Yes. In the West, the evil god of the körmös has commenced

his war. He has chosen to fight in that faraway land because those people have no baqcas to recognise the deceitful evil. The people there are ignorant of the evil god's ways and do not know how to protect themselves."

"Tengri, I fear that you will travel to that strange land that you have spoken about. I fear that their ways will be a danger to you and to our people."

"Yes," he responded, "I must go but not until the second full moon. I must tell this king they call Constantine of the treachery ..."

Tapti interrupted, "their customs, their language forbids understanding. How will you convince him?"

"I will first send to him my sister Pouie. She will weave into his dreams the visions of both the twelfth and the unnumbered sacred stones. He will first see the results of wickedness and to know of them in his heart. I will then appear and show him the vision of the fifth stone. He will understand."

"You have already discussed this with your sisters?" Tapti asked.

"I have. They discussed this matter with me and we agree that this is the best course to take. And, my dear Tapti, I have learned the intricacies of the strange pattern that the stones weave. I know of the substance of which they were made and I know how to journey upon their spirit. Unlike other fibres of the net, their force has a unique flowing quality that adapts to that with which it comes into contact. Its nature is deceptive, but it is more real than reality itself. Its world is Truth."

Tapti and Tengri never parted as they waited for the proper moment. That moment which was close at hand when the fibres crossed and touched to form a reality as real as the spirit home from which he came.

Until it was time for him to leave, they stayed together and concerned themselves with their love. Their second child, a son, was conceived.

7

Tapti awoke before dawn and saw her husband standing naked peering outside into the darkness. Instinctively she reached over to check on their daughter and then sleepily remembered that the day before her sister had come and taken her so as to watch over her for the next few days. Silently, she rose and walked over to Tengri, hugging him from behind.

"Is it time?" She asked, already knowing that it was.

"Yes. We must prepare."

Tapti was worried. Several days before, Tengri had spoken to her of his concerns. He told her that he had never ridden the fibres over such a distance on this plane. It was one thing to travel into spirit worlds because it was only the spirit that travelled, not the body. Even travelling to spirit worlds in other physical universes such as the belt of the hunter, where the body also journeyed was different. There, the threads weren't as complicated and initiation had purified their home in that world. There was a mutual attraction, a perfectly balanced equilibrium. Here, so many variables had to be taken into consideration. There were so many disruptive forces interweaving through and influencing the natural harmonious fabric of the universe. It would be easy to move onto the wrong thread or to not notice its subtle shift as it accommodated for an interfering energy.

She knew that Tengri's dance had to be perfect. He had to be lighter than the clouds in the sky and more powerful than the wind of a storm. To muster such energy, she thought, and to keep the ability to direct it would be very draining to him physically, emotionally, and spiritually. She remembered when her husband had taught her and the other baqcas of the net and how to travel its threads. It was extremely difficult and only two others had been able to demonstrate a small degree of proficiency. She was not one of them. Yes, she thought, all could make it to their special place, but for *that* journey, one *only* had to stay on a *single* thread. She was worried ...

As if reading her mind, Tengri interrupted her thoughts. "If one rides a fibre the distance of an arrow's flight, one must balance a hundred shifts in the fabric. If one fails to balance even a single of those shifts, one would fail to reappear at the desired location. Perhaps, to *never* reappear due to becoming hopelessly lost in the ether as each wrong move would cause tenfold as many times a new pudak."

He continued, "The distance I must travel will be a challenge. I have no idea how many shifts I will encounter. I have never travelled a distance greater than two flights of an arrow."

"Could you not break your journey to make it safer?" She asked.

"No. Each break will use half my energy. I would be exhausted and would have to rest a day and a night before I would even lose sight of my yurt."

He turned around and looked into her eyes. She saw, in their blueness, the faint flashes of silver light and knew that already he was seeing into other worlds. Without a word, she broke the embrace and began to prepare. He went outside and made a fire so he could burn the bark of the fir tree.

8

The sun had just cleared the horizon when she walked out of their yurt. She looked at the sky. There were no clouds; she felt no wind. Already it was hot and she thought she heard the god of the sky say that the heat would climb to unbearable heights before the sun reached midday. But she knew it was not him that spoke but only her own thoughts that she heard. Still, she knew that the day would be long, hot, and dry.

She carried with her in one hand the special wolf skin pouch she had made for journeys such as these. It was special by virtue of the fact that it had no metal ornaments and was sewn together by a special weave that had once been unique to the Old Ones. She had packed it, smiling at the thought of what might have happened had she forgotten to place his clothes inside. There he would be, standing before a great king inside of a marvellous palace swarming with hordes of people. And there he would be, naked! It wouldn't even bother him, she thought, but then she thought of all those strange women ... She checked the pouch again just in case.

She also packed some familiar food -- dried horse meat, because she had no idea what tastes such strange people would have and she was concerned that Tengri eat well. She packed a skin of water as well as a larger skin of kymyz. Perhaps, she thought, Tengri and this king would become friends and would want to sit, well into the night, drinking. And finally, she packed three small clay offering bowls she had made as gifts for the king's wives -- she hoped that he didn't have more than three. In her other hand, she carried her kobuz.

She looked at Tengri sitting by the fire. He was holding his knife -- the knife he had fashioned from the black rock of his spirit world. She took pride in the fact that her husband was a master stone smith, a flaker of stone, and had made many things. She knew that the hardness and sharpness of that strange stone would protect him in case of danger ... and then suddenly, as if the sound of thunder had just been sent racing across the heavens to wake the gods from their reverie, Tapti heard as Tengri began his chant:

"Kagak! Kagak! I am here Kam."

Good, Tapti thought, he is taking a helping spirit with him. The goose has entered into his body and can be called forth to carry him in case he gets lost.

It was time to begin, so she sat in front of him with her legs crossed so that their knees touched. She looked into his eyes. The colour blue was almost imperceptible because of the intensity of the flashing silver lights that shone in its stead. A normal person would not see that, of course, but she could because she, too, was a baqca. She knew that Tengri was now seeing into many worlds simultaneously. This world, Tapti knew, would be seen by him as a dim twilight. He would not notice the intense brightness of the sun nor would he feel its heat. But *she* most certainly would!

Tengri sang:

> "udesi-burkhan, guardian of the gate,
>   breathe open to the sky, I am here Kam!
> I have climbed a blade,
>   I have reached a realm,
> I have attained to tapti's breath,
>   I have risen beyond the moon!
> Beak of ice, talon of copper, sister märküt,
>   Spread far thy wing,
> The sun sees not, the moon is dark!
> I have been reborn through the ground above,
>   I have climbed beyond the blue cloud,
> I can see below, where all is darkened,
>   I am here Kam!"

Tapti watched as her husband entered into a deeper trance. She swayed to his rhythm. She, too, entered into the second state but would go no further. It was imperative that she remain in contact with this realm. Her threads must remain attached. She listened as he continued to sing and rise higher and higher. As in a dream, his voice was far, far away ...

"I am here Kam! "

His eyes glowed with another sight of another place. She watched the flight of a goose. She saw the leap of a stag. She heard the screech of an eagle. She felt the breath of a wolf and touched the wing of an owl. She was going much deeper than she should, and could not stop.

He touched her. She felt his finger slide as would a ghost across her breast. He was marking her with the sacred ash. Her skin tingled and it crawled with shivers ...

> "I am here Kam!
> I have risen,
> See below, all is splintered ... "

As he sang, he marked her face, her arms and legs, her back, buttocks, and hips. She in turn marked him. She knew his marks well and made them properly for they were his, as were hers, protection in the world of the dead. They were disguises so that other spirits would see them as spirits also; so that they would not be interfered with as they travelled their worlds. She had finished but then became vaguely aware that he was doing something new. He had taken his knife and cut into his palm allowing it to bleed freely. He then cut her between her breasts and touched her there, thereby allowing their blood to mingle.

He is bonding our souls through eternity, she realised. She knew she would be proud of the scar that would remain.

He began to walk to the West, chanting as he went. She followed after picking up the pouch and the kobuz. She remained nine steps behind him at all times. She anticipated they would be walking all day and all night until he found the sacred place and the thread that he sought. She knew that when they stopped, she would sit and sing the song that he had taught her and play that haunting melody with her stringed kobuz that she knew so well. She would play it for three days and three nights until he returned -- *if* he returned. If he did not, she would die there. Perhaps she would die anyway, she thought as she walked. She knew she would be unprotected from the harshness of the sun. She could not eat nor drink. She dare not stop the ceremony. It was his protection in case he got lost. She walked on. She was deeper into her trance than she should have been. It was hard for her to concentrate. She couldn't help it. His power had overcome her.

9

The Buryat warrior sat atop his pony. He had been travelling hard all day and both he and his pony were drenched with sweat. He had given up trying to swat away the flies and allowed them to crawl over his face unmolested. Only occasionally he cursed when one bit him -- mistaking the rider for the horse. By the smell, the flies couldn't tell the difference.

He surveyed the steppes to the East. Now that the sun was behind him and would set in an hour, the lighting allowed him excellent visibility. The light was in his favour but the heat was not. Today, he thought, was hotter than normal. It would be a scorching summer.

He patted his pony. He knew it had served him faithfully this day and realised that it needed rest. But he also knew, even though it was small, it was also extremely strong and well suited for this harsh environment. It could continue to run until it dropped dead from exhaustion or until it wore its hooves down to its fetlocks. He decided to walk to the watering place, about an hour away, to allow his horse to cool down so it would not drink itself to death.

He began to turn to the West, but out of the corner of his eye, he thought he saw something in the distance far away. He looked closer. Indeed! There is something out there, he thought to himself, this day may not be a waste after all.

He cautiously approached making sure the sun was behind his back. It was the luck of the gods, he thought, I'll be almost upon them before they even know I exist. At least within bow shot range. He was deadly with the bow and he knew it! That is why the chieftain usually sent him out to scout the borders between Buryat and Kazak-Kirghiz lands. The two tribes had been feuding for three summers and he, personally, had killed ten Kazak-Kirghiz scum who had the misfortune to cross over into his territory.

As he approached closer he saw that it was two figures walking. They were without horses. He knew this would be easy.

Closer still and he could make out that it was a man and a woman.

"By the gods of the sky," he said to his horse, "the sun must have touched their heads. They're naked!"

With that, he kicked his pony and at a dead run, he readied his bow. One arrow is all I need, he thought, the man dies and the woman will live until I am satisfied.

As he closed in upon them and was about ready to let loose his arrow, he suddenly caused his horse to veer to the left with a slight pressure with his right knee. He circled around them making sure that he kept a proper distance. He put away his bow and slowed his horse to a walk and maintained a distance behind the woman of about one hundred paces.

She was beautiful, he thought. He watched her naked body with intense desire. Indeed, they were Kazak-Kirghiz, but he knew that he couldn't touch them. They were baqcas and they were on a spirit walk. In fact, he thought, the man could be a deathwalker. He appeared to be marked as one, but he wasn't all that certain about Kirghiz markings.

Spirit walkers of any tribe could cross any boundaries and go anyplace where their dreams took them. No one was allowed to harm or bother them in any way. It was Law! To disrupt anyone on a sacred journey meant a sentence of death to the disrupter. No one considered such people to be trespassing while on their journeys. After all, only their physical bodies walked the earth.

The Buryat warrior knew he should leave them in peace. But, he thought, they are Kirghiz and their magic is not as powerful as Buryat. Besides, he wanted to feast his eyes on the woman. He knew that if they re-entered our world on Buryat land, he could still have her. He followed.

10

As if in a dream, Tapti saw the Buryat rider approach. She saw the energy emitted from his groin and knew what he would try if she were not in the spirit world. She also knew that Tengri saw him as well and what he would do if the rider chose to break the Law. She shuddered at the death he would feel at the release of the ghost wind.

She felt him behind her and knew he would respect the tradition. She wondered why he did not leave them in peace. She wondered why he chose to follow them and take such terrible risks. He wasn't prepared. He was not marked. Tengri would not help him and she couldn't.

Tapti soon got used to his presence and forgot about him.

11

The Buryat warrior saw them stop shortly after sunset. He decided that he would watch their ceremony. In his own tribe he had status. His mother's brother was a shaman. He could have been a shaman himself if he had wanted. But he chose not. He preferred to fight.

He watched as the longhaired man traced a circle in the ground with a black knife. He wondered what type of stone that was. He had never seen the likes of it before. He observed the woman enter the circle and walking around in a spiral toward the centre. He hoped she would stand facing him. She was beautiful. Long legged, firm breasts, beautiful face, and eyes of emerald green. He abandoned all caution and approached within a few steps of the circle. He felt that he could reach out and touch her if he wanted. Fortunately, he wasn't that careless. He knew better. He still thought that he remained in the bounds of respect for the two shaman.

The man stood at the far end of the circle facing West -- away from the warrior. The woman had placed a pouch around his neck and then returned to the centre of the circle. He was in luck. She was sitting down facing away from her companion and facing him!

He heard the haunting melody of the kobuz as she began to play and he heard the man begin to sing:

"Mighty bull of the universe, the horse of the steppe
   has shied away from your bellow!
Mighty bull, the horse trembles at your awakening!
   But I fear you not and rise above all, for I am man!
I am the man who has been gifted!
   I am the man created by the Lord of Law!
Come to me, horse of the steppe, I will listen to your wisdom!
   Appear, mighty bull of the Universe, and answer my heed!
Bai Ülgän, command my spirit skin!
   My sister, the Owl, show me my faults,
And the fibres I must travel!
   Fly before me, prepare my way!
O spirits who dwell in the West,
   May your shadow guide me on my way!
Wise Mergen, my ancestor of fearful powers, be with me!"

What was to be the last sight that the Buryat warrior ever saw, was the sudden disappearance of the Kazak-Kirghiz baqca, and then a blinding flash of light that burned the image of a spider's web into his eyes. For the rest of his life he remembered the chilling feeling of having his soul touched by the deathly cold hands of a hundred ghosts hungering for his soul. For the rest of his life he could hear the haunting melody of Tapti's song and the words she sang over and over and over again:

"Under the white sky,
Over the white cloud,
Under the blue sky,
Over the blue cloud:
Rise up to the sky, bird!"

The now blind Buryat warrior was a warrior no more. He had stumbled to his horse, mounted it, and let it find its own way home. He wished he had never laid eyes upon the two Kazak-Kirghiz baqcas.

The Buryat people have a song about a warrior who one day returned home from a hunt. He returned blind with the image of a web burnt into his eyes. They tell of his hair that had turned white and the story he told of his encounter with two spirits not of this world.

After several generations, that story changed to recount the adventures of a Buryat shaman who fought with a powerful demon and lost. Several generations after that, the story told that he had defeated the demon. In time, he became the Buryat people's greatest shaman.

But the Kazak-Kirghiz story tells of a foolish Buryat idiot who lusted after Tapti, the wife of the baqca Tengri.

12

Tengri felt the familiar tingle upon the soles of his feet as he leapt upon the thin silvery thread. In the instant body and fibre touched, he turned his head and saw Tapti sitting in the circle with her back to him. She appeared to him as if a ghost. As if he was looking at her through murky water. The water rippled, and she was gone. He couldn't shake the sense of loss.

He was now completely engulfed into the ether between all worlds. He did not exist in, nor could he see into, any of the other multitudes of worlds -- be they spirit or physical. He now existed in that space before creation and after annihilation. He was deathwalking.

Tengri quickly adjusted to his new environment. Only moments before he had felt the confusion of consciousness brought about by the awareness of multiple realities as the trancelike state consumed his intellect, thereby making it difficult to function consciously. But, his training allowed him to act with the instinct derived from the wisdom of intuitive insight, thereby bringing a condition of clarity that was unfettered by physical, psychic, or emotional densities. It was a type of clarity he wished all could have while existing in physical reality, but he also knew that could not be as such clarity would drive the uninitiated insane.

He surveyed his environment, comparing it to his observations of the night sky. He thought of this world as being similar to the blackness of night. He thought of it as being what he imagined it would be like far above the sky where there existed a large, deep, and black void between the points of silver lights. Only, he knew that this place was not the depths of space, but rather, the depths of nothingness. The depths of the void.

In the night sky, Tengri knew that the hunter and his dog chased the seven sisters across the heavens. He also knew that the hunter was being hunted. He was being stalked by the scorpion. He knew that they were real entities living in their own dream reality and within their own span of time. A time which could *only* be understood by the gods and observed by men.

My lifespan, thought Tengri, is brief, compared to the seemingly eternal existence of the hunter. But here, it is different. There was no hunter and his dog. There was no scorpion. Indeed, there were no stars. Here, he thought, there was only blackness, myself, the fibres whose weave connects all realities known as existence to each other, and the son of one sister -- the messenger of God.

Tengri also understood that such concepts as time and space did not exist in this essence. There was only a type of motion that caused an illusory sense of time to manifest to an observer. He knew it was that illusion which fought his spirit for possession of his soul. A perpetual war which existed in an attempt to defeat his soul. To steal it, to mould it, to obliterate and then absorb it, into the non-reality that existed before existence and which was the stuff used by God to create.

Movement! Thought Tengri. One really couldn't tell. I feel as if I stand still. I feel as if the blackness *is* stillness, and it is only the silvery threads which dance, sway, and dart all about me.

He knew that the motion was not really motion. But he didn't know how to accurately describe it. He knew only how to dance with it. He knew that his sense of time was not *really* time and it only appeared as such. Perhaps he only described it that way because he had the experience of entering and leaving this void, thereby knowing that time had passed in his world while he was gone. Certainly, while in the void there was definitely no sense of time. It was only his memories of a vague dream of worldly reality that allowed him to think such nonsensical thoughts.

Suddenly, he jumped, danced, and alighted. He had sensed a fluctuation, a change in the nature of the thread on which he stood. He sensed it before it happened and took the appropriate steps. He watched as the thread split, following its natural weave. He watched as the portion on which he once stood disappeared off in another direction. He did not know where it would finish *its* dance.

Tengri listened with the soles of his feet:

> *Under the white sky,*
> *Over the white cloud;*
> *Under the blue sky,*
> *Over the blue cloud:*
> *Rise up to the sky, bird!*

He had landed on the proper thread! He was glad he had taken the proper precautions and in his ritual of making the woven pattern that would take him to his destination, had decided to have Tapti sing. Her singing at the point of origin of the thread he wove, enabled him to feel the vibrations of her sacred song, thereby knowing he had remained on the right thread. He had planned to be gone for three days so had asked Tapti to remain in the second state for that length of time, continuously repeating her song. This would allow him the security of knowing he followed the correct pattern to his destination, as well as following the correct weave home.

Tengri had never previously remained in the state of deathwalking for more than a few moments. Though when in that state, as far as he knew, it could have been eternity. To travel physically through this world, he estimated that it would only take a short time to walk the distance. That is, if he didn't get lost. When he travelled the distance of the flight of two arrows, the *real* time it took was less than the blink of an eye. But the *appeared* time in the void was the time it took to leap twenty four times and to remain on each thread long enough to regain one's focus and contemplate the next jump.

That time when he remained in the void for the briefest of moments was during his period of apprenticeship under the guidance of Mampüi. Then, it *seemed* as if he were dancing here for half a day.

This would be a long journey, he thought....

... another leap, dance, and landing. He felt ... *Rise up to the sky, bird!*

Immediately, again ... *Under the white sky,*

"Yes, all is well," he said, but there was no sound that any ears could hear.

Then Tengri thought, there is no real point in having Tapti sing. For either I will remain within the proper weave or I will not. If I do not, then I will be lost and it is doubtful that I would find the correct fibre within the three days -- or even until she dies as

I know she would. She would continue to sing until she died or I returned.

He vowed to himself that he would be certain not to stay more than three days. Less, if possible.

Tengri then allowed himself to continue with his previous contemplations. He compared the ease that it took to travel to the hunter's belt and compared it with the present difficulty. To travel to his spirit home, a special sacred ritual of making wove a single thread that would never split or follow its own pattern. It was a secret thread that only those who knew *his* True Name could ever see or travel upon. It was a single thread that never interfered with or intercepted other fibres.

However, to travel the *natural* threads as Tengri was now doing, involved an understanding of the natural flow of an *endless* number of fibres. All of which danced and intermingled with each other.

He recalled Mampüi's teaching when he described the fibres as having an unique quality about them. They were like water, he had said. When a pudak, or obstacle, confronted them -- whether it be another fibre or something else -- the nature of the thread would usually follow one of two courses of action. Its energy would become confrontational thereby creating a conflict, a war of forces. If two intercepting threads *chose* a direct conflict, which fortunately was extremely rare, they would both annihilate themselves, creating an explosion which would send waves of an ethereal wind storming throughout the void.

Normally, his teacher had said, the other condition usually prevailed and was quite a common occurrence. The threads simply redirected their energies like water and flowed around each other. They would mix with each other briefly and, perhaps by their interaction, would cause each other to split into two or more threads hurtling off in different directions. Or, they would simply remain intact and continue upon their own, albeit diverted, course.

If a baqca, he had said, was able to stand apart and watch the dancing fibres from above, as perhaps a god could, he would see a beautiful pattern created by the intricate weave. That is how the various worlds were formed. Each world, each reality, adhered to the nature of each individual fibre and its innate quality. Each world manifested as a whole and would be identified in its completion as a finished garment. It was beautiful. It was *more* than beautiful!

Another shift, a dance, and landing; ... *Over the blue* ...

Tengri continued to remember his teacher's words:

The only danger, he had taught, inherent within the dance of the indirect forces playing with each other lay with the unwary deathwalker. If he did not flow with the fibre on which he walked, he would end up on the wrong thread. He would not be able to go where he intended and would not be able to find his way home unless perchance he was able to find that same thread again.

Tengri remembered asking Mampüi those long years ago when he was first being taught of the fibres of what would happen if one became lost. Mampüi had given him two examples.

First, he had said, his teacher had once become lost. But fortunately had found his way home after many experiences on many different threads. Not all threads concern themselves with our physical world manifesting as a completed garment. In fact, in comparison, only a small number do. There are threads which are ideas. There are fibres which are dreams. There are fibres that manifest as raindrops, or butterflies, or lightening, or fire. Or perhaps as diseases, death, wind, or other things which are unknown to us. Not every fibre connects onto a place where a traveller can reappear. The beauty of creation is that it abides by Law.

My teacher, he had said, was fortunate that he found the *single* fibre that would allow him to re-enter his true world and time. Even those fibres, he had discovered, that could take him to a place would not allow him to enter that place unless it was the *identical* fibre on which he departed. The reasons could be varied, he had explained. If one landed on a thread that existed almost immediately or even longer after he left, and if he were allowed to somehow get on and then off that other thread, he would find that his world would have two of him existing. Such would change the weave of the fabric. It would be an impossibility. It would be against Law.

A single thread will take a deathwalker to any world or place depending upon how the deathwalker sang the songs that would cause its weave. But only that thread would allow him to reach his destination and to find his way back home.

Mampüi had also taught him of the *golden* fibres that only allowed the threads of sight to flow upon and which disallowed the transportation of spirit or body. Tengri had remembered that it was a result of his travelling upon that quality of thread that caused him to take this journey. He had travelled into future time and saw the man called Ossius. He wondered how Ossius had felt his presence -- for *feel* it he did!

Another leap, and yes Tengri landed correctly. He felt Tapti's song ... *bird! Under the white ...*

His teacher had told him that *his* teacher managed to find the lost thread and he returned home. However, two seasons had passed while he travelled the void. And his teacher had indeed *aged* as if he had never left his world. So indeed! Time could not be escaped. We will age and we will die as our individual threads do have a determined existence.

The second instance that Tengri recalled his teacher telling him about also involved his grandfather teacher, who *also* happened to be Tengri's seventh oldest brother.

He had a student, Mampüi had said, who fell *off* the thread that they both travelled together. The student was seen grabbing onto another thread and when he did, he disappeared. He was never seen again. He had lived his life and died in the void.

Tengri wondered if he would one day find that unfortunate soul's bones, collect them, and give them a proper burial. He wondered how many lost travellers were presently existing in the void and if he would ever meet them. He wondered if it was possible.

Again, a dance properly performed ... *under the blue sky,* ...

It is strange, thought Tengri as it suddenly occurred to him, I am remembering events of long ago, but it is as if Mampüi is standing next to me and actually speaking.

Tengri recalled their discussion about conflicting fibres:

Mampüi had said that when they do conflict, a tremendous explosion occurs which creates an ethereal wind. He had responded, upon Tengri's inquiry, that on those rare occasions when such had happened, a baqca who either slept or who was in the spirit world would have a prophetic dream of a catastrophe. He would see a future or a past event, depending upon the related time fabric when the conflict occurred. And indeed! That event would or had occurred. Depending upon the strength of the forces that confronted each other and depending upon where in the fabric they collided, the nature of the physical manifestation would be determined. It could be a plague, a drought, a shaking of the earth, or even the end of the universe. It will happen one day. That is Law!

Suddenly, Tengri remembered that Mampüi had once said that ... *whether it being another fibre, or something else* ... which caused a confrontation. Tengri wished that he had asked what that something else might be. He had absolutely no idea.

However, he did know that each time a collision occurred, a demon was born. And if and when the corresponding event happened upon the earth, that demon then entered the earth reality and had to be contended with by either shamans or the poor people who would severely suffer....

Suddenly, without warning, he felt that something was happening. It wasn't wrong but there could be a potential for disaster, thought Tengri.

No -- a disaster *is* happening! He focused his entire being onto the single thread on which he rode....

13

Even though Tapti's back was to her husband, she could feel the instant he entered into the void. She could feel his gaze upon her back and she was happy that he thought of her while he was in other worlds.

She didn't realise it, but as she sang, she also thought. If she had realised she was doing so, she would have *forced* herself to concentrate her entire attention upon the single task at hand. But, she didn't and she continued to daydream as she sang and played that haunting melody on her kobuz. Dreamily, she carried on ...
"Under the white sky,"

Tapti was vaguely aware of the anguish the Buryat warrior was feeling and wondered if he now regretted his lust for her. Even though she was in a trance, she remembered only a few moments before as she was beginning to sit. She saw the eyes of the warrior widen with the desire of lust as he stared at her parted legs. He *knew,* she would be his for the taking.

At the time, she feared that his lust would cause him to break the Law. She feared the disaster that would be created as the result of the interruption of rape.

She feared no longer, for Tengri's entrance into the void caused the warrior excruciating pain. She forgot him ... *"Over the white cloud;"*

Tapti thought about the previous night. Gods! It seems so long ago since they last made love ... and she allowed herself to enter more fully into that waking dream -- the dreams by day. *"Under the blue sky,"*

She brought forth the memory of each and every sensation of the night before; each and every heart beat; each and every caress. So *vividly* did Tapti evoke those memories ... *"Over the blue cloud;"*

Tapti knew with certainty she conceived their second child last night. Even now, she could feel its life, *his* life growing inside of her … She recalled her dream after, finally, falling asleep. She dreamed of their son and that his life would be unique, different, even for a baqca.

She knew his name would be Mergen, so called after the all knowing god Mergen Tengere. Somehow she knew their son would have experiences that no one could truly understand or fully appreciate. She knew that their son would know hardship. But she also knew that he would truly be loved. And one day, after he left she and Tengri, he would always know and remember that. She *knew* it! She *felt* that truth as if it had already happened. … *"Rise up to the sky, bird!"*

Tapti felt a ripple in the thread to which she was connected. She felt a brief sense of absence as perhaps a small branch would feel when a bird left it to fly amongst the clouds. Then she felt the bird land again.

With a sigh, she knew her husband had danced as the fibre changed its course. And he safely alighted back to where he belonged. She smiled.

As she continued to sing, her thoughts again began to wander upon their own threads. She wondered if Tengri could see them. If he noticed that they flew along beside him.

Tapti knew it would only take as long as it took for a large cloud to pass by the sun on a still day, for her husband to reach that strange land. Then, for three days and three nights, she would scnse his absence while he re-entered this world so far, far away. She imagined her joy when she again felt his presence on the fibre. And then his reappearance in the circle behind her.

She knew that even if she couldn't maintain the three gruelling days of singing, it only mattered that he get to where he was going. If, upon his return, he couldn't find the proper thread, he wouldn't risk travelling the void. He would walk home.

How long would that take, she wondered? A year? It would be

lonely, but he would arrive and be surprised with a son.

During these thoughts, she had felt Tengri's change of fibres a number of times. Each time, he had landed safely. Tapti felt confident even though she hadn't even finished a second complete verse.

Her thoughts returned to her dream of their unborn son. He had a second name, she remembered. But it had strange sounds. Something like Gere-em-eyee. It must be a spirit name. Maybe even a True Name.

As Tengri was doing, Tapti's thoughts danced and flowed. Lighter than the air.

I only have to worry for a few more moments, she thought.

But as she finished the fourth chant, barely a breath later, she felt a tug at her belly and knew that her husband was in danger. There must have been fifty changes during the space of a blink of an eye. A dance of lightening during an ethereal storm. At one instant he was there, the next he was gone.

If she were not a baqca, she would have panicked. But she knew that their lives depended upon her. She allowed herself to go deeper. She entered the *fourth* state even though Tengri warned her never to go past the second. She had already been in the third, so another wouldn't matter, she tried to convince herself.

But because of her deeper trance, she no longer had random thoughts. She was completely focused … *"Under the white sky,"* …

There! She felt him regain the balance! He was safe.

But she felt strange as his power surged through her. She knew that she was delicately balanced.

14

Tengri realised he had come to a critical juncture, but he skilfully and artfully performed the proper dances. After about fifty changes of threads, he landed and felt the familiar song that Tapti sang.

93

It had more strength, more conviction, but Tengri had other matters on his mind at the moment. He realised he had become more proficient in the art of deathwalking and after the last incident, acquired a new confidence. Still, he decided to sing another song:

> *"My body is all eyes.*
> *Look at it! Be not afraid!*
> *I look in all directions!"*

Immediately, his entire perspective of the void changed. Instead of being focused upon merely one fibre and its sudden variances and changes, he became aware of *all* fibres around him.

This new perspective, he thought to himself, allowed him to see the other threads as they wove themselves toward his own. He clearly saw in advance the appearance of all critical junctures before they arose.

This new view was spectacular! At times there existed only a single thread. The one upon which he rode as it danced its way through an area of silence contained within the midst of the void. At other times, the weave of the fabric was so tight that Tengri felt that he stood on a *hundred* threads. In spite of that, he always knew where he was. He always felt the song that Tapti sang.

To an untrained shaman or an inexperienced baqca who somehow happened to find themselves within the void, they would only see the silvery light of the threads. However, to Tengri, he could distinguish colour.

The colours were beautiful! They were beyond beauty! The hues were subtle, yet pronounced. And many of them were incomprehensible to Tengri. Such colours could only exist in this strange world and in no other.

First, there was the familiar silver. The colour which gave contrast to this world of blackness. Which gave it a life of its own. The silver fibres were the fibres on which one travelled. They connected all places and things.

Second, there was the golden thread. A single strand for each universe that connected all times into one time. Tengri was amazed at how many different universes there were. The void appeared, when properly seen, as the glow of sunlight with all its warmth. There were so many different colours, but Tengri only knew the meaning of six others. Only eight out of all eternity did he know how to work at this time.

They were the colours of the principle gods: the bluish thread which took one to the heaven of Bai Ülgän. That god was the god of the atmosphere; the greenish thread of both memory and the god Yaik Khan, the Lord of the sea; the whitish thread of Mergen Tengere, the all knowing god of eternal wisdom; the reddish thread of Erlik Khan, the god of the underworld; the black thread of Kaira Khan, the Emperor of all the heavens; and the indigo fibre of dreams. The black thread was the hardest to see and the most difficult to attain. One could only approach with the purest of hearts and the most lofty of motives.

Not all colours could be seen at all times, Tengri noted. They flowed in and out of the fabric as his silver horse galloped through the universe. He felt as if he were the hunter eternally crossing through the sky. Surely, this is the substance on which he walks, thought Tengri.

By now, his dances were automatic. He no longer listened for Tapti's song. He had mastered the art of walking death.

But then he noticed a flash far into the future of eternity. Two golden and two silver threads had battled a great conflict. The destiny of his world would drastically change, he knew. And that destiny would be determined by the thread on which he now stood. When would it be? He thought as he prepared himself for the coming storm. His thoughts turned to Tapti.

The wind hit him as if he were struck by a thundering and panicked herd of wild horses. There was no way that he could stay on the thread and ride it through such a storm. He instinctively sang as he felt himself falling ... endlessly falling through eternity:

> *"Kagak! Kagak!*
> *I am here Kam."*

Tengri felt the helping spirit, that of the goose which he just released, grab him and stop him from his endless fall. But as suddenly as it grabbed him, it dropped him. As if in a dream he floated in a white mist. His last conscious thought was to wonder what would happen to the goose. Did it truly know where it was?

His last feeling was to feel a tear in the fabric. Of something being swallowed. And then the fabric, once again, becoming whole.

And then he slept. He dreamed of eternity.

15

It's almost done, Tapti thought as she sang. But then, the demeanour of her thoughts changed forever. She felt the *strangest* sense of foreboding as it swept through her being, causing her to enter into a vision of the fourth state. It caused her to see and feel the panic of doom.

She saw the conflict of two forces. One was good, the other evil. Sixteen hundred summers into the future she watched as time and place battled with a force that demanded supremacy. A force that *screamed* for its survival -- for its theft of powerful control over the multitudes. It willed into being its very nature. It willed into being its greed. It fought a great war. It was in the throes of its last battle. It manifested its existence after it subtly crept through the centuries and caused a time ravaged by deceit.

Tapti did not know if it won or if it lost but she knew the outcome could be either situation. She was denied the completion of her vision when she suddenly awoke to the realisation that she had unwittingly gone far too deeply into the spirit world.

With a start, she felt herself being pulled into the void. With the shock of horror and panic, she wished upon the gods that she was wrong, but she knew she wasn't. Tapti realised that Tengri had fallen off the fibre. He would be lost -- and her *own* delicate balance had been disrupted!

It was his power and her mistake of entering the fourth tapti that caused her to be swallowed by the void. She realised now that she, too, was lost. She felt herself falling, falling, falling, endlessly falling....

16

The Buryat warrior had just begun to grope for his horse. Had he not been blinded, he would have seen the Kazak-Kirghiz woman disappear into nothingness only a few moments after the man. But, he didn't. He was far too absorbed in his own predicament, his own anguish, and with his own terror.

17

After what seemed an eternity, Tapti opened her eyes. She was still falling, but had finally adjusted to the dizzying sensation of weightlessness.

When her eyes opened, she felt sickened at what she saw and repulsed by how it affected her soul. A demonic wind had just passed and with it the disgusting stench and hideous sight of the birth of a demon. She shuddered to think of where it would eventually manifest. She hoped it would not be upon her own world. Nevertheless, she feared for her people.

With the passing of the wind and demon, the void resumed its normal beauty. The storm was over but she had no experience or ability in this world. She began to weep because she knew that she would never see her beloved husband again. She did not even know if he, too, was forever lost in this ether.

In a way, that thought gave her some comfort for if he were lost too, there might be a chance that they would somehow meet. Then, maybe together, they could find their way home.

All around her was the silver weave. She reached out and touched a fibre and she managed to get onto it. She no longer fell.

But what she saw caused her grave concern. She knew she had been falling for many moons because her belly was swollen with the life of her unborn child.

Then it struck her! She had been in the void for nearly eight passings of the moon in her own world. Her husband, if he had found his way, not only would have *completed* his mission, but would have *returned* to the circle only to find her missing!

Perhaps, she thought, he would think she had left him. Perhaps he wouldn't even know where she was. Frantically, Tapti grasped and jumped onto new and different threads. On each of them she tried to listen to their songs. She tried to listen to Tengri's songs so she could find her way home.

But, she couldn't hear. She didn't know enough. She could only start to cry.

After a while, she concerned herself with watching her belly grow. Soon, she would not be alone.

Her life was passing by so quickly. She knew that she would die here. And then her son would die. She so desperately wanted to tell Tengri about his son. But he would never know. He would never know to sing his song. No one would ever know.

The time came. Even though the illusion of consciousness made it seem she had only been in the void for less than a day, her body knew differently. It told her nine moons had passed -- and she gave birth.

For the first time since entering this unforgiving world, she felt joy. For the first time in what must have been a very a long while, her tears were formed from happiness. Indeed, her dream was true. She had a son. She held him in front of her eyes and saw that his eyes were as green as her own.

She looked at her baby and said, "You are to be called Mergen after the all-knowing god of eternal wisdom. You are the son of the union of Tengri, your father, and Tapti, your mother. Never forget. *Never,* my dear son, forget!"

Mergen looked into his mother's eyes and Tapti saw in them that he truly understood. He smiled and she held him close to her breast, never wanting to release this little life for fear that they might become separated.

She had a sad thought. She wondered how much her daughter had grown and she worried about the broken heart that Tengri must have as a result of her absence.

As she held Mergen tightly, she could feel his bones grow. She could feel him getting bigger as if his growth did not correspond to time. She held him out to look at him, her hands around his waist.

By the gods, she thought, I have been in the void nearly eight seasons. My son has had his first birthday!

She began to sing to him and watched playfully as he smiled, giggled, and kicked his feet. She wondered if he experienced the passage of time the same as she did....

Then it happened! She saw what Tengri had told her about. It was barely perceptible, but nevertheless, she could *see* colour! Right next to them was a golden thread. She could sense its glowing warmth and it fascinated her.

Mergen was fascinated, too. He giggled in delight as the thread danced, and with childlike wonderment, he reached out to touch the shimmering golden thread with his tiny hands.

With a sense of urgency, Tapti saw the look of delight in his eyes turn to a look of surprise. The next expression that she saw on his little face was the look of sadness which seemed to say: Goodbye mother. I shall never forget you or the father I have never seen. I will love you both throughout eternity. But most of all, mother, I love you.

Horror set in as Tapti realised what had just happened. She

had become so fascinated with the golden thread of time that she allowed her grip upon Mergen to relax. He had grabbed it and it *tore* him away from her with such quickness that she only had the briefest of moments to see her last sight of his small, naked body. As it disappeared into the void, the two threads parted forever.

She held her own body as if she was still holding that dear life to her breast. Again, she was alone. So quickly, she was alone. But she thought not of herself, only of Mergen.

She held herself and she cried. She cried for the rest of time.

18

When Tengri awoke, his head throbbed, his vision blurred, and his mind clouded. He felt as if he had awakened after a night of drinking kymyz. He felt awful.

He suddenly worried about his pouch, wondering if it had survived the journey. He felt relief when he saw that it still hung around his neck.

With concern, he wondered if he had fallen asleep. He didn't know if one could fall asleep in the void. He knew that eating, sleeping, or breathing were not concerns to deathwalkers while riding the fibres. He did know, however, that aging was. If he had slept, perhaps he did so for many seasons.

He examined himself and he noted he appeared to be the same age he had been when he entered this world of darkness. He was still marked, he was still naked, he still had the owl's feather braided into his long hair, and he still wore the necklace of wolves' teeth.

Satisfied that all things about his person were in their proper order, he took a few moments to survey his surroundings -- which certainly didn't appear to be what he was expecting. He was now sitting upon a hard, smooth surface and all about him was a dense white mist which made it impossible to see distances greater than an arm's length. It was cold and he shivered.

He stood up and began to explore the only way that he could -- by groping. After a few steps, he felt a hard, smooth wall before him. He followed its shape and soon realised he was enclosed in a square room in which the length of each wall was about ten paces.

He jumped up against the wall in an attempt to find the top, but it was higher than he could reach. The white mist forbade him from seeing its true height.

"I'm imprisoned," Tengri said out loud.

"Dear brother," a voice from behind whispered, "*we* are imprisoned."

Startled, Tengri spun around ready to strike with the black knife that he still held in his hand.

"Is that any way to greet your sister?" Said the voice.

Cautiously, Tengri approached the place from where he thought the sound originated. One step ... two steps ... and then the mist became less dense and he could see a figure standing before him. He allowed his hand which held the knife to drop to his side.

Standing a short distance away was the naked figure of a woman whose eyes were the same colour of emerald green as those of Tapti's, but whose beauty even surpassed that of his wife. Her straight black, hair was shorter than his Tapti's, but this other woman's legs were longer. Her legs reminded Tengri of an owl's flight through infinity. He knew those legs well.

"*Pouie!*" Tengri exclaimed. "Where ... how ..."

"Remember, dear brother. Close your eyes and enter that secret place in your heart...."

Tengri did, and he remembered. He remembered the storm. He remembered falling and then releasing the goose spirit. And then he remembered a stench that brought forth the birth of a demon from the depths of the lowest hell.

"See it and remember," demanded Pouie.

He did. Even in the cold, he could feel a separate chill rising in his spine. He saw clearly what the monster looked like: the head and split hooves of a goat, the horns of a ram, the upper body of a woman with voluptuous breasts, and the lower body of a man. Its legs had long, matted hair. Its genitals were huge. Its perpetual erection was as long as Tengri's arm and its testicles hung to its knees. He not only remembered, there was no possible way he could ever forget!

"That demon," said Pouie, "was born from the conflict created far into the future. The conflict between the fibre on which you rode and the evil of its twin. That nameless horror that you saw will soon, within two moons of your present time, be born and manifest in the subtle realm of your world. It is in your destiny and the destiny of those of your blood to deny its *physical* birth."

Tengri understood.

"Where are we?" he asked.

"You're a baqca. You tell me," she replied.

He considered her caustic remark and decided that it was just her way. He ignored it.

"What are you doing here?" he asked. "And why do you say you are imprisoned as well?"

"My brother, I am bound to you. If you are imprisoned, then so am I."

Tengri considered her responses with irritation. This was her way of chiding him into not giving up and resolving his own dilemma. She had always behaved like an older sister. But then again, she was....

"Pouie, I haven't given up! I simply..."

"Then, why do you ask?" she interrupted.

"All right. I would suspect that we were in the world of Mergen Tengere because of the white mist."

"Suspect?"

"Yes Pouie, suspect! I have never been here before and until I *know* for certain, I will suspect." Tengri was getting aggressive.

"Good!" Pouie responded. "If you are to stand before the gods, then you must do so with assurance. Gods do not like weak mortals. They *must* be approached with strength."

"Why are you here, sister owl? Do not delay my journey with your big sister tactics of reproach. Say what you have to say and then let me continue."

Tengri knew that referring to his sister as an owl would change her attitude. He knew she didn't like to be reminded of her totemic race and preferred to be thought of as human, but she was a spirit owl nonetheless. He didn't know why, but she could be quite sensitive about that fact.

Pouie looked at her brother. Her eyes penetrated deeply into the depths of his own blue eyes and she felt saddened. Saddened by what she had to do and by what she had to say. Saddened by what she *couldn't* say and she felt the pain that he would soon know. She looked at his strength and it reminded her of the Old Ones. He was not small in stature as most of the people of the Mongol tribes were, nor did he have the features that were peculiar to their race -- neither did Tapti, nor his daughter, and neither would his unborn son -- a son he doesn't know will be born.

She looked at her brother and knew his beauty. The beauty of his soul that shone through to his body. Of all her brothers, she loved him the most. She would miss him the most. She envied her sister Kaltak -- but he required the spirit of the wolf, more so than that of the owl.

At long last, she responded, "I am here, dear brother, to say goodbye..."

Tengri was silent.

... "as I must leave you and you must release me from your heart. You must weave a fibre of dream on which I must fly."

"I know not of dream making," he replied.

"You will learn," Pouie whispered, "or you will die here. If you die, the reason for your journey will die with you and destiny will be lost and overcome by a new weave ..."

Pouie paused. She allowed herself to think of what her brother would never learn. The golden thread behaved by a law that he would never know. That law controlled his life as well as her own. She continued, "... our father has given me another direction to fly. It is my destiny. It is necessary to our work. I can no longer be of you again for I must be the guide of another. Still, of your blood and still, I am your sister. But never again will we meet."

"And what of our sister?" Tengri asked. "Is she to leave me as well?"

"No. She stays as both your sister and as your familiar spirit. She must ride, with me, upon the dream that you weave but she will return to you. In her, dear brother, look deeply for my essence and memories. Always, I will be there for you."

Tengri looked at her, "I will never know of you again."

"You will hear of me," was her response.

Pouie looked at her brother and then reached out. They embraced. Closely and for a long time, they embraced. Each felt the warmth and life of each other. Each felt and remembered their touch. Tengri had dropped his knife and Pouie kissed him. Not as a sister, but as a lover.

As Tengri embraced his sister, he felt her breasts and legs against him. He closed his eyes as her lips and tongue found his. The kiss was long. He hoped it would never stop, but it did. As it did, he felt her skin become soft and feathery. He felt as she shapechanged whilst still in his arms. He opened his eyes and arms at once and released an owl. He watched it fly away.

In the white mist of Mergen Tengere's domain, Tengri watched as his sister left him. Pouie was an 'attack owl' -- a type of owl known to his people that flew the night with great resolve. That truly described her personality. Her facial dish was almost a near circle and unmarked, its off-white colour being a bit more white than her greyish white plumage. The streaks of dark brown on her body and the grace of her flight gave her the elegance of eerie ghostliness.

Tengri continued to watch long after Pouie disappeared. It was fortunate that he did because he saw the brief image, or perhaps a vision, of a creature the people far to the South of his land sung about -- those people who lived high in the mountains that touched the sky. Those people who called their beliefs 'bon' had stories about a creature called a dragon -- only their dragon, Tengri remembered from the songs, had four legs. He noted that *this* creature only had two.

At long last, Tengri concerned himself about the matter at hand.

19

Tengri reached down to retrieve his knife which he had dropped while embracing his sister and was astounded at what he saw! His knife was floating in the white mist about four hand widths above the ground. About the same distance above the first, was a second. And another above that. And another ...

There was a ladder of knives rising and disappearing into the mist far above his head.

Tengri wasn't sure what to think but upon closer examination, he could tell that it was not his knife, nor were the others his knives. Only the blade was present, was replicated, and hung suspended in nothingness.

He touched one. It was real. It emulated the sharpness of his own knife as he could tell by the thin line of blood left on his finger. He quickly searched the ground to see if he could find his knife. But his search was to no avail.

It was obvious, at least to himself, that a ladder was formed somehow and that ladder was the path which he must take. There was only one problem. To climb the rungs of blades would not be kind to the soles of his feet.

The shoes Tapti had packed in his pouch would be of no use. The marks on his feet would be covered if he wore them and that would be a serious, irreparable breach of Law.

His options were limited, either climb as he was or stay and spend the rest of his life thinking about it. He chose the former option.

He felt himself as lightness, as if he danced from fibre to fibre, and he took his first step upwards toward the heaven world of Mergen Tengere.

He felt the sharp edge cut into his foot as he rose to the first rung. He knew that he bled. But as he stood there, he recognised a contrast. There was the pain of being cut, but with that pain there appeared a sharpness of mind. For the first time, he understood the true nature of questions. He understood how to properly inquire into truth.

Tengri took a second step and now his other foot bled, but with it came the peace of understanding how to know.

A third step resulted in a deeper and more painful wound as well as a deeper and more comprehensive understanding of the void.

And so he climbed. Ever upward. Each step disfiguring his feet and each step taking him closer to the god of eternal wisdom. As the ladder of knives spiralled upward, so did he. Always retaining the wisdom of each rung.

Forever, or so it seemed, he climbed. Perhaps it was the tenth or fifteenth rung, it no longer mattered, when Tengri noticed that he lost the little toe of his left foot and had felt the blood gush out. But it was on that rung, he remembered, that he finally understood the true nature of the fibres that made the net of the universe. That is, except the golden thread of time. That still remained a mystery.

Finally, he reached up to grasp the next blade so as to pull himself up one more step, when he realised that the blade he touched with his hand felt different than the rest. He looked and saw that it was his own knife, complete with its bone hilt. It came loose from its suspension in nothingness and he held it in his hand. He need no longer climb.

He looked down and saw that he now stood on solid ground. He looked up and saw, through the whitish mist, the blackness of the void. He looked at his body and saw that it was completely drained of blood and his feet no longer bled. He saw that his body was as white as the mist of this world. He knew that never again would he be of the same blood of his sister the owl.

Pouie had been released!

"Who is this mortal who *dares* stand in the heaven of eternal wisdom?" Boomed a voice from nowhere and everywhere.

"I am called Tengri," he responded without hesitation. "I am the ninth son of Tengere Kaira Khan. The ninth son of the eagle and a Kazak-Kirghiz baqca."

"Weave your dream so that the owl and the wolf may ride its indigo fibre into the sleep of your journey's end. Weave your dream so that by the next full moon's rise in your time, the owl and the wolf may enter into that sleep mind so as to prepare your way."

Tengri began to sing:

> *"Ghostly owl, no longer of my blood,*
> *Black wolf with yellow eyes,*
> *Bay at the full moon!*
> *Greyish wings, block the sun!*
> *See the world of no substance,*
> *Be the reality of dreaming time!"*

As Tengri sang, he danced. His fingers moved in a careful pattern. As his left hand emitted an indigo fibre, his right caught a golden thread. He merged them together and threw them outward with force. With power, the dreaming fibre flew across the universe to the sleeping mind of one man. The bridge could be crossed the next night in real time.

"As your father was gifted with the tongue of men," said the voice of Mergen Tengere, "so shall you be gifted with the tongue of one man."

Tengri could now think in another language. It is called Latin, he thought in that tongue.

"You are gifted with the toe that will keep your travels on the threads true."

Tengri felt a life fluid fill his veins and saw a toe appear where his other toe had been severed. A silver fibre appeared and Tengri leapt upon it. True enough, his new toe felt the subtlety of the fibres and he knew that never again would he become lost in the void or be forced off the thread upon which he travelled.

20

It was dawn in a strange land. If anyone happened to be nearby at that exact moment, they would have seen the sudden appearance, seemingly out of nowhere, of Tengri. But no one saw.

He looked to the sky and noted that he had been in the void for about a third of a day. The sun had not yet risen. It would only be a few more moments until its reddish fire would begin to show itself over the horizon. Soon, the chill in the air would be replaced by the warmth of what promised to be a clear day.

The moon and morning star were still visible and both gallantly fought the encroaching fire for predominance of the heavens. A battle never won and never lost. It was the futility of conflict; the illusion of distinctive separateness.

This is a deceptive time, thought Tengri. It is the time in each day when the greatest contrast between lightness and darkness became absolute. It is that moment in time when light is at its strongest point of power. Not midday as the uninitiated erroneously believed, but now.

He waited until the sun fully revealed itself, until the morning star disappeared from view, and the moon, which would be full that night, began to take on an elusive quality to protect itself from the day.

He waited until the right moment before he began to assess his situation.

He listened and soon heard what he waited for. An imperceptible sound to one who had not been trained in the ways of the goddess Nature. It was more than a sound. It was a feeling, a knowing. It was the speech of nature telling him where he could find the necessities required for his survival.

Tengri walked the approximate distance of an arrow's flight and found the small stream hidden away from the eyes of men. He tasted the water and then proceeded to wash the sacred markings of ash from his body. Normally, he would have left them on, thereby allowing them to wear off on their own -- which was custom. However, he did not think it appropriate to appear to a strange people any more noticeable than necessary.

He dressed, ate a bit of the dried meat that Tapti packed, and drank the water from his homeland. It tasted better. He sat for awhile and rested.

Shortly after sunrise, Tengri rose and proclaimed out loud ...

"Tapti, in three days I will return. Be patient. Be safe."

In this land of hills, he saw one that towered above the rest. He chose to go there to survey this new land and to get his bearings for the day's adventure.

When he stood on top of the hill and gazed to the West, he was astounded by what he saw. There was no way he could describe the view. He never knew that such sights could possibly exist!

To the North, Tengri saw a great expanse of water. To the Northwest he could see a faint outline of a coast, but to the North was only water. Such *vastness!* He thought.

He recalled many summers before when Mampüi sent him on his first sacred journey. He had, at the time, only seen fifteen summers and alone he journeyed through the steppes and deserts of the Kazak-Kirghiz lands, the deserts of the Oirat, and deep into the forests of the Buryats until he reached the shores of the sacred source of all water. The earth home of Yaik Khan. The sacred expanse of water called Baikal. He was impressed then, but this! There was no comparison.

To the South was land, but to the Southwest was a smaller

expanse of water but still much more impressive in size than his sacred Baikal.

What concerned Tengri was the wide river that connected the Northern and Southern bodies of water. But water was water no matter what its size and could be contended with when the necessity arose.

However, he knew that his experience wasn't sufficient to effectively handle what he now saw. His own language couldn't identify it so he searched his new tongue to find an appropriate word. The word that he arrived at was *city*.

Before him, on the other side of a vast river (which he would worry about crossing when he got there) was an enormous walled city. It wasn't movable, Tengri could tell that. So it must be permanent. Why?

Then he looked into the Northern water and even from this distance, he knew the answer.

The water is not alive, he thought. It has been abandoned by the gods. It has been abandoned by its own life force. The evil gods of the East have taken this place and have deceived its people so they would forget who they are. They think they are free. They do not know that they have been imprisoned by deceit. They do not know that their lives are controlled for they have freely given themselves away and have replaced true life with false life. I can see that they think their structures are permanent. But they are not! They build a wall, but for what reason? Protection? I think not. I think they are insane. I think they have forgotten all that is sacred. I can now understand their religion. As they have built their cities, they have built their god.

Tengri continued to look at the walled city and noted that on this side of the river there also existed what appeared to be a lesser city. Not as magnificent, but ominous nonetheless. It was there that he must first go, and so he looked for a suitable path.

He saw that at the bottom of the hill on which he stood was a road leading to where he wanted to go. It was travelled. He saw people walking and riding. He saw carts and wagons. Not many, at least not yet. But he suspected that when the day grew longer the road would grow busier.

He chose his path and began to walk. As he walked, he thought. I only have less than a day until my sisters enter the sleep mind of Constantine. I wonder if I could be there by then?

Tengri figured that it would take until the sun was full in the sky to reach the outer city. How long it would take to reach his final destination, he did not know. He was tempted to stay where he was and ride the fibres but he decided against it. It would require too much energy, energy that he would need if he were to show Constantine the Truth. Though he might have enough anyway, he decided not to take the chance.

As he walked down the hill, he thought of what Pouie had said to him. She had said that she must leave him to guide another still of his blood. He was beginning to wonder what she truly meant ... when he became distracted and forgot those thoughts.

Half way down the hill he crossed a path that before had been hidden from his view. To his right it veered off back into the hills. To the left, it bisected the main road. As he looked to the right he saw, in the distance, four men wearing greenish brown robes riding small horses with big ears. A *vulture* circled high over their heads.

Tengri was momentarily distracted because of a goat, which he hadn't noticed before, that suddenly appeared, bleated once, and then scampered off. It made him remember the vision he had of the demon.

When he again looked up the path, the men had disappeared from view having turned behind a hill. The vulture must have found something dead or dying, for it, too, had disappeared.

He considered that what he saw was an omen and felt pity for the four men.

Tengri paused for the briefest of moments and then turned to the left toward the main road. He had dismissed and forgotten what he saw, but later, many times, he remembered this moment buried deep within his dreams.

21

Diana, still groggy from the depth of sleep, *burst* into her uncle's breakfast room.

"Uncle!" She excitedly exclaimed barely able to contain her excitement and hoping that her uncle was present. She spoke as she flew open the doors and before looking....

Good! He was there.

"Uncle, I dreamt again of the Mage! Only this time he rode on the back of a huge, black wolf with yellow eyes and a white owl sat upon his shoulder..."

Her uncle looked up from his plate.

"... and he promised to show you and I wondrous sights!"

The Emperor Constantine smiled at his niece. She was seventeen years old, reddish blonde hair and blue eyed. She was a beautiful young woman, lovingly compassionate, and keen to learn. She hadn't quite grown out of her tomboyish ways, but she reminded him so very much of his departed sister. He thought of this girl as his daughter and when her parents had died fourteen years before, he had sent for her and she came to him all the way from the land of the Britons.

It is partly because of her, he thought, that he became so tolerant of the various religions and so proclaimed their free expression throughout his empire. She saw the good in all of them and she always pointed that out to him whenever he became frustrated by their silly squabbles.

Here she was, so excited and enraptured with a dream. So innocent and so willing to share her experiences. She could not even conceive of the danger that she wrought. That damned Bishop Ossius had even suggested to him that her prophetic propensities were the work of Satan! And he wants us to be Christians, he thought.

Soon, she would have to marry. She should already be married by normal standards, thought Constantine. But he couldn't bear to lose her. Not yet. It wasn't because she would leave him to spend her life with another man. No, that wasn't the reason. He wanted her to be happy. He wanted her to live a fulfilled life. He knew his reason for delaying her inevitable marriage was because he *wanted* her to be happy. It was due to her relationship to him that her marriage was destined to be arranged. It was purely political and there could be no happiness in that -- only duty -- duty to a senseless and fabricated existence.

The time in which they lived was changing. It was becoming more dangerous. There were plots and intrigues. There were scandals and murders. And he couldn't do anything about it. He only hoped that at least he could protect his niece. To give her a life that wouldn't destroy her compassion, her freedom, and her inquisitiveness. He was proud of her pagan heritage even though it was different from his own. To force her to become a Christian would be ungodly. But he saw no real alternative....

"*Uncle!* Are you listening?"

"Yes ... Mage ... I heard."

"But he didn't look," Diana continued, "like one of the three wise men that Bishop Ossius has described to me in my lessons. He looked more natural somehow. Like I would imagine ..."

Constantine interrupted, "... the Priests from the forests of your land?"

"Not quite. His skin was darker but his eyes were the deepest blue. And his hair was very long. Not like the Druids. He had no beard. Do you think I will *really* meet him?"

"It's a dream, Diana. Dreams do not come true."

Constantine thought that he had better start to harden her even though her look of disappointment when she heard his words saddened him terribly.

Had she come to him the next morning instead of this one, he would not have uttered those words. That night, his view of the reality of dreams would drastically change. But for the time being they, the Emperor and his niece, sat and spoke. They were enjoying each other's company and each had a couple of hours before they were needed elsewhere. Constantine would later have to attend to the routine matters of court, and Diana would later go to her daily lessons in Christian theology.

22

As he had expected, the sun was high overhead when Tengri finally reached the outskirts of the lesser, but no less impressive, city. His journey to this point was more or less uneventful. The road he was on became more travelled and now that it was midday, it had become quite crowded. At first, he had dreaded the slowly increasing masses of people. They had stifled him with their strange ways and with their rudeness. At first, Tengri was acutely aware of the stares that were directed toward him. He knew that he was the cause of whispers. He saw children hide behind their mothers. At one point, a rock was even thrown at him but it had missed. He never saw who threw it.

What really bothered him was the look of fear in the eyes of those who stared. There was something terribly lacking in those eyes. They expressed defeat, death, and a lack of wisdom. These people had no memories of ancient ways. They knew not of true freedom.

Now, he welcomed the crowd. It was still overpowering and made him nervous, but at least most people simply ignored him and went about their own business. Only occasionally was he aware that he was an object of curious attention.

Perhaps it's not them, he thought. *Maybe I'm too self-conscious.*

Tengri still wished he had brought a blanket to wrap himself so as to cover his rather distinctive clothing. But then again, it would be too hot.

As he entered the lesser city, he knew he had to remember every sight, sound, and smell. He had to remember every detail so he could tell his daughter when he returned. She would pester him incessantly to hear his stories of a *city*. Tapti would put her up to it, he knew, but she would never admit that it was really *she* who wanted to hear. With that thought, he began to take special note of the clothing and their colours worn by the women. That got him into trouble....

Tengri's first mistake was to pay careful attention to the dress of a woman who approached him. He was entirely engrossed by the unique design and the carefully woven pattern of reds, blacks, and golds. Particularly the gold which glistened in the noon sun.

His second mistake was to stop, turn, and reach out to touch the fabric as the woman passed. When she shied away from him, Tengri woke up to what he was doing. He didn't know the customs of these people and in his desire to please his wife, he forgot where he was. It was too late!

Tengri heard a bellow from behind and before he could turn his head, he felt a shove. Not a simple little shove. There was enormous strength to it. Tengri went flying ...

Instinctively, he dipped his right shoulder and with his left hand he made his third mistake. As he started his roll, he pulled his knife.

Gracefully, he began his roll as his shoulder touched the ground. He gave the appearance of floating in time as his body flew and then harmonised with the energy of the push. When Tengri regained his feet, he was slightly crouched, legs apart, and with his right foot ahead of his left. He was facing his opponent and his left hand held his knife so that the butt was pointed toward his attacker and the blade against the under part of his forearm.

Tengri saw who stood before him. A giant of a man who had upper arms the size of most men's thighs. He figured that this man must wrestle bulls for entertainment and he could tell by his eyes that he must have the temperament of a bull as well.

By now, the many people who were standing around began to comprehend what was going on. Tengri felt, rather than saw, that a crowd was beginning to gather. He could feel running feet approaching. He could feel the vibrations in the earth. It looked like he was going to be the day's entertainment. He wished he had decided to ride the thread.

Tengri saw that his opponent had seen the knife and watched him intently. He saw him cautiously step back several steps and for a moment, Tengri thought the fight was over. However, whatever hopes he had, disappeared. The man had backed up to a table and picked up a blacksmith's hammer.

Tengri noted for the first time that the man must be a blacksmith because he saw, in his stall, an anvil, tongs, bellows, and other paraphernalia associated with the art of smithing. Now there truly existed a conflict in his mind.

Tengri knew that only a smith could defeat a shaman because they, too, had magic. They were of the god Boshintoi, the celestial smith, and were of the nine families to whom the art had been taught. The true smith was also born of an eagle, not the same eagle as he was born of, but an eagle nonetheless. That made baqcas and smiths cousins. So why was this man fighting him? The confusion evoked old memories …

Tengri recalled his first spirit walk to Baikal when he was fifteen summers old. That journey had taken him three summers. The reason for that length of time was because of a smith. The smith who had forged his powers.

After he had arrived at the sacred lake and had seen its vast and living beauty, he met the three spirit nymphs. They had manifested to him as three young and beautiful women and since he was young and unmarried, there would be no jealousy on their part. Had he been married, they would have stolen his children.

However, they appeared to him for a purpose. As he was a virgin, they would teach him lovemaking and the power of sexual union. For three days, they seduced him. Individually and collectively they

made love to him in all of its forms. On the third day, it stopped.
Each had become pregnant with Tengri's children -- the union of
man and spirit.

On the sixth day, each child was born. The first was a stag. It
became his helping spirit and gave him heart and grace. The second
was a hare and that helping spirit gave him speed of body and mind.
The third and last child born of the nymph was a goose and it gifted
him with a soaring spirit and a sense of freedom.

The three nymphs then took him to the mouth of a cave which he
could only enter by walking backwards. After doing so, he turned
around and saw a naked man working a bellows. Upon the fire was a
huge cauldron. Between him and the man was a river. The naked man
saw Tengri and caught him with a pair of giant tongs. Once captured,
the man cut off Tengri's head, removed his bones, throwing them into
the river, and then chopped his body into small bits, throwing the bits
into the cauldron where they boiled for three years.

After three years, the naked smith retrieved his head and began to
forge it on a golden anvil. Afterwards, he put the rewoven eyes back
into the head so that Tengri could see into the spirit world when
shamanising. He pulled the bones out of the river and assembled
them. Then he put his boiled flesh back onto the bones thereby making
Tengri whole again. Finally, his ears were pierced thereby allowing
him to understand the language of plants. He was now a shaman and
released to begin his journey home ... suddenly remembering he
was in a fight, Tengri broke away from his momentary reverie ...

So why was this man fighting him? Many shamans were smiths,
although Tengri was not. He preferred to work in stone rather
than metal. A baqca was forbidden to work metal. But still, he
and this man were cousins.

And then it occurred to Tengri, the smith was from a different
land. *He* didn't know that Tengri was a baqca. Of course! It's
simple, he thought.

As the smith began his advance wielding his hammer over his
head with both hands, Tengri shouted: "Boshintoi, I am baqca. I

am your cousin!"

But the smith advanced and began to run holding the hammer over his head and starting another bellowing roar.

Not only are these people insane, thought Tengri, they're stupid. They don't know how to fight! No longer was their conflict in his mind and he readied himself with resolve.

As the man neared, Tengri stood quiet. At the exact moment when the smith reached a certain point and he had started his downward swing with the hammer, Tengri moved his left foot forward and placed his weight upon it thereby allowing himself to pivot, resulting in a move which sidestepped the smith's lunge. At the same time, he struck out with his right arm lightly pushing upon the smith's right arm and causing his swing to veer downward toward the left.

Since the smith had almost halted his rush when he got into striking range, he no longer had any forward momentum. If he had, Tengri would have let him dash on by. But he didn't. Tengri's next move was to strike out with his right foot which was still suspended in air. It struck the smith's right leg slightly above and to the side of the knee. Tengri felt and heard the bone snap....

As the man began to fall toward Tengri, he placed his weight on his right foot, now on the ground, and moved backward to maintain his distance from the falling smith. At the same time, he brought his left hand and arm forward allowing his pivoting body to determine the arc. In his left hand he held the knife. Against his forearm was the blade. At the present motion, the blade would slice deeply across the falling smith's throat and he would collapse on the ground behind Tengri thereby allowing Tengri the advantage and readiness to take on another attacker if one appeared.

The entire manoeuvre took less time than that required for the blink of an eye.

But Tengri changed his mind. Instead of killing the man, he checked and adjusted his swing so that the knife would miss the throat. Rather, the point of Tengri's elbow crashed into the side of the smith's head with just enough force to knock him out.

The man crumpled to the ground in a heap. The hammer hurtled off into the crowd but miraculously did not hit anyone. Tengri was absolutely embarrassed and didn't know what to do next.

"It is all a misunderstanding," he said in his newly discovered language. "He is not too badly hurt."

Some in the crowd began to mumble and soon words began to be thrown at him, but they were the wrong words. They were not in the language of Latin! Tengri had trouble reading the crowd. No one seemed terribly upset. No one moved to help the smith. No one moved to attack him. No one did anything.

Again Tengri spoke, "Do any of you speak Latin?" At this point, he wasn't sure if he did.

A man of middle years stepped forward and said, in Latin, "I speak that language but it is difficult to understand your accent. Do you speak Greek?"

Tengri had never heard of Greek but he doubted if he spoke it. Some people began to approach the downed man.

"Come with me," said the man, "you must leave here before the authorities arrive. You are a stranger and will undoubtedly be arrested if you are found."

Tengri understood the words but not the concepts. Still, he decided that the man's words were wise and he followed.

The man had taken him to his shop which wasn't too far away. He was a merchant, he explained, and mostly dealt in pottery, cloth, and jewellery. Some of his wares were imported from long distances. He further explained that the smith wasn't well-liked because of his temper and because he overcharged for his services. He seemed quite pleased that Tengri had defeated him. The woman, it was explained, was the object of his attention but she had different ideas and consequently no harm was done.

Tengri explained simply that he had heard about the great city called Byzantium and had travelled a great distance just to see it. He had asked how to get there and the man told him he had to take a ferry. During the course of the conversation it was discovered that Tengri not only did not have any money, he couldn't fully appreciate the concept. Subsequently, a bargain was struck. The man, who was named Alexis, had seen the three bowls Tapti had made. Tengri had shown them to him after seeing the various pieces of pottery in his shop.

In exchange for the bowls, Alexis would escort Tengri to the ferry and see that he got on as a passenger. He would also trade enough of the same cloth that started the incident with the smith so Tapti could make herself a garment. It was agreed....

As the sun was setting, Tengri stepped off the ferry and onto the other shore. He had enjoyed the company of Alexis and had shared the evening meal with him. They had mutually agreed that Tengri didn't like the food and Alexis didn't like kymyz.

People, Tengri thought, are basically the same everywhere. But here, they had the tendency to be more insane. I look forward to going home.

Instead of going into the city, Tengri decided to head South. He had seen the gently rolling hills and thought that perhaps after a short period of time he would be able to find a secluded spot where he could sing the song to ride the thread to his ultimate destination.

He did find such a spot. Later that night, after Pouie and Kaltak would have completed their dream journey, Tengri would start his own.

23

Constantine did not look forward to this so-called emergency meeting with Ossius. That fool bishop had *demanded* an urgent audience with him as a result of the day's lessons he had with Diana. The Emperor supposed that it was Diana's fault, he sighed. After all, he did tell her to not tell him of the dream.

The Emperor had a few moments to himself. Not really, he considered, but I *am* going to take a few moments for myself. He needed them. He needed to consider how he was going to approach the anticipated dilemma before it was presented to him.

"Your Excellency," said the Quaestor of the Palace, "I do not mean to be insistent, but the bishop is waiting and he is quite impatient."

Constantine broke from his thoughts and looked up at the man by raising his eyes without raising his head.

"Your Excellency, I will not interrupt again." The officer remained standing quietly.

Constantine continued with his thoughts. Just moments before, Diana had spoken to him. She had been hysterical. She had run all the way to see him after her lessons and she had come via the secret passage and entrance into this room. He figured that Ossius had also run to see him so as to ensure that he was the first to tell him. Diana was quite athletic and Constantine would have enjoyed watching the footrace between the two. But, she had taken the shorter, more direct route. At least Ossius would not know that Diana had already told him her story. At least I know the truth, thought Constantine.

Apparently Diana, in her excitement, had recounted her dream of last night to Ossius. She had also told him of her other visions not already revealed to the bishop. It's ironic, thought the Emperor, my niece enjoys her lessons in theology very much. And she tries very hard to emulate the life and deeds of this man they call Jesus. Had it been one hundred years earlier, he considered, she would have made an excellent adherent to the Mithraic Mysteries or, even more appropriately, a High Priestess of the Isis Mystery Schools. The way *he* thought of her, she *should* have been a goddess. If this Christian cult would leave well enough alone, Diana would naturally absorb herself into its doctrine. But as it is, they push and shove. They force and they conspire.

After Diana recounted her visions, Ossius apparently became quite agitated. He had told her that she was allowing Satan to influence her and that if she wasn't careful, she would burn in hell.

Diana should have shut up then and there, but she didn't. She had argued that the man in her visions *had* to have been one of the Wise Men, one of the Magi who was equal to Jesus in ability.

Constantine concluded that it must be the word 'Mage' which had caused the conflict. It was then, Diana had told him, right after she had uttered that word, that Ossius excitedly and aggressively responded, stating that he exerted great spiritual power over Constantine and that they had been discussing sending her away to be fully indoctrinated into *proper* Christian thought and practice. In fact, thought Constantine, he had told her that it was my idea and that *he* had advised against it! *Then*, Ossius added that he knew that to send her away was the correct decision and that it was necessary for the good of her soul that it be done. Unfortunately, Diana half believed him. At least enough to make her become highly emotional. She had thought, perhaps because of what was said to her that morning over breakfast, that I, her uncle, doubted the truth of her visions. That was the real issue as far as Diana was concerned. She would not allow her confidence in herself to be shaken just because of a theological dispute. It could only be because she was concerned that I doubted her.

To send her away, thought Constantine, would have the same effect as if she were to be killed. It would kill her spirit and for her, spirit and life were identical. Ossius and his Christian brothers thought of her as merely a woman and they did not really care what she thought. But, they know of my love for her, they know she is my weakness. They are after me!

Still, one thing bothered Constantine -- the *real* issue. Why would Ossius so overtly lie to Diana by proclaiming that it was *my* idea to send her away? Did the bishop truly think that his influence over Diana surpassed mine? Did he truly think that she would trust him over myself? No, thought the Emperor, Ossius had a plan -- a trap! And that bastard has no doubts that it will work!

Abruptly Constantine proclaimed, "Quaestor, show that bastard Ossius in!"

The Quaestor smiled. He had no love for Christians. He opened the door and announced: "The bast ... um hm ... The Bishop Ossius of Cordoba, your Excellency."

Ossius *glared* at the Quaestor but said nothing until he had closed the door and left him alone with the Emperor.

"What is so urgent", asked Constantine, "that interrupts my dinner with my niece?"

"Your Excellency, the Quaestor is quite rude ..."

"I will speak to him." Constantine was skilled in diplomacy. "But Ossius, answer my question. I'm *not* in the mood for pleasantries. Diana is probably wondering what has become of me."

Good, thought Ossius, he has yet to speak to his niece. "This concerns Diana, your Excellency. I fear she is in danger of losing her soul to the dark evil of a sorcerer. I fear that she is a recipient of magical attacks and the reason those attacks are directed at her are for the purpose of undermining your involvement in important matters of court."

"What on earth are you blabbering about?"

"Your Excellency ..."

Too many excellencies, thought Constantine ...

"... Bishop Eusebius and I concur ..."

Very good, thought Constantine, a very good political move. He knows that I know they are enemies. And now I know that he has discovered that I'm considering Eusebius to replace him. Ossius does have a plan and it will be well thought out and dangerous.

"... that witchcraft, sorcery, and the dark arts of evil are being used to create chaos in your empire and that there exists a foul plot to disrupt your goodness and purity."

"Are you telling me," replied Constantine, "that you have consulted with Bishop Eusebius and that you both agree that Diana is being attacked magically?"

"No, your Excellency, I have yet to consult with my dear brother Eusebius directly concerning *this* particular instance ..."

He really is trying to convince me that they are on the same side, thought the Emperor.

"... I was speaking, ... ah, ... more loosely, let us say. But I believe, your Excellency, that you are *acutely* aware that Eusebius has been more than merely vocal about his bitter complaints concerning the use of witchcraft by that tyrant Maxentius in his struggle against you. Indeed, I give full credit to Eusebius for exposing that foul evil and countering it with the love of Christian Faith and the Love of our Lord Jesus Christ." Ossius hoped to play upon the perceived superstition of Constantine with that last statement.

Constantine missed that innuendo but did catch the Nicene slight on Arianism. "Nonsense, Ossius, I defeated Maxentius in battle at Milvian Bridge twelve years ago ..."

"True, your Excellency," Ossius interrupted, "but who is to say that if it were not for the Love of our Saviour and Lord God, that *you* would have been defeated."

This is getting us nowhere, thought Constantine. "Get to your point, Ossius. What does this have to do with Diana?"

"Well, your Excellency, who is not to say that your enemies are continuing to direct evil forces against you with the intent to undermine your Empire?"

"Diana, Ossius. What has this to do with Diana?"

"I know for fact that evil forces are being directed against her person!"

"What facts?"

"Her dreams, your Excellency. She is receiving pagan and foul symbols originating directly from Satan, Himself. Today, your beloved niece told me this ..."

"Diana told you that she is receiving dreams from Satan?" interjected Constantine.

"No. It is not that simple. Diana is too young, too naive, too impressionable to realise the truth. She thinks her visions are consistent with our Faith. She thinks that a Wise Man is causing her to have blessed visions. She truly believes the person she sees is a man of God. There is no doubt that her heart is pure. But today, the evil slipped. The man in her visions told her that he was a *Mage!* A *magician!* Already, he tries to twist and pervert her innocence. I truly and deeply pray for her soul!"

There was a moment of silence. Constantine thought and then responded; "If your Lord God can, by virtue of prayer and love, cause the defeat of an army, why not simply pray and thereby defeat the demon who haunts the dreams of a little girl?"

"Your Excellency, in case you have not noticed, Diana is not a little girl. That is part of the problem."

Here it is, thought Constantine. A case for an arranged Christian marriage!

"By all standards, she should have been married at *least* two years ago. Had she been, a demon could not have taken possession of her soul. She would have been too occupied with matters befitting a wife and mother and would not have been susceptible to such adverse influences."

"You know as well as I," replied Constantine, "that her marriage must be arranged for the good of the state. At present, an advantageous alliance through marriage would be premature."

Good, thought Ossius, he is on the defensive. "I beg your forgiveness, your Excellency, but an arranged marriage with one of the many Christian Princes would be *extremely* advantageous and timely to your Empire. I am very fond of Diana, too, and I would miss her challenging mind as much as you if she were to leave this court for another. And, by the way, I do have a marriage in mind, but I fear that it would be a grave error if she were to marry now; maybe in two years, but not now ..."

Constantine was confused and he feared that it showed. He was so certain that the marriage was the real purpose of this meeting, but Ossius, in principle, was agreeing with him.

... "No," Ossius continued, "If she had married two years ago as I advised, all would be extremely well at this time. But under these extenuating circumstances, much more serious matters must be attended to first."

"What matters?" replied Constantine.

"Because of her vulnerability to demons, she must be purged and purified of the foul evil that presently haunts her. She must consent to Baptism immediately! Further, because damage has already been done, she must be properly re-educated at an isolated Christian retreat where she can also be protected. There is one within a three day's journey from here, I am told. It is highly recommended and is operated by a Christian Brotherhood of high esteem. Perhaps you have seen these esteemed brothers? They wear greenish brown habits?"

Constantine couldn't recall having seen them and shook his head no.

Ossius continued undaunted, "I also advise that *you* convert immediately as well. Who knows, you may be attacked next! Above all else, your soul *must* be saved."

Constantine now understood *perfectly* what was being proposed. They wanted Diana to be held hostage so that *he* could be controlled. However, one item was missing, he thought, and it bothered him. The merits of Ossius' arguments may work on already converted Christians. He knew that was an already existing tactic they frequently employed. However, either Ossius did not have any greater leverage to *force* the issue, which he doubted -- he never underestimated these Christians -- or the final convincing argument had yet to be revealed. Whichever, Constantine realised that he would either win or lose. This was a decisive battle! Not a preliminary provision for a future victory, but the final outcome of the war for the possession of souls. Constantine decided to intensify the battle.

"Ossius," Constantine said, "You speak of your faith as if I and the Empire have accepted it as the state religion. You forget that Christianity merely enjoys free expression as do *all* religions and beliefs in my domain. Do not confuse the absence of Christian persecution for complete and total acceptance. It could very easily happen that your faith may once again be repressed. Even exterminated! Your arguments presuppose that I believe in *your* truth. As you know, I am merely interested. However, it would be very easy for me to lose that interest if attempts to control and manipulate are observed. As I see the situation, I am beginning to think that *you* are attempting to control the state by taking my niece hostage thereby exerting undue influence over myself. *Prove me wrong Ossius!* Otherwise you and many others will join that bantered about list of martyrs that you are so proud of."

Ossius also knew that victory or defeat was imminent. Suddenly, he realised that the entire future of his Faith rested in his next choice of words. He must continue with confidence. He had to maintain the certainty of the Emperor's weakness for his niece. But he just couldn't come out with the threat of her death ...

"Your Excellency," he finally said, "You misunderstand. Please forgive me but I must accurately describe the present climate. The Christian Church has, unwittingly and unsought, found itself in a very sensitive predicament. Many kings and princes have already unequivocally embraced our Faith and subsequently look to the Church, and Pope, for spiritual advisement and blessing. The Church is *required* to serve them in the name of God. Unfortunately, many of the secular authorities of *considerable* influence only understand very little of our dogma. One could say with accuracy and conviction that *their* only concern is that their eternal salvation is guaranteed. They do not fully appreciate nor are they capable of fully understanding the intricacies and nuances that such salvation entails. The Church can *guarantee* their salvation and it does not require that they fully comprehend how it is done. They know that. It is simple for them and that is how they want it to be. If it were to happen, for example, that a small kingdom or province *denied* God and the Church, many larger kingdoms would see to the eradication of the heretics. Especially, if they felt that the Church was in danger of being suppressed by the forces of darkness."

Ossius continued: "If anyone, particularly if someone of

importance, were *known* to be or was even merely *suspected* of being in a position to influence, let us say, a king, to enforce Satan's evil work, I fear there would be a terrible, but necessary, war to preserve the goodness of God. There would be a mighty rally to depose the evil doers. I ask that you recall history, your Excellency, recall the Bacchanalia affair of four hundred and fifty years ago. Rome had exerted her powers, after the Second Punic war, over those cities subordinate to her. They had caused the persecution of all people suspected of importing alien magical practises. Of course, at that time Rome was pagan and wrong in her beliefs. They did not yet know of God, but the fact remains that their erroneous religion supported and caused the complete persecution and annihilation of people's rights based solely upon accusations. Just *think* of what would happen now if it were to be known that magical and satanic practises interfered with the *true* Faith!"

"Ossius," replied Constantine, "*you* consider history. Recall Nero's persecution of the Christians. Remember very clearly that he had them suppressed because he thought they conspired against the state by making the similar magical claims that *you* now make. That was less than three hundred years ago. What makes you think that *that* history will not repeat itself?"

"Your Excellency, I am merely pointing out such instances in the hopes that undesirable situations do not repeat themselves. However, our present condition is quite different. We are not superstition, we are truth. We are opposed to superstitious beliefs. We are different today than we were under the insanity of Nero. Different not by virtue of belief, as God's word is unchangeable. We are different today because our way has finally demonstrated the truth to the people. The Church is vast and no longer will everyone unite against us. An attempt to suppress us will only result in a war that God could not possibly lose."

This man is a fanatic and he is dangerous, thought Constantine. He speaks of truth and righteousness but he is blind to his own attempts to manipulate. Or is it intentional? But in many ways, he is right. If anyone of power attempts to renew Christian persecution, they would throw the entire world into chaos and ultimately the Church would win and be in complete dominance. They are very cunning. Very cunning indeed ... "Ossius, what has all this to do with Diana?"

"Your Excellency, your niece has compromised your authority. Not intentionally, mind you. No one more than I recognises her true purity. But nevertheless, her indiscretion has indeed compromised your position. She speaks without reserve about her visions ..."

That was dangerously true, thought Constantine.

"... and many people in this court consider her words as heresy and the work of Satan. They rumour that you continue to condone her behaviour. If it does continue, they may believe that you had either encouraged or had even *caused* it! Be very clear, your Excellency, my motives now are personal. I only want to protect her ... and you ... from the inevitable accusations. Accusations that could cause history to repeat itself. Accusations that could result in the mass removal and death of officers in the imperial court. Accusations that could result in your defeat by your enemies. If such were to occur. If accusations were made against you that were based upon heresy and satanic involvement, the Church would have no choice but to side with the accusers because those accusations would be true! I ... we ... want to keep that from happening. I do not want to see Diana's life become *forfeit* as a result of her own naive beliefs. I pray. No. I *beg* you to accept my proposal to have her converted, trained in seclusion, and then married to a Christian Prince. It is for her own good. It is for the good of the state. It does not benefit the Church, only the state. It is your duty as Emperor, and it is her duty as your niece."

There was a long moment of silence finally broken by Constantine. "Give me a week to consider your request."

Ossius smiled. "As you wisely request, your *Excellency.*" He bowed and left the Emperor to reflect in solitude. He *knew* he had won!

Constantine was not a fool. He knew precisely what had just happened. He lost the war. It was clear that if he refused Ossius' scheme, there would indeed be accusations. The Church would make them and they would also create the hysteria that would either demand the denial of the rights of the accused and their deaths, or open revolution. In either case, the Church would ultimately acquire the power they sought. They would stop at nothing. They would unleash demons if necessary. Perhaps they already have.

Constantine considered his options. He could not simply dispose of Ossius because it was obvious he was merely the voice of a deeper and more sinister movement. He could not ignore the matter or even fight it overtly. The Church was too powerful. Besides, he would then make enemies inside of his own court. Already, they understood his weakness. Diana! She was the crucial key. If he refused the request, she would eventually die and the empire would eventually crumble. If he accepted the request, she would die inside and this damnable faith would become too powerful, too quickly.

However, if Diana were no longer here, they would not have the leverage they now enjoy. Their whole plot is centred around Diana. Unfortunately, to simply send her away was useless. She could still be used anywhere she happened to be inside of the Empire or Christian world. There was no place to send her where she could still be happy. There was no way to undo her headstrong and vocal outbursts. She either had to die or to succumb to their whims.

Finally, Constantine reached a conclusion. He had no choice. He had to make his decision based upon what was best for all, not just one person regardless of how much he loved her. Diana would become a Christian as Ossius demanded. But, he thought, afterwards Ossius will be gone! His decision was best because it would allow him time to delay the inevitable. They may eventually acquire domination over the world, he thought. But not while *I'm* Emperor! At least Diana has a week to enjoy what little free life she has left.

Constantine left the dignitary meeting hall and met Diana in their private dining room. Her eyes were red and puffy from crying but at least she was no longer sobbing. She confronted him about having her sent away and he replied that it would only be considered if she chose to become a Christian. He also told her that if she left, he would miss her terribly and probably would not be able to bear the hurt. He also told her that to be realistic, one day she would leave. She would marry and embark upon a new life. If she was happy, Constantine had said, then he would be happy, too and that was all that really mattered.

Diana had surprised him at that point. She said she knew that one day she would be expected to marry and that she, in some ways, looked forward to it. However, she would only marry someone who lived in the city and who would not take her away. She wanted him to see and know his grandchildren. She also said that she never had any intentions of becoming a Christian because there were too many inconsistencies in their theology -- at least in the manner in which Ossius taught. Subsequently, she had assured her uncle that he never need worry about her leaving.

At this point, Constantine became very sad. In his own way, he almost wished that Diana wanted to convert and looked *forward* to going away to study. But then he realised that such wishes were nothing more than mere selfish indulgences. He told her not to worry. He said that the entire matter was resolved. Constantine also suggested that she take a week for herself and forego her theology and all other lessons. She had delighted at that prospect and her delight had lifted the Emperor's spirits as well.

He even asked her to tell him, again, of her visions and to recount the story of the wise man. He was truly intrigued and even found himself wishing that the fantasy were true. It allowed them both an escape from the harsh reality of what would soon occur. A reality that he understood all too well, and a reality that she had yet to suspect.

After a long while, Constantine retired to bed and left his niece to her own thoughts.

Elsewhere, Ossius rejoiced in his victory. When he retired to bed that night, he was jubilant. He had no idea that on the following morning he would be taking a journey to the same retreat which would soon be the temporary home of Diana. He would be met by a mysterious messenger riding a donkey. He, himself, would ride a donkey for three silent days until he arrived at that secluded spot that would change *his* life for all eternity. When he would return home, he would be wearing the greenish brown robes of the Brotherhood for whom he now worked.

However, for now, he wrote in his diary of the day's victory over the Emperor.

24

Shortly after her uncle had left to retire for the night, Diana sighed and decided to do the same. The day was physically and emotionally draining and she was exhausted. Still, she doubted she would be able to sleep. As she walked through the hallway that led to the stairwell ascending to her room, and as she climbed those steep and endless steps, she reviewed the day's events in her mind. First, her uncle had said her dreams would never come true. That was at breakfast. Now, of course, she realised he had only said those words so the future would not disappoint her. But when Ossius proclaimed that it was her uncle who conceived the plan to send her away, for a brief and insane moment, she believed him.

Diana now wondered how she could *ever* doubt her uncle. She trusted him implicitly and without question. At dinner, he explained everything to her -- how he would *never* send her away; how he would be terribly hurt if she left. She even let it slip that she wanted to be near him so he could watch his '*grandchildren*' grow. Diana loved him so much that in her mind he truly was her father and not just her uncle. Now she worried she may have betrayed her trust in him with her doubts.

As she entered her room and quietly closed her door, she realised her uncle would never make her leave. Would never hurt her, and would always protect her. Tomorrow, she thought, I will ask him if he minded terribly that from now until the end of time, I call him father. He *is* my father! And his son, Crispus, not those other three, is my brother. Why haven't I thought of this sooner?

For the first time that day, Diana felt completely safe and secure. It was her room which gave her that sense of security. Ever since she could remember, since being three or maybe four years old when she first arrived at the palace, she fell completely in love with this room. Even though she could barely remember the journey to Byzantium, she clearly remembered the day of her arrival. She remembered being frightened of this huge and fabulous place and of the many people whom, to her, haunted it. She had heard stories of ghosts in castles and fearfully thought that *this* castle was the source of such legends. Therefore, everyone in it simply *had* to be ghosts. That is, except her uncle. To her he was real and everything she had hoped him to be.

When they first met, Diana remembered thinking at the time that he could read her mind. She had tried to be brave and wouldn't *dare* let anyone even suspect that she was terrified of her new surroundings. But her uncle simply looked at her and said they had chased all of the ghosts away the day before she arrived and that they were not allowed to return because he, as Emperor, had said so! She felt better after hearing those words and her sense of dignity was restored because she had noticed the nods of agreement of everyone present. It was obvious she wasn't the *only* one who was frightened of this place!

Her uncle then told her that he would *personally* escort her through the entire castle and that she could choose *any* room she wanted for her very own. But, he had said, she could only choose one. He then took her by the hand and together they toured the entire and intimidating palace. She inspected each and every room thoroughly. After all, she was a little girl with a mission and a great responsibility.

Diana remembered thinking many times since that day that her uncle *must* have been thoroughly exasperated by her search because it lasted for hours. She had found fault with every room. That is, until she found a lone iron enforced wooden door in one of the secluded hallways leading to the back of the kitchen. She asked her uncle if she could inspect this room. He only looked at her, smiled, and then opened the door....

Her eyes had widened at what lay behind. Not until she was much older was she able to count the steps, but there were *three hundred* of them spiralling upwards into the spooky semi-darkness of too few torches. Since all the ghosts had been banished and they were no longer a threat, she simply *had* to see what was up there -- so she and her uncle climbed. She with trepidation, and he with amusement.

Finally, and at long last, there was a second iron enforced door and when her uncle opened it, Diana was not prepared for what lay ahead. She expected to see a dark and musty room complete with scary spider webs and hordes of rats! Instead, she saw a room that was bright and airy. It was spacious, but not too large. The room was circular in shape and had four fairly large windows that were crisscrossed with iron bars. The wooden shutters were open and allowed more than enough light into the room. There was also a fireplace, several chairs, a desk, a carpet, and then she saw it … Another door!

Her uncle then said he wanted to show her something. He opened the door and they both climbed the few covered steps which led to an open air roof the same size as the room below. The area was enclosed by a wall that rose to the height of her uncle's chest. He lifted her up and she saw that she was on top of the highest tower in Byzantium and could see the entire city, the sea, and the surrounding land of gently rolling hills. It was the most *beautiful* sight she had ever seen!

She asked who the room belonged to and her uncle replied that it was *his* special place. A place where he went to meditate upon his many duties. Well, that did it! This *was* a magical place, made magical by being special to her uncle ... *and it was going to be hers!* Diana had chosen. He had asked her if she were not afraid that the ghosts might return to the stairwell and she had responded by saying no. Her uncle had said so, and that was that! Even *if* they tried to sneak back, certainly they wouldn't be dumb enough to go where they would be expected! No, this was the *safest* place to be in the entire castle! Her uncle simply laughed and said the room was hers on the condition that, until she was ten years old, she would not be allowed to be in the room by herself, climb or descend the stairs unaccompanied; and that Helen would live in the room with her until then. Also, she had to accept the fact that it would take another week before the servants could ready the room and she could move in. Diana was elated! Every time she went up or down those steps would be an adventure! Readily, she agreed. But it was the *longest* week of her life.

Diana smiled when she thought of Helen. Indeed, she lived with her until her tenth birthday and her bed, even now, was still in the room alongside her own. Of course Helen never used it anymore. Still, though she was getting old, she climbed all those steps everyday just to see if Diana needed anything. Helen was a servant, but to Diana, she was more of a mother and a friend. When first leaving Briton those many years ago, Helen had travelled all that way just to fetch her and to be with her on her journey to her uncle. Now, only Helen and her uncle were ever allowed into this room -- except for her best friend, and even then, only with an invitation.

As Diana stood in the doorway, she surveyed her room. It had become quite comfortable over the years and was filled with various odds and ends indicative of her personality. She liked pillows and there were many different varieties laying about the room which had been imported from many different lands. She was also quite fond of wood carvings, especially of animals, and there were many of those as well. A number of them she had made herself after having learned the art. But her *favourite* object was the one given to her by her uncle on her thirteenth birthday. It was a full length, finely polished silver mirror mounted in a dark oak frame, intricately carved with various scenes, mostly, having to do with animals. But one strange creature attracted her attention over all the others. Over the top of the mirror was a serpent-like creature with wings and two legs. It *almost* looked like a dragon ... Her uncle had the mirror made to fit the frame, which he had found in the bazaar. She wished she knew who had carved it.

Diana moved to the heavy deep blue curtains which covered the walls from ceiling to floor and gently pulled one aside. The one which covered the door to the roof. She decided to observe the heavens as she did on most nights before retiring.

As she stepped out onto the roof, she gasped. It was astoundingly beautiful that night and even though it was a full moon, she could clearly see the stars shining brightly overhead. They told her of their stories. They whispered them to her via the cool wind that now gently blew across her face. Pegasus, the winged horse, was her favourite. Diana had always wished that she had one. Orion, the hunter, was intriguing. She had once dreamt of the hunter and his dog but couldn't clearly remember the dream. She thought about the heavens and recalled, for a few moments, what she had been taught about Greek mythology.

Diana carefully walked to the South wall. She walked carefully so as to not step upon the many plants growing in her garden. She had decided to grow a garden up here about five years before and had chosen an odd assortment of plants. She wasn't sure what kind of plants they were and wasn't interested enough to find out. She simply took pleasure in helping them to grow. It was like having her own little kingdom. At least those were the thoughts she had when she was twelve.

Normally, the wall rose to the height of her shoulders so that only her head could appear over the top. But on the South side, which was her favourite view, she had built a small platform on which she could stand and safely lean over the edge. She did so now but instead of looking at the moonlit sky, she looked down. This was her favourite view because she could see the more secluded areas of the kingdom. To the South and East were the rolling hills and woods that were untouched by the city.

Diana realised that she belonged in the city and knew very little about surviving in the wilds. But something inside made her long for the experience. She felt she needed to learn the secrets of nature and to discover the innate beauty of harsh environments. Somehow she knew there would be something there that was *needed* to be known before her life could become complete. That drive had been so strong that when she was twelve she had actually pestered her uncle until he relented to a camping trip.

It was intended to last a week. Her uncle couldn't go but had arranged for her best friend, Helen, a trusted woodsman, several palace guards, and for some reason, Bishop Ossius, to accompany her on the adventure. The trip was a disaster! Her best friend was attacked by every imaginable insect that had ever been known to live -- and probably some that anyone had yet to learn about. And Helen had fallen into the river and was whisked a short distance down stream until two guards managed to catch up to her and pull her out onto the muddiest section of the bank. That was only the first day!

On the second day, Ossius used poison sumac leaves to wipe himself and by the third day, he could barely walk. When their guide discovered what Ossius had done, he laughed so hard he cried. Ossius threatened to excommunicate him which only made him laugh that much harder because he wasn't a Christian! However it did end the trip. On the way home, the guide taught

Diana about the plants that they saw and it inspired her to start a garden. It was because of Helen's discomfort that Diana never asked to go on such an outing again, because even though she truly wanted to, she knew that her uncle would demand that Helen go as well. She wouldn't do that to Helen.

Diana, dismissing her memories, looked down from the tower mostly out of habit because she really didn't expect to see anything in the dark, even though there was a full moon. However, she did notice that in a secluded area far to the South, there was a faint glow from a campfire. She envied the campers, whomever they were. She noticed the chill and thought to herself that it was pleasantly strange that the days could be so hot, and the nights so cool. Silently, she descended the steps to her bedroom.

She felt warmer now that she was in her room and the outside door was closed. She proceeded to prepare herself for bed and started to undress. As she was undressing, Diana noticed herself in the silver mirror and watched as she finished removing her clothes. She blushed because ladies were not supposed to look at themselves in the manner that she was. They were supposed to be modest and shy, she thought to herself, or so I have been taught. Still, she was curious. She was curious to know if men would find her body exciting. She had been told that she was beautiful, but she wasn't certain. She wanted to know.

Diana began to brush her long, thick reddish blond hair, noting it was that part of herself which pleased her the most. Then, looking at her eyes, she saw that they were still a bit red and swollen from the day's crying. She suddenly felt embarrassed. How could she have been so silly to have believed that trite and foolish Ossius?

"Sometimes I hate being a girl," Diana said out loud to the mirror.

She became sensitively aware that her skin was very fair, very white. When she cried, her face remained a blotchy red far too long. And when she blushed, that was the most embarrassing of all. She turned a deep crimson red that she *swore* glowed in the dark! When she was younger, the other children used to make a game of seeing who could make her turn the reddest. That game lasted only a short time. She had responded by beating up the culprits, at least until her uncle got a hold of her.

And then, it was only six months ago when *that* young man from Nicomedia had visited her uncle's court with his father. He was two years older than she and he was truly handsome. As they were being introduced, she had wondered if they were visiting for the purpose of prearranging their marriage. When she realised what she was thinking, she remembered suddenly feeling her skin turn hot and she *knew* that her skin changed from white to red as quickly as a chameleon adapted to a sudden change in its environment. The worst of it was that it only got worse and not better! She had entered into an endless cycle and the only way she could think to gracefully get out of it was to suddenly exclaim that she had acquired a bad sunburn!

She blushed now and watched her body turn red in the mirror as she remembered the young man's innocent response. He had immediately asked her where she could have possibly found any sun *because it had been raining every day for the past two weeks!* He had been right, of course. It *had* been raining in Byzantium, and naturally, if it rained here, it would also rain in Nicomedia only a short distance away. At his comment, the only response that she could think of was to run from the room. He probably thinks that I hate him, she thought. He thinks that I am a fool and an idiot! She had avoided him for the rest of his stay and had yet to ask her uncle about the young man because she knew it would cause her to blush -- a blush that would betray her secret. She liked him!

"My skin is too white," Diana said to the mirror, "it makes me *ugly!* It betrays my innermost thoughts!"

At least I'm not fat, she thought. She wasn't. Being tall for a girl and somewhat wiry and athletic looking, she was by no means masculine in her appearance. Her legs were long and well formed as a result of years of climbing the stairs to her room. Her hips were shapely and contoured to her satisfaction. She was pleased with the way that her hip bones moulded her lower body. She was, however, self conscious about her behind. She didn't know why, it just made her self conscious. Her waist was slim, her body supple, and her muscles toned.

Diana looked at her breasts and then turned her body sideways to examine them from the side. They were large, but not overly so. They curved in an appealing way and the nipples seemed to be the right size and in the right place. She noted that they always hardened when she blushed.

When her breasts first began to develop, she had tried to hide them by wearing clothes that would make them appear to be nonexistent. Finally Helen had told her that she should be proud of them. They were firm and well formed. Helen had even said that she wished that she had breasts like hers. That had pleased Diana and she no longer attempted to hide her changing body. She looked at her breasts now and even *she* had to be satisfied with how they turned out. She put down her brush and lifted them with her hands, (she wondered if her fingers were too long, but her uncle had said that was a sign of artistic ability and intelligence), and then released them. Their resilience was just right! They were indeed firm and she hoped that they would stay that way. Next to her hair, her breasts were her favourite part of her body.

When she looked at her pubic hairs, she wondered how her hair could be one colour on one part of her body, and another colour on another part. They were a kind of light brown! It wasn't a problem, it was just an interesting question. Diana was thankful they were not thick like the hair on her head. Rather sparse in comparison, she thought.

She put her legs together so that the ankles and knees were tightly pressed against each other. The upper thighs didn't touch and that pleased her. She ran both hands down the contour of her pelvis until her fingers grasped her inner thighs. She liked the feel of her shape. Then, releasing her thighs, Diana looked. Still ...

... She wanted to know. She had been told she was beautiful, but she was still uncertain. Since she was grown, no man had ever seen her naked, not even her uncle, and she thought that the only way she could ever truly find out if she was indeed beautiful, or at least pretty, was if she could *see* the response in a man's eyes as she stood thus before him. Not her uncle, of course, but a man! She also wanted to know what a man, a real man and not a painting or a statue, looked like. The young man from Nicomedia?

Diana watched in the mirror as her nipples hardened and her skin turn red. *Not again!* She thought and then sighed. I guess I will know soon enough when I am married. Somehow she knew that it wouldn't be for a long time and in a way, it made her sad. Slowly, she turned away, put on her night dress, and got into bed leaving the oil lamp lit. She knew she wouldn't sleep. Not yet. She wanted to think.

Diana didn't realise it but she fell asleep almost immediately. Now, she *jolted* awake from a dream she couldn't remember. She was strangely alert, not groggy as she normally was when first waking up, and she knew that something important had just happened. Her lamp was still lit but she did not concern herself with it. Intense with concern, she *jumped* out of bed, threw open the door, and darted past. She hurriedly ran down the stairs holding the hem of her gown up to her knees, forgetting that the flimsy white cotton nightgown which revealed more than concealed her body was the only thing she was wearing. Heedless of this and due to her fast-growing concern, she ran. Never once did she stop and consider the scandal that it would cause if she were to be seen or the embarrassment that it would cause her. Had she considered what she did, she would have blushed, but she never once blushed. She only knew that she must run immediately to her uncle's room because something important was happening. So she simply ran.

Fortunately, it was late and the route she took, more out of habit rather than instinct, was the private one. Diana encountered no one, and no one saw or heard her run through the palace. When she came to her father's door, she felt a strangeness in the air. As if some type of residue lingered. As if a type of density pressed upon her. Her nostrils flared! There was a peculiar smell. A smell of fire? It was somehow a clean smell. She would never forget it.

Without hesitating and without knocking, she burst open the door and flung herself into the room -- only stopping her momentum after she was inside.

As she stood there, she screamed,

"Father!"

What she saw when she realised that she was seeing, made the blood rush from her head causing her to faint! She collapsed in a heap on the floor. As she fell, her last thoughts were both confusing and terrifying. Then only blackness....

25

Tengri was exhausted. He looked at the moon and knew that its dominion over the night sky would soon end. It is nearly dawn, he thought, the second dawn I have seen without sleep. He seriously wondered if he would be able to successfully walk the net into the Emperor's room.

He had two problems to consider. First, to travel the fibres required a lot of energy. Energy that, once expended, would leave Tengri exhausted and vulnerable. Already, much of that vital life-giving power had been used just to reach this strange land in the West. Soon he would have to once again, call upon the shaman's power to access the void in order to locate the silver thread that would take him to his destination. Coupled with no sleep and the day's events, he knew his energy might not be sufficient. That, in itself, could be extremely dangerous. Also, his helping spirit had already been released during his journey to Mergen Tengere. Now, he wished he had had the foresight to capture at least one other spirit. But, it was too late. He dared not use what little power he had left.

Second, Tengri wasn't quite sure where he was going. Had it not been for his toe, he realised there would be absolutely *no* chance for success. For unless travel was intentionally random, some type of *prior* knowledge of one's destination was usually needed to successfully navigate the fibres -- either by having been there before, or by having acquired a clear image through hearing the proper songs. He had neither. What he *did* have was a sense of connection with the man named Constantine, felt when his mind travelled the golden weave of time several years previously. That connection was the result of *feeling* the essence of Constantine through the man known as Ossius. Tengri wondered if that would now be sufficient.

But there was also something else, Tengri noted. There was another source of attunement. He wasn't sure of its source or point of origin, but it felt as if an essence had reached out to him. Not the other way around as was normally the custom of a seeker.

It should be about time, he thought, and he checked to make certain everything was properly prepared. Tengri was properly marked and his clothes had been placed in the specially made pouch -- the pouch made by Tapti by her special weaving and her special songs. Only material objects made in such a manner could travel the void with its owner. Only sacred objects made sacred by special consecrating ceremonies were capable of surviving the ordeal. Those that were not had to be completely encased in a sacred pouch.

Tengri began to sing:

"Silver moon bird ..."

He suddenly stopped! Even though he had entered the second mystical phase, he still stopped.

Tengri had heard a crashing sound. The sound of a quickly moving ... animal? ... human? racing without heed nor care of the bushes and trees blocking its path. It came from the North and it was on a course that would intercept his present position.

The fire! Thought Tengri, it is attracted to the fire.

Closer …

Tengri pulled his knife from the pouch …

Closer it came … More loudly and quickly did the sound reach his ears.

… I am in the second state, he thought. I am more dangerous as a warrior. I can call the ghost wind …

Closer!

… but to call the wind would certainly drain me …

Louder!

… I must fight with knife or forsake the mission! Tengri rose and turned to the North …

Leap!

… a *manbeast!* By its sound and its feel, it is both man and animal. A demon?

It lands!

Tengri relaxed as he saw a black wolf with yellow eyes carrying a silver light in its mouth,

"Kaltak!" Said Tengri in a voice betraying his anger. "Why do you interrupt? You know that what I do is important!"

He watched as his sister shapechanged into human form. Like he, she was naked. Her fair hair was mussed and her skin shiny with sweat. She smelled of lovemaking and as Tengri looked into her yellow eyes (he was the only person who was capable of seeing them without having doubts of their colour), they indeed betrayed her unfulfilled excitement of recent sexual union.

"You disapprove brother?" She said noticing Tengri's glance at her pubic area.

"Of what?" He replied. "Your interruption or your lovemaking?"

"Both."

"Kaltak, the answer is yes on both counts. I wove the indigo fibres so that you and Pouie could enter into his dreams for a

Baqca

purpose other than fulfilling your human desires."

"I am not fulfilled, brother, your sister pushed me away and as we now speak, she makes love to him still. She makes love to him in future time."

"*What?* Are you two crazy?"

"Don't be so judgmental," she responded, "you certainly did not hesitate with the three spirit nymphs ..."

"*How did you ...*"

"How did I know about that?" Kaltak interrupted, completing his sentence while slowly approaching him. "Did you really think that your big sister would let her little brother take such a long and *treacherous* journey without protection? Did you really think I would willingly *miss* your first lessons in love ...?"

As his sister spoke, Tengri reflected. He didn't know that Kaltak had watched or that she had watched over him during that journey. Had he known then, he would have been mad, embarrassed. But now, it didn't matter. Both his sisters teased him terribly and he wondered if they were like that with his older brothers. He doubted it. Pouie was more serious than Kaltak, and even though she worried, she would never think of doing what she would consider, intruding. Kaltak, on the other hand, would tease him mercilessly about anything. However, he knew that she did so simply to cover her worry. She worried much more about him than their sister. If she teased him now, it was for a reason.

"... My dear brother, I saw in your eyes the pleasure that you enjoyed. I *saw* that it took *two days* before your hardness softened for the first time ..."

"Dear sister," Tengri interrupted teasing her in kind, "your words and your eyes betray your arousal. You are disappointed because you have not been satisfied."

Kaltak, now close enough to her brother, quickly reached out with her hand to grasp his penis. Tengri was quicker, he backed up and grabbed her wrist with his hand before she could touch what she was after.

"*Kaltak!* You're my sister!"

"I know," she said with a pretended pout, "I merely jest."

She suddenly became serious. The sense spread to Tengri and they both responded to the gravity of the situation.

"Tengri," she said breaking the brief silence, "the spirit memory of our mother entered into the dream of the man called Constantine even before we did. He had to have his fibres rewoven or he would not have been able to withstand the workings of the smith. We did what was required, no more. Still, I fear more should have been done to strengthen his weave. His spirit flows along a path of great importance and is delicately balanced. The force of his actions is extremely powerful. Let us hope that his power flows the proper channel because he has weaknesses. Weaknesses that we could not strengthen without causing his death. You, dear brother, *must* cause a greater equilibrium in his life for he will need to rely upon you, to *trust* you with more than he can bear. Pouie and I have planted that seed into his dream, into his very being. He will ask of you, suddenly and without prior thought, to do something, to perform a task of grave necessity. You will not want to do it, but you must. You must appear to him to be willing because if you hesitate, he will doubt the trust he has placed in you and what he will ask, he will not have the strength to ask again. Rather, his life and our hopes would be lost. Even so, even *if* you succeed, his pain will be felt throughout the centuries."

"What is this task?" Asked Tengri.

"I speak only as the net flows. The weave does not flow into your awareness prior to being asked."

Suddenly, Kaltak stiffened with distraction, she listened to voices that only she could hear.

"It is time, dear brother."

She opened her hand and revealed the silver light that, when in wolf form, she carried in her mouth. She threw it to the North and the light unravelled to form a thread.

Kaltak looked at her brother and said, "I knew you were tired so I captured the fibre you needed. Go now."

Tengri looked into her eyes and then tenderly touched the side of her face. With that, he jumped onto the fibre and danced through the void. He did not need to sing any songs.

Kaltak watched as her brother vanished in a flash of light. She was one of the few who could watch a 'leaving' without fear of blindness. It was a quality of her eyes that protected her vision. It was that same quality which prevented her from forming tears ... but it did not prevent her from crying.

She now cried without tears because of the pain her brother would soon feel. If he accepted Constantine's request, it would fortunately prevent him from making a serious error which, if made, would devastate the future of all people. If that mistake were to be made, it would start a war between the Kazak-Kirghiz and Buryat peoples. It would prevent an event which a golden thread had revealed to her a thousand years hence. However, she also knew that such a war between two Mongolian clans would be nothing compared to a future war that would be caused.

26

Constantine's eyes opened before his mind woke from its vision. It was a strange sensation. It was strange to have the mind enveloped in darkness while the eyes could see the dance of shadows. A dance resulting from the flicker of the dying fire still hanging onto what little life left to it in the fireplace.

As his mind began to awaken by striving to attain equality with his sight, he grimaced with the pain he had felt in his third vision. The pain that overcame him just prior to his succumbing to the darkness.

But as sleep overcomes wakefulness, wakefulness, in turn, overpowers sleep. The pain left and consciousness brought forth memories -- memories of two women, lovemaking, war, and betrayal.

"By the gods!" Exclaimed Constantine, "That was *not* a dream! That was life itself."

He wondered if Diana's visions were like the one he just experienced. He wondered if she experienced lovemaking. He reached down beneath his covers to feel for a dampness that would betray his wet dream, but his nightshirt was dry. He wondered how that could be because he *knew* that he came at least twice. He could still feel his softening erection which even lasted through the horrors of his third dream.

Then Constantine noticed that the smell of the third vision still lingered in the room. The oddly clean smell of Greek fire.

His attention focused as the hairs on the back of his neck stood on end. In the semi-darkness he watched as thin silver threads began to dart about the room. He watched as the darkness appeared to tear and a deeper darkness hidden behind the fabric of reality showed through. He watched with fascination as the silver fibres formed a pattern not unlike the web of a spider.

A sudden flash of light temporarily blinded the Emperor and when his vision returned a heartbeat later, the hidden darkness and silver web were gone. In their place stood a man with long black hair. Except for a necklace of animal teeth and a feather braided into his hair, he was naked -- unless the marks of what appeared to be ash could be considered as covering for his body. They couldn't.

"Wh ... wh ... who? ... Wh ... wh ... what? ..." Stuttered Constantine more amazed than alarmed.

"I am Tengri, the ninth son of the eagle, Tengere Kaira Kahn. I am Kazak-Kirghiz. I am a baqca, a deathwalker. I am the weaver of your vision, your vision of the owl and the wolf. I am here to warn you of betrayal."

"I know you!" Shouted Constantine. "You are the Mage who has appeared to Diana, who has given her the gift of second sight. You are the man that the owl just told me about! You are here to help me!" He started to get out of bed.

"I do not know this Diana of whom you speak, nor have I ever appeared to her. But the owl is my sister." Tengri opened his pouch, pulled out his shirt and pants and began to get dressed.

"Diana is my niece and she has had dreams of you. She has described you to me in detail. You are indeed the one in her visions. How could you not know of her?"

"Your Diana, must have the gift of your gods. It sounds as if her spirit, or mind, has learned to travel certain fibres. If what you say is true, she has travelled to me. Not I to her. Indeed, she sounds to be of a truly rare quality."

"Fibres?" queried Constantine.

"The threads which make the net of the universe. They make the fabric that manifests as our material world. The quality of the thread and the manner in which it is woven will also determine the nature of other realities, be they dream, spirit, thought, time -- it makes little difference except to the reality itself and those who live in it. Ultimately, the fibres are created by God by virtue of the eternal song that he sings. Motion is caused by his eternal dance. We must learn to be in harmony with the sound issued from his mouth. That is why he wove the fibres to make shamans."

"And Diana *knows* of this?" questioned Constantine.

"You must ask her. I doubt it, though. Shamans do not live in your land. I can tell that your kind, those who people the West, do not understand these things. Your land has spoken to my feet as I walked and told me that its people have forgotten the ancient ways. They have replaced sacredness with a man-made god who has been made as one makes a city that cannot move. Without movement, the land underneath dies and becomes a place of the dead. A place suitable only to demons who do the bidding of the nameless. This is why I am here. To warn you and to tell you that your land is dying."

"I can understand you," said Constantine, "something inside of me is different. I see and feel differently. But oddly, I know that I can trust you."

"I have journeyed long and far. I have not slept and I have spent too much power to get here. May I sit?"

Constantine nodded his head and Tengri walked to the fireplace and sat so that his back was to the fire and he faced the Emperor. Constantine sat on the edge of his bed.

"I have much that I need to tell you," continued Tengri, "and much to show you. However, I have only a short time left, but I need, first, to sleep."

"You are a welcome visitor to my palace and my land, but I fear that you must be hidden from view and I further fear that you will be in great danger if you are discovered. Because of my fears I will not be able to afford you the hospitality I would like."

"It is of no matter," replied Tengri, "your ways are strange to me and I would be out of place if I were to meet many of your people. I take no offence at your wise precautions."

"Then it is settled. We must find you a secluded place to rest ..."

"Before I sleep," interrupted Tengri, "I must tell you of *your* danger. I do not know the words that were spoken, I only understood the emotion. But I *do* know that men named Ossius, Nicholas, and Athanasius conspire an evil plot. They intend to betray you and attempt to cause an evil to manifest in your land that will control the beliefs of your people. I fear they have already succeeded to such an extent that they cannot be truly stopped. Rather, their deeds can only be fought at a time far into the future. What *we* do now will determine their success or failure."

"How do you know of these men? Because you describe a truth that I have begun to suspect."

"I have travelled a fibre with my mind and have *seen* them. The one called Ossius *sensed* my presence. Be careful of him. He is very dark and very dangerous. Tomorrow, I will show you the weave of the fifth, twelfth, and unnumbered stones which describe the present and future times that the owl and wolf revealed to you during your vision dream."

Suddenly Constantine, without thinking, blurted out, "Tengri, I

must ask you a favour. I must ask you to do something for me that
will hurt me deeply ..."

Tengri knew this was the request Kaltak had told him about.
The request that he would not normally have agreed to, but which
was absolutely necessary.

"... but if you refuse me as I fear you might, then I fear I
will be *hurt*, no, *destroyed*, by what is destined to happen. I will
understand if you refuse because what I am about to ask will
sound so impossible ..."

"Ask!" Interrupted Tengri in a tone of authority. He already
knew that he would consent -- *must* consent to the request because
he now, for the first time, realised the truth of why he came on this
journey. It was for no other reason than to *fulfil* the Emperor's
demand!

"Tengri, when you leave here, you must take Diana, my niece,
with you." Before allowing Tengri to answer, Constantine fully
explained the situation that Ossius was forcing. It took some
time to explain, but Tengri only superficially listened. He was
considering the hardships that would be experienced by Diana as
well as the great responsibility that would be thrust upon Tapti,
their daughter, and himself. When Constantine finished speaking,
and answering without hesitation, Tengri said, "Yes. Your niece
will be safe in my yurt. She will be the daughter of Tapti and
Tengri, the ninth son of the eagle. She will be the sister of my
daughter. Diana will become Kazak-Kirghiz."

Constantine relaxed ... his niece would be safe.

At that instant, the door burst open ...

"Father!" Screamed the young woman in the white nightgown.

Tengri and Constantine both watched in surprise as Diana's
eyes widened when she saw Tengri, the man she knew from her
visions. She collapsed before either of the two men -- brothers --
could react.

27

"Diana ..."

She heard a voice, so distant, so far away. She knew the word but wasn't sure what it meant. She recognised the quality of the sound ...

"... Diana ..."

... but it was from another world. It didn't matter here. It is so far away ...

"I think she is coming to, *Diana*. Can you hear me? ..."

... Diana? That is me. That is my name ... so far away, let me go.

"... Are you all right? Diana, listen to me. I'm your uncle. Diana wake up!"

... My uncle? Yes, my uncle ... Emperor ... Diana, I'm his *daughter* ...

"... *Diana!*"

... I remember now, I had another vision! Her eyes opened and she saw her uncle looking down at her. She was in her bed and wrapped in her blanket. Why is my uncle in my room? She thought.

"You had me worried," said Constantine, "what ever made you come down here?"

"Down here?" Responded Diana confusedly. "Why are *you* up here?"

Then she noticed. She wasn't in her room. She was in her uncle's. She was in his bed, looking up at his ceiling above his face.

"Oh," she responded, "now I remember."

Remember! Yes, she remembered! She had had another vision. She had seen the Mage again. It seemed so real, she thought, but *how* did I get down here?

"Father," she said, "I dreamed of him again, the Mage, I saw him with you."

She is calling me father, thought Constantine, and it caused him to feel warm inside.

"Diana," said Constantine, "I was wrong yesterday when I said your dreams would never come true ..."

"What?" She interrupted. "I understand ..."

"... No Diana! Listen! I, too, have had one of your visions ..." Her eyes widened. She was now fully awake.

"... I understand what you have been experiencing now. I know your visions are important and it would be terribly wrong to force you to deny them."

"But ..."

"Diana, there is something I want to show you. Someone I want you to meet."

Constantine pointed to the fireplace where Tengri still sat. Diana sat up and again her eyes widened as the strange man stood and walked toward the bed where Diana lay.

Diana wasn't quite sure what to think. She knew he was real and had expected that one day she would meet him. But she never expected it would be today. And now, she had to do something but didn't know what. She considered fainting again, but that was no good.

Meekly, she said, "Hello. My name is Diana."

"I am called Tengri."

"Are you," Diana started speaking with excited enthusiasm, "a Mage?"

"Your tongue," replied Tengri, "is very new and foreign to me as I have only learned it recently by virtue of a gift from the gods. But as I search for words in your tongue, your word 'Mage' is inappropriate. In my language I am a shaman of sorts and that word may adequately compare to your *Mage* except there are still major differences. However, in my own tongue, I am known as a baqca which transcends the abilities of a shaman. It is like being a shaman except that it is more than being a shaman. A translation in my language would also be deathwalker."

"Deathwalker," Diana pronounced the words out loud.

"I find in comparison," continued Tengri, "that the word cannot adequately be defined in Latin. However, the phrase *Master of Moonlight* is adequate."

"What does deathwalker mean?" asked Diana.

"It is one who is at home in the world of spirits. One who can freely move through that world and other worlds by riding the fibres of the net."

"Fibres, net? *What* is that?"

"Diana," interjected Constantine, "Tengri has travelled a long way by a means we don't understand and to explain would take a long time. He is tired and has not slept in two days. It is almost dawn and I think we all need to rest. Let us wait until tomorrow evening and I'm sure that Tengri will try to answer your questions."

Turning to Tengri, Constantine continued, "you may sleep here, but be careful not to wander outside of this room in case you would be seen. I will ensure that no one enters while you are here."

"No," said Tengri, "I cannot rest in a yurt that cannot move. I must be able to touch the sky so my energy can be renewed. I will return to the forest."

"That will not be possible," he replied, "you would have to travel through the palace, the city, and you will surely be seen. That is neither safe nor wise." Nor was it necessarily true.

When she heard what was being discussed and understood, Diana excitedly interrupted. She had *a brilliant* idea.

"Father, if he is not to be seen, it is obvious he cannot stay in your room. Even if you tell the servants not to enter while you are absent, they will suspect that you are hiding something. It is also obvious that Tengri cannot leave the palace as he will be noticed. And, Tengri, you say you need to be outside. There is only one possible solution. Tengri must stay in the tower. Or, rather, *on* the tower. The walled forecastle above my room."

The three discussed the matter and it was decided that Diana's suggestion was the only logical solution. Quietly, they sneaked

through the back corridors and safely made it to Diana's room
and settled Tengri into his temporary residence. He was satisfied
with the arrangements.

When Constantine and Diana closed the door to the roof and
were alone, Constantine said, "Daughter, there is something of
grave importance that I must tell you."

They sat and spoke until well after dawn.

28

When Diana awoke, she waited a few moments before allowing
her eyes to open. When they did, she noted that it must be mid-
afternoon. The angle at which the sun's rays entered the room
through the cracks of her closed shutters betrayed the length of
time that she slept.

Betrayed she thought, such an ugly word. Such an ugly concept.
She felt that *she* had been betrayed, but not nearly as badly as her
dear uncle -- no, father! She corrected herself and smiled at the
feeling she had -- that warm, soothing, feeling that flowed through
her very soul when she heard her father call her 'daughter'. That
made everything all right. That made her life up to this point
worthwhile and would make the rest of her existence worth living
no matter what difficulties she may encounter.

Still, she was angry. Angry at Ossius and what he represented.
Never! Even if it meant torture and death would she *ever* become
a Christian. What they did to her father even after he *allowed* them
their freedom could never be forgiven. Never would she convert
even if it meant burning in their eternal hell!

She could not have possibly known it, but torture, death, and
worse awaited her if she had gone to that secluded retreat as
Ossius planned.

She was sad. Her father had told her early that morning what
had transpired with Ossius and what it meant. He had told her
of the necessity of her leaving with Tengri. That surprised her at

first and she vehemently protested. But after all was explained, she realised that there was no other choice.

Now, the idea intrigued her. In a way, she looked forward to the adventure. Her father had told her that Tengri could teach her about her visions and that he had said to him that she was special. Her father related *his* vision although she had suspected he left parts out. Probably because it was late, Diana decided. And he had said that Tengri *caused* it. He used words like weaving dreams and travelling along fibres. He told her that Tengri had sisters who were owls and wolves. She liked that idea. It somehow made sense to her. She remembered, when the three of them came into her room, that at first she thought Tengri vain because he stared at the mirror. Then she realised that it wasn't himself he looked at, but rather the carved dragon-like creature. It seemed important to him but he said nothing about it. She mentally made a note to ask.

Her father told her that Tengri would adopt her as his daughter. But she would never think of him as such. Perhaps as a friend or teacher, she had said, but she only had one father as far as she was concerned. What she *didn't* express aloud were her timid thoughts that, perhaps, Tengri could be a … husband? She was disappointed when she found out he had a wife named Tapti and a daughter. Still, she wasn't too disappointed because she realised her thoughts were not really realistic, they were only curiosity. She wanted to know more about Tapti. Maybe they could be good friends, or maybe even as close as sisters?

Diana knew that when she left she would cry and would probably do so for a long time. She would miss her father and it would hurt. They both talked about that, but she was grown up now. No, she thought, one *never* grows up this way. Feelings don't go away. But there was one consolation. In a few years, when she learned to be free, when this present mess was over with, she would return and again be with her father. They both agreed and her father asked her to do him a favour. He wanted her to start a diary. To keep it and let him read it when they were reunited. She would.

Diana remembered confiding in her father about things like marriage, love, her insecurities about herself, and she was glad she did. Somehow, it made her more mature. Somehow, there seemed to be more love in their relationship. He told her that the young man from Nicomedia, though handsome, was an idiot and he hadn't come to discuss marriage. Just like a father, smiled Diana, he wasn't *that* bad. However, she also realised she was thinking more ... physically.

She was sad, happy, excited, apprehensive, everything all mixed into one. She knew it would hurt to leave, but it would hurt even more to stay. Her father would die inside if she stayed. *Damned Ossius!* She was also sad because she knew that she and her father would not talk again, maybe even for years, because tomorrow night, she would leave and there was still much to be done. However, tomorrow evening there might be a little time. They had concocted a plan.

Her disappearance would cause a lot of trouble so together they worked out a scheme in which late tomorrow afternoon she and her father would have a public fight. He would demand that she convert and submit to baptism and renounce her dreams as the work of the devil. She in turn would throw a tantrum, run to her room, and in a fit of anger and depression, kill herself. She would have a *glorious* funeral and her father would demand that Ossius bless and baptise her closed coffin. She and Tengri would then sneak out in the middle of the night....

She didn't quite understand how they would travel, but it sounded like living in a dream. She wanted to comprehend *desperately* all of this new knowledge.

Knock ... Knock ... Knock ... The door opened.

"My, my, my, young lady!" said Helen as she entered the room carrying a tray with two portions of food.

Diana was happy that Helen and her new brother would be told of the plan the next day.

"... Already it is mid afternoon and you are *still* in bed!" She said as she set down the tray and flung open the shutters letting in the sun and fresh air.

"Good morn ... err ... afternoon, Helen."

"Your uncle said to wake you and to give you *two* portions! You must truly be hungry. He wants me to do something else immediately so I can't stay to help you get dressed. I wouldn't anyway because if you sleep all day, you have the strength to do it yourself." She teased.

"Thank you Helen. Oh Helen, I love you very much."

Helen paused at the door and looked at Diana before leaving.

"I love you too, dear. Now get dressed and eat." With that, she left and silently closed the door.

Diana threw off the covers and got out of bed. She walked to the mirror as she normally did each morning and looked at herself.

She gasped in *horror* at what she saw!

It suddenly occurred to her that the night before she had run through the palace and spoke to her father and a strange man while wearing only her nightshirt. As she looked in the mirror now, and with the sunlight behind her, she could see through the thin material. Even when she blocked the light by closing the shutters, she could still see the darkness of her nipples and pubic hairs showing through! Also, she could clearly see the contours of her breasts, hips, and legs as well as the colour of her skin. Although not totally revealed, her body was revealed enough! She was embarrassed and began to blush. Quickly, she got dressed in her most conservative clothes. Perhaps they hadn't noticed, she hoped -- *she wished!* If Tengri had seen, she also wondered what he thought. Would men find me attractive?

Knowing the food was meant to be shared with Tengri, she picked up the tray and proceeded to climb the steps to the roof.

She peeked her head around the corner hoping Tengri was awake. Good, he was.

"Tengri, are you hungry?"

"Yes," he said looking up.

"Unless I am disturbing you, may I stay?" Diana asked meekly.

"Yes, please sit," he responded pleasantly.

"Tengri, father told me that I am to leave with you tomorrow and that I am to live with you and your family. I'm scared and I don't want to be a burden. Are you sure it is all right?"

Tengri looked deeply into her eyes. Diana became self conscious at the silence and feared he would ridicule or otherwise deride her. She didn't expect the warmth and compassion in his answer.

"Diana, you will be *more* than welcome. You will be of my family. I will be a second and lesser father to you, but I will also be your teacher ... I am willing to teach you because *you* have the inner spirit to become a shamaness if you so desire. You have a unique quality that is rare even amongst my own people ..."

"I *very* much want that," she interrupted.

"... Tapti, my wife will, I think, be more of a sister than a mother. She is not much older than yourself and in many ways, you are both alike. You both have the makings of being close friends."

Diana noticed Tengri frowning at his food and sympathised with him because she knew that soon her own tastes would have to adjust. She said, "You try our food, for soon I must eat yours."

Tengri smiled, reached into his pouch, pulled out the dried horse meat and said, "Sooner than you think, Diana. I will tell you what it is after you eat, and then you can tell me what I ate."

Diana frowned but agreed. She frowned more after tasting.

"Tengri, can I ask some questions?"

"Yes," he replied while picking at his food.

"What is your land like? Will we live in a city or a village?"

Tengri looked up, glad to be distracted from his food. "Our summers are very hot, much more so than here. Our winters are bitterly cold with frequent strong winds. We mostly live in the steppes, but sometimes in the desert. That is where I prefer to live. And, sometimes we live in the forests further North. Unless, of course, we are feuding with the Buryat, which is often. We do not know cities as our yurts are frequently moved to new locations. You might say that we are a village, but I do not live near it because I am a baqca. Even so, I live farther away than normally and always choose to live on sacred land."

"Why?" asked Diana.

"A baqca must live with forces people don't understand and if we live too close to our clan, they can sometimes be hurt by spirits and even our ceremonies if we are not careful. Also, I choose solitude. Tapti, however, often goes to the village and you will go with her and can make many new friends. Our people are very friendly and you will be accepted. Perhaps even popular because you are so different. But understand clearly, Diana, your life will not be easy. We live in balance with nature and every act that we perform affects that balance. You must learn our ways while you are with us, and not rely upon your own. It will not be easy."

"Tengri, what must I take?"

"Only what can fit into this pouch. But, I will leave behind everything I have so you can fill it with whatever you like."

Diana frowned at its small size, "can I bring my own?"

"No, the way that we travel is through the void. The only things that we can take are items that will fit into sacred pouches. I will explain this to you later and, tonight, I shall show you fibres so that you can better understand. I suggest that you bring only one dress. Tapti will make new clothes for you when we arrive. Anything else that you bring is entirely up to you as we will give you all that is needed, or teach you how to provide for yourself."

"What should I wear to travel the void?" She asked.

"Wear?"

"Yes, what should I wear that is appropriate?"

"Oh. You will wear the marks of sacred ash so that the spirits will not recognise you and which will trick them into thinking that you are one of them. I shall prepare you tomorrow night."

"No Tengri, I mean, should I wear a dress or some other garment? Will it be hot or cold in the void?"

"It is neither hot nor cold in that world, but you cannot wear *any* clothes, only marks. That is Law."

Diana was shocked to hear what she thought she heard and with indignation, almost aggression, she blurted, *"law? whose law!?"* And then bit her lower lip for fear she may have offended by her unintentional caustic response.

Tengri merely looked at the young woman who had, without provocation, just spoken with a tone of indignation. Then he remembered his mistakes of yesterday with the woman and the smith. Perhaps, he thought to himself, it is the custom of these people to be ashamed of their bodies. Or maybe their clothing had some spiritual significance. He didn't know but decided to approach the subject delicately.

"Diana," he said, "the question is not *whose* law but *the* Law. I speak of the Law of Creation. The Law of God that has set the worlds into being and motion. I have discovered that in your land, your people have learned to make cities and permanent dwellings. With their *making,* you have also learned to make your own laws, all of which seem to be associated with the *ownership* of things. The earth has spoken to me and said that your kind have also learned to make your god so that it conforms with *your* making or reality. The earth has told me that here it is dying. The cities built upon it cannot move and so the spirits leave. Your people have forgotten the ancient Law. I speak not of your illusory sense of reality or your man-made laws. I speak only of the Law of the universe to which all creatures are bound whether they remember or not."

Ashamed that she may have been rude with her exclamation, Diana attempted a more docile response, but she realised her voice still betrayed a hint of her shock. She asked, "but what possible difference could it make to the Law what one wears?"

"What is worn in your material life does not matter. But in sacred work, it does. You can enter into the spirit world without marks. But your soul will be captured and eaten. The spirits care not about your custom or law. They only care about their own. If you travel to a far away land, you would find that their man-made laws are different than they are here. If you inadvertently break one of their laws, you are bound, without choice, to their justice. It is the same in spirit worlds and other realms. Only their laws are far more difficult to understand. That is why it is so dangerous. However, the Law of the universe supersedes all other laws, and *all* are subservient to it. Regardless if they are believed or not. That is why our people would call your people insane. It is because your people have forgotten about the ancient ways and, consequently, have chosen a path demonstrative of a lack of respect and total disregard to universal Law ...

"... Also, Diana, you can enter the void and dance along the fibres whilst wearing clothes. But if you do, you must also understand that within moments you would be destroyed. Clothing is not the only Law. There are many others. You must not only know the words to the song that you sing, you must *also* know all of the subtle variances in tonal qualities and be able to properly emulate the correct sounds. The dance you must perform is not arbitrary. It is exact. The motion must be in perfect equilibrium with the universal dance. The words of our songs are not just mere words. Each word represents a sacred name, and within that sacred name is power."

"Tengri, you said that wearing clothes in the void would cause one to be destroyed. Why is that?" Diana asked, now more curious than concerned.

"Each person is a product of the flow of forces determined by the way things are. Each spirit, soul, and body unite to form one eternal identity and those three elements interweave with each other so as to cause the manifestation of one being upon one or more planes of existence. You, for example, are composed of a body which gives you reality on the earth. But you also have spirit and soul. Those three elements unite in a special pattern which we call a weave and identifies you as a person, a living entity called Diana. When your body dies, you no longer walk the earth. But still, your spirit and soul dance together to maintain your true life in other worlds. Later, their dance will weave a density, another body that will be born into flesh again. Perhaps, next time, you will be a man living in another land. But you would still be as much Diana as you would be a new person with a different name. Simply, your body is merely clothing for the real you.

"After many centuries," he continued, "your spirit dies, or I should say, is reformed and evolves into a higher being living in a new world or reality. But you are still Diana. But Diana is not your true name. It is merely an earth name. Perhaps the hundredth or thousandth earth name that your soul and spirit has had. Your *True Name* was determined when your spirit first moved into this reality and had taken on the clothing of flesh. Your soul, which is the real essence of the one known as Diana, never dies unless it has violated or come into conflict with Law. But this is extremely rare. This only happens if one truly chooses to join forces with what we call the *Nameless*. An unspeakable evil arising from the depths of chaos and which has a power to create its' own Law. It is not really separate from *the* Law. Rather, it appears to be an opposite function of the One and which is locked in eternal conflict for domination. As there is goodness, there is also evil. This is what I mean. Its' creation is destruction and a movement backward in time to a beginning of no existence. Our creation is progression to a greater and expanded awareness. One must choose one or the other path. If one chooses the path of the nameless, then one seeks to destroy and to ultimately dwell in a primitive state. If one chooses to learn True Names, then one seeks enlightenment to the true nature of God so that Creation progresses to greater glories. If one chooses the evil way, I had said that the soul is destroyed. I don't mean that literally, because it cannot truly be destroyed in the sense that we think of destruction. I mean it in the sense that the soul finds new existence in the torment of losing what it has gained. Truly, such would be torment because the nature of things cannot fully accommodate a forgetfulness of loss. One path is Truth, the other, deceit."

Diana was so intently listening and enraptured with what Tengri was saying, she had forgotten her question. It no longer seemed significant. She felt a strange flow of energy swirling about them and a pronounced sense of awe.

Tengri continued, "to answer your question more directly, Diana, you are in a state of pureness when your three elements are allowed to flow in their proper dance unhindered by the dance of other manifestations. Remember, earlier I told you that everything you do, be it an act, a thought, or a dream, affects the balance of the way things are. You exist by virtue of the way your essence is woven together. That, in itself is sacred! Perhaps more sacred than you realise. You are made up of threads of creation which cause you to be as you are. If you enter into sacred worlds such as the void, your identity must be in its purity because you visit a realm of pure essence. If your fibres were to be mixed, confused, or burdened with the weave of another substance, such as unsacred clothing, you would not be recognised as a living being, but rather, as a mere material manifestation. Somewhat like waste. The nature of Law is to make everything useful and anything wasteful would be rewoven into something else that is of the nature of the void. The natural tendency of the fibres is to change the nature of that with which it comes into contact to conform to its own intent. To enter the void improperly would cause you to become something other than what you are. Since you *are* a living entity, you would not want to become embodied into a non-living shell destined to be lost in that ether for eternity. Your soul would be trapped, it cannot be changed or made nonexistent, but you *would* be unable to function as you are supposed to. However, the real danger transcends that imprisonment. Because also in the void travel the nameless. Those nameless entities will recognise the life force which is trapped and, they in turn, will capture you and take you into the depths of their chaos. We call them 'eaters of souls' or körmös."

Tengri looked to ensure he hadn't lost Diana and was pleased
to see she was absorbed with his words. She will do well, he
thought.

"Not all people can withstand visiting the spirit realms or
the void because their individual weaves are not strong enough
to adjust to the intensity of power. Indeed, there are even many
shaman who are incapable. Always, in our training, one's fibres
must be rewoven, usually by the smith. But there are also other
ways. You have a unique weave although your fibres are weak.
I have no doubts that in the future you *will* meet the smith, but
for now, you will be able to withstand the journey, but only if I
properly prepare you. I will protect you so that you will remain
unhurt. Still, I cannot allow you to wear clothing because of the
danger I just explained. But tell me, Diana, is there some custom
that your people have about their clothing?"

Diana, now remembering her question, awoke from her intense
fascination and with that awakening came that all too familiar
and uncomfortable heat brought about by her blush. Oh no, she
thought. *Please* not now!

Tengri, noticing, said, "I'm sorry, I did not mean to pry into
your customs ..."

Quickly, Diana interjected, "oh no, that's not it. I ... uh ...
thought that ... I mean, I um ... Just a minute ..." She tried to
compose herself and thought that if she forced herself to talk
about it, it wouldn't be so bad. She continued, "it's just ... uh ...
that for me ... I mean, in our ... um ... culture, one's nakedness
is private. We are taught to be modest and that men and women
shouldn't be seen ... uh ... without clothes unless they are married.
I mean ... it's just so embarrassing!"

"It is the same in our culture Diana. We do not normally walk
around naked and we understand modesty. Very seldom will you
see someone unclothed, but if it happens, we do not concern
ourselves about it ..."

"No," Diana interrupted. She decided she might as well come

out with it. If he were to be her teacher, she supposed that he had to know what she thought and was really like. "It's not that, Tengri, this is difficult for me as I have never told anyone this. Especially to someone whom I've known for less than a day, but, I'm scared of what people will think of my body. I've never been seen by a man before nor have I seen one ... er ... man that is. I'm afraid that you ... oh God! ... *they* ... people I mean, will think I'm ugly."

"Diana, you are not ugly. But even if you were, why would you care what people think? It is not your body which defines beauty, it is your inner weave. Allow yourself ..."

"Diana, Tengri." They heard Constantine's voice as he climbed the steps to the roof.

"Please, Tengri," she whispered, "don't tell him of our conversation."

Constantine arrived carrying a role of bound parchment, a vial of ink, and several quills.

"These are for you," he said handing them to Diana. "They are for your diary." He noticed she was blushing but thought better than to mention it.

"Thank you father," she said smiling as she took them.

"I need to speak to you, Tengri, about a plan my daughter and I developed this morning."

"I'll leave you two alone," said Diana, "besides, I need to decide what to take with me." She rose to leave.

"Wait," said Tengri. He emptied the sacred pouch. "This knife, smaller pouch, and red fabric which is a gift to Tapti, will need to be taken with us, but you can fill it as much as you wish with your things. Just remember that it must be able to be completely closed." Tengri gave her the pouch with the fabric still inside, but kept the smaller one and his knife.

She took them and left.

As she sat alone in her room, she wrote briefly in her diary. Then she rolled it up and put it, the ink, and quills inside the pouch. It doesn't leave me much room, she thought.

She spent the next hour going through everything that she owned trying to decide what she should take. She tried a number of combinations, but nothing seemed to work right. Ok, she thought, what will I need? The diary is from my father. That goes. This wooden horse that I carved will be a gift to Tengri's daughter. That goes. That leaves room for my shoes. They go. And now, which item of clothing shall I take? And then she saw it! The wood carving on the mirror of the dragon like creature. Something inside said she had to take it with her. She had forgotten to ask Tengri why he had stared at it … later, she thought. On a whim, she knew it had to go as well.

She examined it and discovered it could be broken off without too much damage. She knew she would be able to fix what little damage that would be done. She took her knife and carved it off. It only took about five minutes to safely detach it from the mirror. She decided to take her carving knife as well and put them both into the pouch.

At that moment her father entered her room from the roof, "Tengri is resting and I have a couple of things that need to be done. Will you join me for dinner in about an hour?"

"I would like that," she said.

"Oh, it's very odd," said Constantine, "but Ossius seems to have left and told no one where he is off to. He was seen with another man and both left the city riding donkeys heading East. Probably off to that damned retreat to prepare for your arrival. Won't *he* be surprised!" He kissed Diana on the forehead and left.

Diana went back to find a solution to her present dilemma. Not a lot of room, she thought. She packed, one by one, every piece of clothing she had into the pouch with the other items and she couldn't make any of them fit properly. Then it struck her … If he is giving all of the space to me, she thought, except for the knife, little pouch, and cloth, then what will *he* wear when we get there?

Diana felt another blush developing, but this time she kind of liked the idea. She was scared but now, sort of, looked forward to the thought. He was handsome and well built. He will see me naked, she thought, and I him. Maybe I will be able to see if he finds me pretty? How will I know? And then she blushed more deeply at the thought she had.

As an afterthought, she folded her thin cotton nightgown into the pouch and found that it fit. "After all," she scarcely whispered, "if he is going to be naked, what will it matter if I wear this?"

Again, she considered. He said that Tapti will make clothes for me. So what I *really* need is something soft and comfortable to sleep in. I will wear what I have on to wherever it is we go to enter the void, and then leave it behind as I suspect Tengri will do with his clothes.

29

Their timing was impeccable. Diana and Constantine both arrived at the dining hall, via different routes, at the exact same moment. They entered together.

"I have a surprise for you Diana," said Constantine.

"Oh, what?" She replied enthusiastically. She loved surprises.

"Crispus has just arrived ..."

"Crispus!" Diana could barely contain her enthusiasm. Flavius Julius Crispus, she thought excitedly, was Constantine's first born son. He was the result of her father's first marriage to Minervina. Diana and Crispus were very close. He was seven years older than she, but when they first met shortly after her arrival in Byzantium in 311, he treated her as an equal and had spent a lot of his time with her even though his friends teased him endlessly because of it. She was always so proud of him, especially in 317, when he was merely seventeen years old, Constantine had proclaimed him Caesar and sent him to Gaul to rule that province. Now, eight years later, Crispus was not only loved and respected by the army, but by his subjects as well. She knew it was because he cared. It

was because he took the time to listen so that he could make fair decisions. *"Where is he? When can I see him?"*

"Slow down, Diana! He arrived not two hours ago and is extremely tired. He was as equally excited to see you but I told him of the plan and he reluctantly agreed to forego seeing you until tomorrow so that we can spend our last free time alone together."

"What did he say, father? What did he say about the plan and my leaving?"

"At first, he was very upset and threatened to have Ossius flogged while forced to listen to Crispus' renunciation of Christianity. Then, as I convinced him that it would be to our advantage that he keep his faith, at least to all appearances, he argued that you should return with him to Gaul and let him protect you. However, he now understands that will be the first place they will look if they ever find out or suspect that your suicide is faked."

"What does he think about the place where I am truly going?" Diana asked.

"He doesn't know, Diana, and I ask that you not tell him. He and Helen will meet Tengri tomorrow and they will both know that you will be taken East. But they are *not* to know who Tengri really is, nor are they to know about your visions or anything related to them. They are to only know that Tengri will sneak you out of the palace in the middle of the night and that you both will join a caravan heading to Persia."

"I understand, father, and I won't say anything other than what you said. Why did he come here all the way from Gaul?"

"It is because," Constantine started with a tone of sadness, or perhaps guilt, "of my victory over Licinius at Chrysopolis last year. As you know, both Licinius and I shared rule over the Empire until his defeat. Now that I am the sole Emperor, our Empire is once again reunited. Crispus will, one day, replace me as Emperor upon my death and he is here so we may plan for that future event. Also, next year, both Crispus and I will travel to Rome in the attempt to force the subjugation of the Christian Church under our secular rule. You see, Diana, that is why you have become a critical factor in this game of political plots and counterplots. They seek to control me through you. They anticipate my actions to control them and want to ensure that I fail and that the Church controls *both* the Emperor and the Empire."

"But why did you allow that insignificant little cult to gain such power?" Diana asked innocently.

Constantine now knew why Ossius could get so frustrated with her questions. They were *deeply* penetrating.

"That is a difficult question to answer. Suffice it to say the Empire has usually been tolerant of varying religious expression within its borders. That policy has always been a paradox. On the one hand it has caused our greatness. It has pacified subjugated peoples to accept our rule. But on the other, it created division and internal strife. Our present situation is a direct result of such strife. A divided Empire cannot sustain itself and will break up and die. My plan was to first unite under one ruler, that is done, and when that was accomplished, we were to start reawakening our ancient glory by following a tactic of allowing religious tolerance, but with *controls*. However, we would also create a *state* religion to control the others. It would be subservient to the sovereign ruler for two reasons. First, a sovereign could guarantee that an attitude of tolerance is maintained by the state, and second, it would disallow religious fanaticism to acquire control *within* the state ..."

"But what would stop a sovereign from becoming a religious fanatic?" Diana interrupted.

"Two reasons. First, the sovereign would necessarily not belong to *any* religion thereby maintaining neutrality. This is why I have refused to convert and will not choose to follow *any* faith until I am on my deathbed. And, second, one must understand the inherent greed of people. I do not believe that anyone filling my office would willingly relinquish control of that position to another person or entity even if they *were* religious fanatics."

Diana considered what he had said and even *she* could see serious flaws in her father's arguments. What she understood him to be saying could *only* lead to political manoeuvring and intrigues of the *worst* possible kind. In her opinion, *that* was the cause of the Empire's undoing in the first place. Finally, she asked: "But why Christianity? Why not Mithras? That was the religion that rose to greatness with the Empire and it would certainly make more sense for *it* to become the state religion. The *Christians* are the worst political connivers of them all. Just look at what they are doing to me -- to us."

"You may be right, Diana. I may have made a mistake. I chose to attempt to unite the Empire *under the Christians ...*"

Diana was stunned! It had *just* dawned on her, when she heard her father say he *chose* Christianity, that they were *not* speaking in terms of general ideals. Rather, they were speaking in terms of political intrigue. It was a plan of action, a strategy already decided upon. And it was turning on him. It controlled him. He *didn't* control it. Why? thought Diana.

"... because they were, apparently, an insignificant sect. Pacifists by nature, and not very educated. They appeared to be more concerned with their piety than with the circumstances surrounding them. Within themselves, they were divided and very inconsistent with their beliefs. But when I protected them, when I raised the sword in their name, their true nature revealed itself.

"Even though their beliefs are still divided and they argue endlessly, those arguments have taken a new direction. No longer do they argue amongst themselves merely to see who is right or wrong. They do so now with an incessant vigour to become the dominant controller of destinies. They can *smell* power and chase after it as would a dog following the scent of game."

"Father," Diana paused for a moment and then tested, "may I ask you a personal question?"

"Yes of course, Diana. What is it?"

"Why did you divorce Minervina and later marry Fausta, the

mother of your other three sons? And why did you battle Licinius, the brother of your second wife?"

Good, thought Constantine, she is becoming weary of this talk of the Empire. I was beginning to fear that I said too much. She *should* be more interested in family matters.

"When the Roman Legion in York proclaimed me Emperor in 306, two years before you were born, the Empire was divided. Maxentius in Rome ... well, it's not important, just believe that the situation was chaotic. My marriage to Minervina placed me in a very disadvantageous position and I was advised to divorce her so I could be free to engage in an arranged marriage that would strengthen my position when such an opportunity availed itself. I defeated Maxentius in 312 at Milvian Bridge and that victory made me the uncontested ruler in the West. In the following year, Licinius defeated Maxentius' father at the battle of Adrianople. This placed Licinius in a stronger position of influence. To stabilise the Empire, it was arranged that his sister, Fausta and I marry. We did and in 317 she bore our first son. However, Fausta is intent upon acquiring control. As everyone knows, Fausta and I rarely see each other and I do not allow her any influence. She also knows that Crispus is my successor. To make a long story short, as I do not wish to bore you with these unimportant details, Licinius sought to depose me through his sister and so I had no other choice but to defeat him in battle and to execute both him and his son. That is the law under which all rulers are bound."

Diana remembered her earlier conversation with Tengri about Law and she suddenly felt as if she wanted to cry. She felt sorry for her uncle. He had carefully planned his rise to power and disrupted the lives of many people along the way. Her uncle was attempting to *justify* his actions, but in reality, he was little more than a schemer. He was doing the same thing the Christians were doing, and it resulted in his own plot turning against him. He had chosen to use Christianity because he thought such a simple religion to be inconsequential, and subsequently beneficial to his schemes. But he made a seriously grave error. He had underestimated them and now, *they* were in control and she doubted that *anyone* would be able to stop them. She felt as if a demon had been unleashed and that thought *did* make her start to cry. Diana turned her head and looked away from her uncle so he couldn't see the single tear that streaked her cheek. She never felt more alone in her brief life, so *disappointingly* isolated from the once secure belief in one who is loved and trusted. But still, she knew without equivocation, she *did* love her uncle. However, the nature of that love had changed. No longer was it *only* love that she felt, she *also* learned to feel pity -- and *that* was what hurt the most! To suddenly feel sorry for someone who was once thought incapable of doing wrong was indeed a shock. She felt as if a black, horrific pit of incurable defeat was about to open up beneath her feet and swallow her whole.

"But enough of this Diana," Constantine continued without any idea that he was interrupting such grave thoughts or that she hid the silence of a tear, "we only have about one more hour that we can be alone. Tomorrow, we will not have the chance and then you will be gone. Let's talk of happier things because soon, we are expected to see Tengri."

Yes, *Tengri,* thought Diana in an attempt to dispel the dark clouds of disappointment and despair that had appeared over her horizon -- a storm that had developed as a result of her seeing her uncle with the clarity of truth. I want to see Tengri, the man whom I barely know, but whom I am destined to follow. I want to leave with him tomorrow. I want to love him. I want him to see me naked, to hold me. I want to share in his strength, and *I need* him to make love to me!

****

Diana and Constantine did speak about happier things during their remaining hour together, but it lacked that special closeness they once shared. However, Constantine never noticed that the nature of what he and Diana once had was forever changed on that day. He could not truly understand the gravity of his crimes -- but Diana did. She had finally grown up.

After she left with Tengri the following night, she never saw her uncle again. He never read her diary. She *did* appear to him in a dreamwalk twelve years later as he lay on his deathbed and while the Bishop Eusebius baptised him. She wasn't surprised to learn that her uncle stayed true to his word given to Tengri and that he seriously attempted to correct his wrongs. But while they spoke in the dream world, Diana also knew the agonising pain her uncle felt. The remorse and guilt that one feels when it is discovered that they were tricked into committing the most heinous *acts* imaginable. It was during that vision when Diana discovered for the first time that Tengri had found out about those acts the night before she left the city and her uncle. He found out and saw less than a year into the future when they occurred, and he never told her. He never told anyone.

Constantine stayed true to his word as much as he could but he fought a war he couldn't possibly win. He lived to see a valiant attempt at victory, but he died before the war was lost. Christianity did not become the state religion until the year 391. It wouldn't have, even then, if it were not for Constantine. But it did.

30

As Diana and Constantine quietly began to wind their way up the tower, Diana finally released the troubled thoughts she had developed from their earlier conversation. She began to replace them with the excited anticipation of what was soon to occur.

She didn't quite know what to expect. Only that Tengri was going to demonstrate his art for a purpose. She didn't know what that purpose was and, frankly, at the moment, she really wasn't all that interested. What *did* evoke her interest was simply the adventure of the discovery of experiencing, first hand, the magic of a baqca. She knew that his mysteries, at least some of them, would not be revealed until after she got to her new home, and for that, she would have to develop more patience. But this? This was in the now and would be her *first* experience of something she longed for forever in her dreams -- and that was the true measure of her excited anticipation. Her true reason for being here today. Never before had she bothered with how long it took to climb the three hundred stairs to her room. Already it seemed like an eternity and they were still a long way from the halfway mark. Even so, she listened to her uncle pant and wheeze as they climbed. He always did. This climb was indeed strenuous for him and she thought, for the first time, that he was getting old. She recalled earlier when she, her uncle, and Tengri climbed the stairs. It was obvious that Tengri never climbed stairs before and it was somewhat humorous to watch him make the attempt. Although her and her uncle's eyes sparkled as they watched, neither laughed nor said anything.

Oh my god! She thought randomly, I forgot to ask him what type of meat I was eating earlier.

They reached, finally, the halfway point in their climb. Diana trembled with excitement and anticipation of seeing the fibres she had heard so much about.

Then she trembled in the fear of embarrassment, because suddenly she remembered their earlier conversation. Tengri had said that to ride the fibres, it was Law that they be naked. Her sense of fear overpowered the force of her blush. She didn't blush. She was too frightened to be embarrassed as she thought to herself: will I and my uncle *have* to remove all of our clothes … together? What will I do when I reach the roof? Will Tengri be standing there naked?

Diana thought she had come to terms with this problem. Earlier, she concluded if that was the way it had to be, then that was the way it *would* be! But now, she wasn't so certain the issue was resolved. Now that the *real* possibility confronted her, compounded by the fact her uncle was present, she decided if it were to happen, then she would feign tiredness, or *something,* and excuse herself ... She wondered if she really would.

Diana and Constantine approached the door behind the drapes in her room and were about ready to proceed up the final steps, when she broke the silence, "You go first."

Diana at first, stepped back, allowing her Uncle the first glimpse of what was to come; but at the last second, in her eager anticipation to see the state Tengri was in, awkwardly strained for a look, nearly upsetting her balance. Bumping clumsily into her Uncle, she nearly fell.

"Are you all right Diana?" Constantine asked.

"Yes," she replied sheepishly. She saw that Tengri was dressed and had a single mark of ash on his forehead. She was both relieved and disappointed.

Tengri rose from where he sat waiting. He motioned them to silence and to remain standing. They watched as he drew his knife and outlined a circle on the stone floor with the knife's point. He then approached them:

"You are to be marked," he said, "with a line of sacred ash on the forehead."

He began to mark them and both felt a cool, tingling sensation on their foreheads as he did.

"We must then enter the circle and sit facing the centre. I will take care of the rest. Do you have any questions?"

Constantine considered, and looked as though he might have a question developing, but then thought better of it and simply shook his head no.

Diana, somewhat confused, asked, "does this satisfy the Law you spoke to me about earlier?"

Tengri, knowing what she meant replied so as not to betray her request, "Yes. We will not dance upon the fibres nor will we enter into spirit worlds. Instead, you will simply *see* the fibres woven into the stones and I will explain to you what they mean."

With that, Tengri entered the circle first, followed by Constantine, and then Diana. When all were seated, Tengri focused his gaze upon the Emperor -- a gaze that sent chills cascading through his very soul -- and then spoke:

"I have decided to do two things. First, I will cast the twenty-two stones which will be thrown by you. They will reveal the present weave and I will interpret its future potential. Then, I will show you the prevailing effects of the fifth, twelfth, and unnumbered stones. However, I fully expect that those three stones will predominate your casting." Tengri then opened his small pouch and poured the twenty-two stones into Constantine's hands.

Diana looked over to see the stones her Uncle held and saw a number of small, shiny black pebbles, each having a blood red design on one side. At first glance, they seemed ordinary enough, but as her gazed continued, she could inexorably feel her consciousness begin to slip away as she felt herself being drawn into their world. It was as if they were the source of all dreams; as if they epitomized the landscape of that ever elusive world she could only know when consciousness was subdued. And as her consciousness became dulled with their mystery, an almost surprisingly odd clarity of thought began to take dominion over her tamed, sleeping objectivity. She focused upon the blood-red designs and they appeared to her like the letters of some ancient and forgotten alphabet, but she wasn't quite certain. She had certainly never seen such letters before ... or had she? Dreamily, somewhere, hidden deep within her memory was the nagging tug of something trying to fight its way to the surface. It was almost as if there were seventy-two names calling out to her in a language unheard for a very long time ... and suddenly, it was all lost and her drifting mind *snapped* back to reality at the sound of Tengri's voice:

"When I finish my song, toss the stones before you."

Constantine nodded in understanding.

As Tengri began to sing, Diana noted a strangely soothing quality about his voice. It was eerie and it caused her to feel chilly, light-headed, and once again, she began to think in a dreamy, distant fashion. She felt as if she was on the verge of leaving her body ... He sang, in a language she didn't understand:

> *"Ö' Trät ... tree branch flies;*
> *Eighty-one branches hold up the moon!*
> *Undo the skimming frog's wings,*
> *Be not unlike violent wind;*
> *Hammering sand, spreading doom!*
> *Stones ... weave your patterns of black and red;*
> *Frog ... leap onto the golden thread;*
> *born kindly ... or deadly,*
> *of the weaver's loom!"*

As instructed, Constantine tossed the stones he held onto the ground before him. As they landed, both Diana and her uncle watched in amazement, and awe, as six of the twenty-two stones were positioned so that their red markings could be seen. But it was not their positioning which caused them to gasp in amazement. It was the emission of small silvery strands of light from the centres of the six stones.

Constantine saw silver. Diana thought that the colour was somehow golden. Tengri *knew* they were gold in colour!

They watched as the threads danced about the circle and then, above their heads, they twisted around one another forming a single rope of light. At certain points along that eerie rope, the threads tied themselves into knots. In that strange dance of light, seven knots were formed. Then, suddenly, the dance stopped and the rope of light with the seven knots fell to the floor. It still glowed eerily and shimmered as it lay there, but it no longer moved. Tengri picked it up and said:

"The nature of a fibre is unique. Its nature is not unlike the quality of water. Water flows upon its course and adapts its shape and direction according to the shape and direction of that which holds it. Rarely does the flow of water become confrontational. Preferring, rather, to be at peace with that which contains it. Only when unreasonable force blocks and interferes with the peaceful flow, does the water rebel. Always, does it overcome its oppressor, either directly and violently by destroying that which seeks to control it, or indirectly by subverting its attacker so as to conform to its own peaceful, flowing nature. A cup, by itself, can be used for many and varied functions. But a cup filled with water has only one purpose. And that purpose has to do with the nature of water.

"The threads," he continued, "of the void are similar in nature. An ancient baqca captured the threads that form the rope that you see and inserted them into the stones thinking they had been imprisoned there. However, the stones, once free to be as stones are, now no longer have any other function than to serve the threads. The baqca who works the stones may *think* they serve him. But *if* he understands clearly and truly, he will find that the threads work him. He is no longer free to pursue his own course as he has become dependent upon the threads and subsequently follows where *they* take him ...

"... As can be seen, this fibre flows through seven pudaks, or obstacles, and since the larger knot originates from the fifth stone, as can be seen by its red mark -- made from the blood of the baqca who captured the threads -- those pudaks refer to present situations expanding to a relatively short time into the future. As it is the first knot, no past events are revealed."

Tengri then intently stared at the shimmering rope of golden fibres.

Diana noted that the rooftop glowed with the supernatural light and a ghostly eeriness pervaded her senses making her dizzy. She watched Tengri dance as he slowly chanted a droning song ... she watched intently as he swayed in time to its peculiar cadence.

A mixture of emotions and concerns attacked Tengri simultaneously as he penetrated into the elusive mystery of each knot. But also, with that mixture, came a certainty as to why he had come to Byzantium. He suspected it before, but now he was *absolutely* convinced that the reason why he was here had nothing to do with the Emperor and everything to do with his niece, Diana.

What he saw in those pudaks was astounding. Certainly, no one was capable of ascertaining the future destiny for the simple reason that it wasn't predetermined. The interaction of forces with causal events shaped future effects, not into predestined events, but rather, into an infinitude of potential occurrences based upon variances of actions, reactions, and definite intentions. That was the secret of prophecy that he learned long ago. One could never *foretell* the future, rather, one could only ascertain what was most *likely* to happen based upon their ability to comprehend the flow of the relationship between causes and their effects. In other words, one's ability to *flow* with the fibres of the universe and to interpret events with clarity.

The fibres contained within all twenty-two stones were not just arbitrarily captured. They were actually woven and were, subsequently, *causes* within their own right. They were not placed within the stones simply for the purpose of attempting to ascertain the future. They were placed into them for the purpose of *making* the future! They were intended to be an objective, a plan, a course of action to follow. They were intended to be a guidebook to tell *chosen* adepts what to expect as time flowed through the centuries. They were teaching stones that taught the initiate proper *actions* which had to be taken so that the final objective could be achieved. And they taught when and how events were to occur *if* final victory was to be realised!

Even so, the stones held the power to reveal *potential* events when they were cast in the present manner and when only *some* select stones were utilised. But as Tengri began to give voice to their message, he realised what the stones revealed, and was astonished at the force and detailed accuracy of what they sang to him about

Constantine. He decided then he would never tell anyone all that he saw and learned. Simply, because there was no way to avoid the events and, mostly, those events *had* to happen if a future victory was to be achieved.

Constantine was certainly destined to feel a severe anguish that would drive most men insane. It was probable he *would* go insane. However, the Emperor had to learn and accept the workings of the Law. It was essential he take responsibility for his own actions, because it was *only* as a result of those actions that his immediate future was already determined.

Tengri decided he would only reveal one, seemingly impersonal event. He began:

"As I expected, the fifth, twelfth, and unnumbered stones are revealed. Also, the fifteenth, seventeenth, and eighteenth have shown themselves in your casting. The seventeenth and eighteenth stones represent my sisters -- Pouie the owl and Kaltak the wolf -- and pertain directly to your vision of last night and what happened ..."

Diana noticed her uncle fidgeting uncomfortably and thought she perceived a slight redness of the cheeks.

"Can you see the *details* of all that happened?" He asked nervously.

"I can if I choose to ride a fibre into the dream," Tengri replied, "but I choose not to. Besides, Kaltak has already told me."

That most definitely is a blush, thought Diana. *I wonder what happened?*

Tengri continued, focused entirely upon the matter at hand: "the fifteenth stone reveals influencing factors ... I ... can ... see ... two women. One is called Faz ... no ... Fausta. The other ... Ha ... Hel ..."

"That would be Fausta, my uncle's wife and Helen, my servant," interjected Diana somewhat abruptly.

"No, not Helen, *Helena,*" corrected Tengri.

"That would be my mother," said Constantine. He noted with

dismay that Diana had called him uncle. Perhaps, just a slip from habit, he thought -- he hoped.

"Constantine, they are discussing a place called Nazareth and a word called 'netzer'. I do not know either word but it seems extremely important to the Christian religion. Helena is very upset with Fausta and calls her a fool ...

"... Fausta had just told her, at Helena's request, that she had someone research her question in the state library. She was told there never existed a place called Nazareth in Galilee where the Lord Jesus was alleged, by the Apostle Matthew, to have been raised. It was said that an exhaustive search through the Talmud and Old Testament had been conducted and there was no mention of that place. Further, an extensive history written by a Jewish General named Flavius Josephus concerning the wars in Palestine was also researched, and again, no mention of a village called Nazareth was found. It is said that if such a place truly existed, Josephus would certainly have mentioned it because he had been appointed by the Romans to be the governor of Galilee and that he wrote about *all* towns in that province. Rather, it was suggested that the one called Matthew had confused the Hebrew word *'netzer'*, which means roots, and assumed it meant that Jesus was from a place associated with that word. Subsequently, Matthew referred to Christ as being a *Nazarene* and assumed it denoted a place. Subsequently, the word *'Nazareth'* was created to give credence to the assumption and was fabricated to be the town where he was raised ...

"... Helena," he continued, "is *furious* with the report told to her by Fausta and says that a Jew cannot be trusted with *any* matter except for feeble attempts to subvert the true faith and that the palace historian, who furnished the report to Fausta, was a pagan and couldn't be trusted either. Helena further states that she is planning a pilgrimage to Palestine next year and she will *personally* see to it that the home of Jesus, Nazareth, is located for all the world to see.

"I do not know the words," continued Tengri, "but I think the subject of which they spoke was important."

Constantine was momentarily speechless. "Tengri, you could see all that? Indeed, my mother does plan a pilgrimage to Palestine next year whilst I'm in Rome. And indeed, the place where Jesus was raised is an enigma to the Christian faith. Many have looked for that town called Nazareth, but none could find it. It has become an important issue based on the premise that if the New Testament has any errors, then the faith may be in error and subsequently not a result of God's Word!"

Tengri thought for a moment, thinking he might continue along this line, but changed his mind instead and said, "I will require much strength for tomorrow's journey through the void and I must rest."

Diana and Constantine watched as Tengri snapped the ghostly rope of light as he would a whip. The fibres untangled themselves and he made a motion with his hand causing the threads to return to the stones.

He then added, "The fifth stone denotes the present time and reveals that a powerful religious leader will dominate your land thereby causing a forced belief upon all peoples. You must be cautious, Constantine, because your time is very imbalanced. It is a time of power and greed. It is also a time of death. The twelfth stone is seven hundred summers into the future, and denotes a great religious war started for reasons of greed. The war is the direct result caused by events occurring in the present time. The unnumbered stone refers to a time far into the future, sixteen hundred summers from now, when a final decision must be made by all peoples of the earth. Either, they will choose to walk off the cliff and fall into the depths of the abyss into chaos, or they will awaken to Truth. Promise me, Constantine, Emperor of the greatest Empire this world has ever seen, that you will devote your life to Truth and that you will fight this disease of untruth which infests your land and which affects all people on this earth, and our goddess as well."

Constantine looked directly into Tengri's eyes and saw how fiercely they burned. They *glowed* with the intensity of fire ... With sincerity and humility, he said simply, "I promise."

Tengri knew, however, that it was a promise the Emperor couldn't keep. Constantine had created a situation for himself that was now beyond his control....

31

As he watched Constantine and Diana leave, Tengri reflected upon the disturbing visions that he had seen and vowed never to reveal. He saw that Helena and Fausta belonged to an evil brotherhood whose members wore greenish brown robes. They were devoted to the work of chaos and attached themselves to the faith called Christianity for the sole purpose of subverting truth.

Fausta, Constantine's wife, jealous of her stepson Crispus, would conspire to have Crispus killed the following year. She was a sexually depraved woman who had numerous affairs with the palace slaves and who forced those slaves to perform *whatever* sexual fancies struck her. At the exact same time that Tengri looked into the weave of the stones, Fausta was in the stables with four slaves, men who were forced to mount her repeatedly as well as to perform the most bizarre acts upon her and each other for her pleasures. What Fausta did *not* know was that she was being spied upon by an agent of Helena.

The following year, Constantine would hear accusations made against Crispus. Fausta would claim that his son dishonoured her chastity by raping her. In reality, Crispus refused *her* advances. However, since Constantine's mother would refrain from telling her son the truth, at least until it was convenient, Constantine would respond by first exiling his son and then, shortly thereafter, having him executed.

When it did become advantageous to her, Constantine's mother

Helena would produce evidence that it was truly his wife at fault and that the depraved woman had also committed sexual sins with numerous slaves. She told her son these truths only after Constantine had Crispus executed because, simply put, Crispus was not extreme enough in his Christian beliefs to suit her or the brotherhood. The man couldn't be trusted to perpetuate the faith properly as Emperor.

Constantine responded to the news by having his wife executed.

By those acts caused by his own hands, he would be known as the man who championed Christianity and allowed it to evolve from an insignificant sect to a world dominating power. He would also be known as the Emperor who had his brother-in-law, nephew, son, and wife murdered.

He is indeed destined to torment, thought Tengri. He is a man to be pitied.

Tengri slept.

****

Queen Helena did indeed make a pilgrimage to Palestine the following year. And true to her convictions, she did search for the place called Nazareth of Galilee. But like everyone else, she couldn't find it for the simple reason it never existed. But not to be undaunted, she did find a small cluster of ruined houses and named *them* Nazareth! It wasn't until almost one hundred and fifty years later, in 570, that the Christian historian, Antonius Martyr, established fame for those ruined stones named Nazareth by Helena. Finally, the puzzle that bothered many Christians was solved. It was documented by a 'reliable' source.

Incidentally, Helena also managed to find the *cross* on which her saviour was crucified. Needless to say, she was later canonised by *her* Church.

32

Every so often, Diana let out a sob. Her eyes were swollen and her face had turned a blotchy red from crying. It had been less than an hour since she had thrown the pre-planned tantrum and now ... she waited in her room, alone with her thoughts, for the arranged time for their departure.

She had managed a superb performance as could be confirmed by the look of shock on the faces of those who bore witness. That evening they had a family dinner which included she, her uncle, Fausta, Helena, Crispus, and Constantine's three other young sons. Additionally, there was a priest in attendance whom she didn't know but whom, she learned shortly after she was seated, was an assistant to Ossius. He wore robes of greenish brown and his face reminded her of a weasel; his voice sounded like the hissing of a snake; his presence had caused her to shudder and, overall, he was repulsive ... sinister ... dark.

Their dinner was served by several servants overseen by Helen. At the appointed time, her uncle announced they were gathered together to celebrate a special occasion because in a few days Diana would be baptised and would then enter into seclusion for intense religious training suitable to her personality. The priest, Fausta, and Helena looked very pleased, *too* pleased, upon hearing those words and turned to congratulate her. They didn't, of course because they were stunned into shocked silence by her sudden outburst filled with real vehemence.

For the next few minutes, Diana shouted out a monologue of disbelieving denial before she was silenced by an all too real bellow from her uncle. Then ... it started. Ten minutes of shouting and arguing which finally ended with her uncle flatly stating that she was going and his word was final. She responded with an even greater flurry of tears as she ran from the dining hall. The last thing she heard before slamming the door was Helena calmly saying to the shocked audience to let her go until morning giving her time to come to her senses.

Now that she was in her room, she realised that much of her act *wasn't* staged. She had released all of her pent up anger, frustrations, and disappointments during that charade which made it all the more convincing -- but still, she sobbed. She sobbed because she knew she was truly sad and would sorely miss her uncle ... no, *father* she corrected herself, Crispus, and Helen.

Diana frowned at the clothes she was about to put on. Earlier, before dinner, Crispus had come to her room with a gift. He had decided that since she would be travelling an extremely harsh route to Persia, and since she was supposed to be travelling incognito, she may as well be practical and wear clothing that would be suitable for the trip. He had given her padded clothing -- soldier's clothing -- a pair of boots, and a full length, dark, heavy cloak with a deep hood. He had also brought a cloak for Tengri, saying it would help in their disguises perchance they be seen.

Now, she wore her gift instead of the conservative dress she had previously chosen. She wished she would be able to take her brother's present, but when she tried to pack just the pants and shirt, they wouldn't fit in the pouch because of their bulk -- even when everything else was taken out. She did discover that if she exchanged the shoes with the boots, they would fit along with her nightgown, carvings, and diary. So, she took the boots and left the shoes behind.

Crispus had also told her that she should be careful about taking too many clothes because someone, if they noticed, may wonder why they were missing. He didn't know that the only thing she was taking was the cotton gown. Also, Tengri had reminded her that she could not take anything made of metal and when she showed him her carving knife, he merely looked at it and said matter-of-factly he would make her another. Besides, Crispus needed that knife to put the final touches on their plan. After she was gone, he would sneak into her room with a goat and bleed it on her bed. No one would see her body, but they would see her blood. Diana felt pity for the goat.

Another sob broke the silence as she remembered the long hug she gave Crispus and their tearful farewell. They didn't speak at dinner.

She stood before the silver mirror and looked at herself wearing the padded clothes and cloak. If only I had a sword and a spear, she thought, I would be mistaken for a mercenary.

Diana was glad for the heavy clothes because it was dismal outside. It was cold for summer, and now that it had just turned dark, it was quite cold. It had rained heavily all day, but now slowed to a mere drizzle. She looked out the window and saw that it threatened to storm at any moment. The howling wind gave the night a spooky quality. Had she stayed, she would have lit a fire.

The plan was to take the secret passage at the foot of the stairs leading to her room. A concealed trapdoor opened to reveal a long ladder that would take them to a passage that slanted downward until reaching an ancient door. That door opened to a maze of tunnels -- the catacombs -- beneath the palace. Although Diana rarely went down there because the place was filled with spider webs, rats, and other horrible things that preferred to live in perpetual damp, putrid, darkness, she nevertheless knew the correct path leading to a secret door on a remote part of the South wall of the city. It was, her father had explained, an escape route -- just in case. There would be two torches waiting for them when they entered the catacombs.

Diana knew that at any moment, Tengri would descend the steps from the roof. She wondered why he stayed up there in the rain most of the day, under his makeshift shelter, but decided he had his reasons. It was decided that they would leave just after dark so that they could reach their destination about an hour after midnight. It would take about an hour and a half to wind their way through the catacombs, saving them about the same length of time had they taken the streets above. However, they could be lost for days if a wrong turn were taken and, Tengri estimated, another three to four hours walking through the dense underbrush of the forest until they arrived at a proper point of departure. After that, he had said, it would take a good portion of the night to prepare. He hoped they would be able to leave shortly after dawn. Diana heard his footsteps descending the stairs and then the creak of the hinges as the door started to open. Her heart pounded and raced with anticipation! She picked up the pouch and another sack containing two small clay bowls Tengri had requested, and turned to meet his eyes as he stepped from behind the drapes. *Her adventure had finally begun!*

33

Diana didn't know what time it was but she knew they had been walking, or, what seemed more like slipping and sliding, for hours. Upon leaving the catacombs, they discovered that a full scale storm had developed and the rain poured incessantly in sheets. The wind made it considerably worse and caused her face to sting as each individual raindrop *intentionally* sought her out for the purpose of making her life miserable. And indeed, her life *was* miserable. Despite her padded clothing and cloak, she was *drenched* to the bone. Her muscles ached, and her hands and face had been whipped numerous times by twigs, branches, and everything else that the forest hid from her view in the dark. She hadn't the faintest idea how Tengri could see where he was going ... but she didn't concern herself with his problem, she had enough of her own just following! And on top of everything else, she was covered from head to foot with mud as a result of her countless falls.

Diana took consolation in the fact that Tengri was covered in mud as well. As they picked their way down one steep embankment, she had slipped, fallen, and slid right into Tengri before he knew what was happening. He joined her in their slide through the mud ...

Diana was amazed that even though she was wet and she knew it was cold outside, she sweated. She knew it was because of her exertion and she also knew that when she stopped, the cold would set in very quickly. That is why Tengri would not let her stop and rest. She was proud that never once did she complain ... at least out loud!

"Here," Tengri said without warning, "here is where we depart this land."

Diana looked around and saw they had suddenly appeared in a small but sufficiently large, cloistered clearing. She couldn't feel the rain because the dense branches high above them made a natural shelter that blocked both rain and wind. She bent to touch the ground and found that it was damp but not overly wet. Occasionally, a drop of water would strike her but she realised that it came, not from the rain, but from dripping off the leaves high above. They were only stopped for a moment when she began to feel the chill seep through her, causing her teeth to chatter.

"Here," said Tengri handing her the stick he had been carrying for about an hour, "over there," he pointed, "start digging a hole an arm's length wide, deep, and long."

Before she could say anything, she watched as Tengri tromped off through the bush disappearing from sight....

Dig a hole! She thought indignantly. *Why I never ...* She took out her aggression on the hole and soon realised she no longer felt the chill.

Shortly, Tengri returned carrying an armload of sticks and a couple of dead logs. He piled them in the centre of the clearing. He then went to the *edge* of the clearing and dug around under a dense bush with his hands and went back to the centre carrying forest refuse. He sat down and withdrew something from a pouch attached to his pants and began striking it. It caused sparks and soon he was blowing into his tinder. Shortly, he had a roaring fire lighting and warming the clearing.

Tengri walked over to Diana and said, "that's good enough.

Come over to the fire and warm yourself."

"What is the hole for?" She asked hoping it was for some purpose other than to keep her warm. She hoped she was being useful.

"To bury our clothes and all traces of our being here."

"Oh ..." She suddenly remembered they would soon be naked. She felt a surge of excitement at the thought which caused a warmth to flow through her, but was relieved that there was no hint of a blush developing. But just to be sure, she changed the subject ... "Why not just burn them?"

"The art of the fire is sacred and is not to be profaned by burning what is not wanted. It is only to be used for what is essential -- warmth, cooking, and for ceremony. Besides, our things would not burn sufficiently. All that we are to leave behind is the trace of the fire ... Sit before the fire, Diana," he added somewhat abruptly.

She did. He took her cloak. *Is he undressing me?* She thought, and this time, she did blush, but no, he hung the cloak near the fire and sat next to her. She felt silly.

Tengri took one of the clay bowls and poured water from one of the two skins that he carried into it so that it was half full. He set it next to the fire.

"Take four or five large gulps from this," he said while handing her the other skin.

Diana took one gulp and immediately spewed it out into the fire. It caused it to flare. *"What on earth is this?"* She gasped while making a face that could scare any demon!

"Kymyz ...," he said somewhat surprised. "Fermented mare's milk. It will warm your insides. But don't drink too much or you'll become drunk."

She tried again and was successful in taking four large swallows. It's not so bad, she thought, and she drank once more before handing the skin back to Tengri.

Diana watched as Tengri took a couple of swallows. He was right, she thought, I do feel warmer inside and the fire feels really good. *I* feel good! She realised she was feeling a bit giddy and hoped she hadn't drunk too much. Anyway, it made her anticipation melt away.

"You are to receive your first lesson," Tengri started. "I have two immediate concerns. The first involves preparing you for the journey through the void; and the second has to do with protecting you when we arrive at the other end of the thread. Both concerns can be resolved with one simple solution."

"And they are?"

"When one travels the void, they first must have their fibres rewoven so they can adjust to the change of power. However, your fibres are sufficiently strong to withstand the journey so long as I protect you. We cannot reweave your fibres here to make it safer for you and I will not attempt to do so, even later, because I believe you are capable of going to the smith. He can make them much stronger than any baqca could ever hope of doing. Subsequently, a special potion must be made and then applied to your outer skin. It will serve to deflect any forces which may potentially cause you harm if I become distracted by something else and, consequently, am unable to protect you."

"And the other?" Asked Diana.

"Your skin is very fair and soft. The sun in the steppes, very harsh and strong. You will be all day in that sun and without protection, your skin will blister and your body, dehydrate. You could easily die. After you live with us for awhile, we'll teach you how to toughen your skin. In fact, you can start now. Take off your boots."

She did as she was directed and laid her boots near the fire so they would dry. She watched as Tengri took off his own.

"Look at my feet, Diana."

She did and noted that the skin on his soles were leathery and calloused. They had deep cracks and appeared to be very tough, very strong. She looked at her own and compared them with Tengri's. Comparatively, her feet were very soft and tender. Even though she had always played in bare feet when she was younger and did have some calluses, she saw they would not be sufficient to support her without shoes.

Tengri continued, "Fortunately, the same ointment that will protect you from dangers in the void will also protect you from the sun when we arrive."

"Do you have any of this ointment?"

"This will be your first lesson. I will teach you to hunt the plant from which we will make that potion. I have seen some nearby."

"Hunt plants?" Diana said with astonishment! *"If you've already seen them, why not just go and pick them?"*

Tengri just looked at her and smiled, "you have a lot to learn, Diana. Plants can be very useful to humans. They can also be harmful and even deadly ..."

Diana recalled the time that Ossius wiped himself with poison sumac.

"... People will use plants for food, medicine, and other things. But very few people understand how to properly collect them. One cannot just go and pick them. One must *hunt* them as they would if they hunted a hare or a stag. You just don't walk up to a hare and grab it by the ears and walk away. The hare would object and run away as soon as he knew you were after him."

"Yes," said Diana, "but a hare can move and therefore runs away. A plant is just there and cannot do anything to protect itself."

"It is true that you can just walk up to a berry, pick it, and eat it with the result being that you feel nourished. However, by doing that, you will find that the berry was already dead *before* you picked it. Its spirit, its life saw your intent by the way your fibres moved and it left, severing its ties thereby causing the berry's death. You would have only succeeded in capturing an empty shell. True, that shell may furnish you with needed nourishment and if the plant was intended for medicinal purposes, it may still have healing effects. But just think of how much more effective it would be if the spirit were to be captured. No, Diana, we do not hunt shells, we hunt the *spirit* of the plant."

He continued, "the plant we need for your protection is a common weed and is useless to us unless we capture its spirit. Also, a spirit of a plant is not confined to a single shell. Rather, it is capable of moving around an area determined by the type of spirit. Some plants have spirits that can travel farther than you could walk in three or four days and nights without once stopping. Others, only the distance of your arm. The one we will hunt is of the latter type and is not dangerous."

"Dangerous?" Diana repeated.

"Yes, dangerous. Some spirits are capable of defending themselves by capturing *your* spirit, thereby causing your body to die, but there are also those capable of hunting *you* for their own purposes. You must learn of these things and so you will be taught. But for tonight, you will only watch."

Diana watched as Tengri took out his stone knife and struck the edge of its blade with a rock. A very thin sliver broke from the blade.

"I will pierce the lobe of your ear with this sliver from my knife. It will serve, temporarily and until the smith can complete the process, to allow you to hear and understand the language of plants."

Diana thought she had better have another swallow or two of the mare's milk. It might help with the anticipated pain. She drank but soon found she needn't have because she barely felt anything as the sliver smoothly pierced her ear. "Tengri," she said after her ear was pierced, "I don't hear anything different."

"Of course not," he laughed, "you must first enter into the second realm. After awhile it becomes second nature to be able to move freely back and forth between the worlds of plants and man."

"Shouldn't we be marked?" She asked remembering about Law.

"Normally yes, but for the plant we will hunt, it is not necessary. It's a very simple spirit and only a pure mind and sense of sacredness is required on our part. First, I will weave the proper energies. Then, we will hunt. When I find what I am looking for, we will sneak up on the spirit and capture it while it is still attached to its shell. Once I cut the shell while still attached, the spirit cannot escape. Finally, once the hunt is completed, we will thank the earth for allowing us to use her resources. We shall begin."

Diana reached for her boots but Tengri stopped her by saying that she needed to toughen her feet and might as well start in her own soft land. Also, he wanted her to listen with her feet to see if she could hear the earth speak to her.

Tengri started to drone. The sound he made was eerie and it sent shivers through her spine. Then, he waved his hand and Diana felt a very different, odd, sensation. She could *see* Tengri, yet she couldn't sense him. It was almost as if he were invisible, as if he were a dream … As if *she* were a dream. The only thing which appeared real were the plants, the rocks, and the earth. They were strangely real. Differently real. The only things that were *truly* real … She and Tengri had become ghosts!

Diana listened and she heard buzzing sounds. Were they insects? No, *they were plants!* She could *actually* hear them speaking! No, they weren't speaking exactly, *they were singing!* So very beautiful, she thought. So harmoniously melodious.

The earth beneath her feet felt alive. It welcomed her and sung a song of love to her. It was telling her that it was pleased she understood. She wanted to take off her clothes so her body could absorb the overwhelming beauty because now she understood that the weave of her clothes interfered with the weave of … *beauty!*

Then, suddenly, she had a brief glimpse of the most beautiful woman she had ever seen! Diana's eyes *sparkled* in the reflection of her beauty. She was naked from the waist up and her breasts were full and well formed. She wore a sheer black shimmering veil from her waist to her knees, and then appeared to mouth her name, *Diana*, but no sound issued forth.

Diana fell to the ground. She felt so heavy, so dense, and

suddenly, very cold and wet. She couldn't stop her teeth from chattering violently and her body shaking from chills. She looked up and saw Tengri standing over her holding a cluster of weeds in his hand.

"Diana," he said gently, "get up."

She struggled to rise and said meekly, "I'm sorry. I didn't follow you or see what you were doing." Then she looked around and saw that there was no clearing or fire in sight.

"You did follow me. But I did not expect you to see what I did because one usually hunts alone. I only wanted you to get used to this realm. What do you think?" He had brought the skin of kymyz and handed it to her.

She drank several long gulps and didn't take the skin from her lips until she felt the warmth growing from her belly and extending to her toes and fingers. When they finally tingled, she handed the skin back to Tengri and finally spoke.

"It ... was ... beautiful, Tengri. It was like living a dream. Thank you." It was difficult for her to speak because her teeth still chattered but she persevered through her numbing cold and recounted her experience in every detail....

While she spoke with excitement, she noticed Tengri watching her. He was smiling gently. "Is something wrong? Did I do well?" She finally asked.

"No, nothing is wrong Diana. You did much better than I anticipated. You were blessed by the goddess herself. That rarely happens on one's first journey. And, Diana, you have nothing to fear. You are a *very* beautiful young woman and will please a future husband very much."

Diana looked at Tengri with a puzzled expression on her face, and then slowly followed his eyes to look down at herself. To see what he saw.

"Oh ... my ... god ... I'm ... naked!" She exclaimed in shock.

"And your nakedness is beautiful," responded Tengri.

"How ... where ... are ... my ... clothes?" Diana looked around

and couldn't see them.

"You were like that when I returned. You must have taken them off as you walked when the thought struck you. It is not uncommon and it may be one reason why the goddess appeared to you. Had your clothes been on, she never would have. You have received an initiation."

"I'm so very sorry, Tengri, I am so embarrassed ..."

"No, Diana," he interrupted, "there is nothing to be sorry or embarrassed about." He put his cloak around her and held her close to share his warmth.

She felt goose bumps but she wasn't sure if they were from the cold, or his touch. Together they walked back to the clearing and the fire. She was giddy. Perhaps she had drunk too much. It was surprising how far they had travelled for the hunt because it had taken almost a half hour to return.

Suddenly, she realised that she hadn't blushed and wasn't even blushing now. Diana was truly pleased with herself. Now, she didn't have to worry about removing her clothes while Tengri was present. They were *already* gone! But, she thought with a slight smile as they approached the fire, *I* can watch him!

34

Diana sat next to the fire and became absorbed with watching every act Tengri performed. After returning to the clearing, Tengri had taken her cloak which had been left hanging near the fire and put it around her. Having been warmed and dried by the blaze, it felt very good against her body. Her internal warmth had returned and she felt quite good; quite happy. Tengri's cloak was now hanging where hers had been two or three hours earlier.

As Diana sat there watching Tengri, she occasionally sipped from the skin containing kymyz. It has an awful taste, she thought, but it's not so bad after getting used to it. Actually, it added to her happy contentment. She knew that she wasn't drunk, but she also knew that the tingling sensation in her body and the slight difficulty she had in maintaining a focus in her concentration was probably due to a condition that wasn't exactly sober either. Still, Tengri hadn't stopped her from drinking and, she decided, it was keeping her from blushing. Over the past couple of hours, Diana had thought a lot about Tengri seeing her and her curiosity about seeing him. However, now, her attitude about what was soon to happen somehow changed. Now, it seemed, *natural.* She wasn't certain if her new outlook was a result of the mare's milk or from her previous experiences on the hunt. Probably both, she concluded, but still, her curiosity was making her impatient. This whole process was taking *far* too long!

Diana noticed the darkness was beginning to fade. It was still raining and there would be no sunrise in Byzantium that day. Still, within moments it would be dawn.

"Tengri, it will soon be dawn. Are we not supposed to be leaving now?"

"I had hoped to ... but circumstances have caused a slight delay."

"What circumstances?"

"There ... finished." Tengri responded ignoring her question.

He had been sitting there preparing the weeds in a special way that Diana couldn't exactly follow. He had boiled them, then cut special patterns into them, boiled them again, then extracted something out of the bowl, went to get more water and more wood for the fire, and generally was completely absorbed with what he was doing. The only sounds emanating from either of them was the chanting that he did as part of his work.

Tengri rose and squatted in front of Diana while showing her the contents of the bowl. "See ... finished. Touch it."

She looked into the bowl and saw that it was filled almost to the top with a clear salve. She touched it and noticed it caused her finger to tingle as if an energy, a life energy, entered into her. It cleared her mind, made her feel alive, excited. It felt cool and slightly slippery. She looked up at Tengri.

"What circumstances?"

"Two. I have to wait until it is light enough to see so I can find your clothes ..."

"Why didn't you look for them when we were out there? They couldn't have been too far away. Anyway, why not just leave them behind? We can't take them with us. No one will find them."

"They will be easier to find in the light and you needed to get to the fire. I'm not concerned if someone finds them or not. They will never be associated with you if someone does discover them. I have other reasons which you will better understand as your training progresses. Those reasons have to do with actions in relationship to the equilibrium of the universe. Remember, every act that we do affects that balance. Subsequently, our actions must be *needful,* not arbitrary. As we have already set fibres into motion with regards to what has been planned, in this instance, it is far wiser to remain on our present course than it is to change it."

"And, the other reason?"

"The kymyz."

"I am not drunk!"

"You haven't stood up yet."

Now, Diana was terribly ashamed and it showed on her face. She thought she had done something wrong. "But, why didn't you *say* something instead of letting me go on making mistakes?"

"No. Diana, you are misunderstanding what I mean. I would have *made* you drink had you chosen not to. It was *necessary* that you drink because your body was losing its heat and the mare's milk helped you to regain it. Nor, do I care if you are drunk or not. It is of no significance. I now know that the only way I can guarantee your safety while we travel is if I take responsibility of holding on to you instead of you holding on to me. I did not want to take the risk of you letting go of me because of being drunk. Now it is not important ..."

"Why not?" She interrupted.

"Whether drunk or sober, you have demonstrated your ability in shaman's work. In the second realm, you entered that state and were unaware of your surroundings or actions. That is good. It shows that you will go far. But you have yet to learn to balance yourself in both worlds and I will not take the chance that you might, in your visions in the void, let go of me and fly away. Your spirit knows how to soar, Diana, and while we are in the void, *let* it soar. I will hang on to you thereby freeing you from *any* responsibility."

"If that is the case, why does my drinking effect a delay in our departure?"

"The mare's milk, though warming your body, also causes it to dehydrate."

"*Dehydrate!* Tengri, just look around you. There is more chance of us *drowning* than dehydrating!"

"Where we go, the sun is already high. It has baked the earth where we will walk and has scorched the air that we will breathe. In real time, it will only take several moments to reach there from here. By delaying, we allow the sun to spend its fury. I have already decided that we seek shelter when we arrive and wait until nightfall to travel home. It will take one night's travel and perhaps half of the next. Also, I have another concern. Tapti has spent three days singing and has remained in the sun without water. She will need rest as well."

"Tengri, what is Tapti like? Will she like me? Will she be upset to see that I'm with you?"

"Don't worry, Diana. Tapti will like you. She will be surprised to see another member of our family, but not upset."

"Won't it ... uh ... bother her to ... uh ... see you with a ... another woman without clothes?"

Tengri looked at her and smiled. "Diana," he began to tease, "perhaps she will be a little upset when she sees such a beautiful woman."

"Stop! You're embarrassing me."

"It is light enough to begin," he said changing the subject and becoming more serious. "There are some things you must do to prepare. First, you are covered in mud and it must be washed off. About three or four arrow flights in that direction," Tengri pointed, "is a spring fed pool in which you can bathe. It will be cold, but necessary. The dirt must not be present to interfere with the salve. Do it quickly, and take the milk. Also, fill the water skin and drink all of it. Your stomach is one of the best places to carry water in the heat. I think we should leave your boots behind and take the empty skin. It will fit. Take the cloak you now wear and when you return, wear the one warming by the fire."

Diana didn't exactly like the idea of jumping into the water, but she had to agree that she was dirty. She didn't complain and began to stand up.

She plopped back down! "That stuff really *is* potent!"

As she somehow managed to relearn how to walk, Tengri went off in search of her clothes.

35

That morning, in Buryat territory, seven warriors left the site where Tapti and Tengri disappeared three days before. They had arrived the previous night after the blind warrior's horse returned him to tell his story. These particular riders wanted to investigate to ensure it wasn't some Kazak-Kirghiz trick that called for retaliation. They spent the night there and were satisfied that indeed a sacred ceremony had been performed. They were somewhat puzzled, however, because they couldn't find any tracks showing that anyone had left. But, they really didn't concern themselves with their puzzlement because it was obvious that whoever was there would have left the same way they came ... by sacred ceremony. Not even a Kazak-Kirghiz shaman would be so stupid as to leave any other way.

One of the warriors found the kobuz that was left behind and decided that it would make a good gift for his eldest daughter. After all, she did have talent....

36

Diana did as she was instructed although it was the fastest bath she *ever* took! She returned to the fire quickly and with teeth chattering, she wrapped herself in Tengri's cloak. After a few minutes, several gulps from the skin of mare's milk, and a forced drinking of water, she began to feel better, warmer, and anxious.

Tengri hadn't returned yet and that made her nervous. What if something happened? She worried. But she didn't allow herself to continue along that line of thinking. She was getting more excited about what would soon occur. She wasn't quite sure if she was more excited about the void or Tengri. The mare's milk convinced her that it was Tengri ... but she knew otherwise ... at least she thought.

Finally, she could hear Tengri returning and she felt relieved. It was already well past dawn and quite light, although the trees kept them in shadow and the day's greyness still cast its dismal mood upon the morning.

"Did you find them?" She asked.

"Yes." He took the clothes to the hole and threw them in. He also picked up the other items that were no longer needed and did the same. He drank what little water was left and then packed the skin.

Diana followed every move with her eyes wondering when he would come and take her cloak from her, leaving her naked and exposed. He started toward her and checked the skin that she was holding and asked if she wanted any more. She didn't and so he emptied it onto the ground and threw the skin into the hole as well. He returned.

"Diana," he said, "I will explain what we are going to do because when I start the ceremony, I will not have time to speak."

She nodded in understanding.

"We are going to move over to that grassy area away from the fire. I will dump the salve onto the grass and then bury the bowl and the rest of our things. I will take your cloak last. It will be cold for awhile but you will have to bear it. When I return, I will begin to cover your second skin with the salve ..."

"What is the second skin?" She asked quizzically.

"It is your flesh which serves as protection for your spirit. You may talk to me while I do this if you like, but when I am finished and sit so that our knees are touching, you must not disturb me as I will start the songs to commence marking. Watch carefully what I do. I will mark myself first, and then you. When we are finished, I will rise. You must get upon my back and hold on tight as well as to hook your feet together in front. I will then commence looking for the spot where we will jump upon the thread. We may travel for some distance, but when we arrive, I will set you down. Remain standing. I will mark a circle in the earth with my knife and then return to you. I will then pick you up so that you are facing me. Hook your feet around my back, and your arms around my neck. We will travel the void in this fashion. It allows me to hold you better. Do you understand?"

I didn't realise there would be so much physical contact, she thought. She felt a funny feeling in the pit of her stomach ... "Yes."

They moved to the grassy spot and as Diana sat, she watched Tengri move to the hole. She watched as he began to take off his clothes and she began to shiver with a different type of excitement. Despite the mare's milk, she could feel the warmth of her skin begin to spread. She knew she was blushing, but it was a different type of blush and, she realised, it didn't bother her ... she didn't care....

She realised she was becoming aroused. She feared this might happen and that was what caused her embarrassment -- the fear. However, now that it was happening, oddly, she wasn't ashamed.

She allowed her feelings and thoughts to fly as they may....

Tengri was facing away from her and had just taken off his shirt and thrown it into the hole. She noticed the muscles in his back and arms ... not huge nor cumbersome like those of the wrestlers she had seen. His were more wiry. Diana had noticed it before, the way that he moved, so different from anyone else she had ever seen. But now that his shirt was off and she could clearly see those movements without obstruction, she understood. There was a naturalness of grace about the way he moved ... like ... *a cat ... a large cat!* It was as though there was something *different* in the way his bones had formed -- something which would allow them to *bend* differently. The manner in which he moved was strong, agile, and graceful. But ... there was also something else ... That's it! She thought, the word I'm looking for is ... *focused!* Tengri was someone who could be a terrible foe. Not so much because of *who* he was, but because of that innate focus manifesting in his mannerisms -- the focus of grace, speed, and agility that would define his movements.

Diana watched as he removed his pants. His buttocks and legs conformed with the rest of his body and she could appreciate more clearly the beauty of his grace. She felt the wetness of her desires and realised she was already *very* aroused -- but it was different from the sensual feelings she had which caused her to bring herself to fulfilment. She liked satisfying herself and ordinarily if she felt as she did now with her state of arousal, she would. But this was different. She enjoyed her feelings and did not want to be satisfied -- at least not yet!

She was pleased her thoughts and feelings were not just lustful. There was more to them than that. Suddenly, she realised *exactly* what she felt ... *she was deeply in love with Tengri!* She wished with passionate fervour that he would come to her and make love. She would. She knew she would. She wondered if he was … ready. Soon, she would find out. If he was, she knew she couldn't trust herself *not* to make love to him! Diana thought of Tapti. She wasn't jealous of her, she just thought her lucky. Strangely, she didn't feel guilty because she wanted ... wanted so badly to make love with Tengri. Somehow, she thought Tapti would understand. What if, she thought, it is their custom for a man to take more than one wife? She had heard of such things. Easily, Diana thought, I would share him with Tapti.

He was beginning to turn around and more than anything else, she wanted him to be ready ... to be erect. Her own wetness increased ... it was unstoppable ... her breathing was heavy....

He faced her and Diana fell more deeply in love with the man whom she now looked at. She wasn't disappointed ... he was *not* erect ... but she was not disappointed. Right now, she wanted to get up ... run to him ... hold him ... kiss him ... taste him ...

Diana watched as Tengri approached. His body was beautiful ... even that oddly shaped scar on his shoulder -- had she seen it somewhere before? She recalled it was not unlike that dragon-like creature....

He took her cloak ... and now, together, she thought, we are naked. Diana watched as he threw it into the hole and buried it. She watched his movements as he worked. When he returns, she thought, I will reach up and touch him ... kiss him....

But she didn't. He arrived and she tried to ... but she couldn't. Her body went limp. It fell over and lay on the ground. She was alert and she knew she wasn't drunk. She didn't know what happened. She could only feel an intense arousal ... if she were to be touched, she thought, she would explode....

"It has started for you," Tengri said. He moved her gently so that she lay on her stomach.

Diana sighed at his touch. "What is happening?"

"You have the ability. You are feeling the flow of forces. It is you, not I who have called them into being."

"I can't move."

"Don't worry. It is natural. I see that you do not have the strength, so I will take all responsibility. Do not concern yourself with anything but your feelings. Allow them to flow. I sense your arousal...."

He knows ... he understands, she thought ... and she wasn't the least bit ashamed.

"... they are natural and it is often how your body interprets the flow of the energies in which we work, at least in the beginning until you get used to them. I will place upon you that salve. I must touch and massage your entire body. Do not be ashamed if you climax ... allow yourself to enjoy ... The salve that you require is sometimes also used to intensify lovemaking since it causes sensations that excite the body."

As Tengri began to apply the balm, Diana understood *exactly* what he meant. However, she thought his touch caused her more excitement than the spirit of the plant that he captured. His touching and massaging her head and hair ... shoulders ... arms ... back ... her buttocks ... legs ... feet ... and then he turned her over! As he began to massage her breasts, she felt the hardness of her nipples touching his palms and fingers ...

"Tengri," she whispered, "I am hopelessly in love with you."

"It is good to love," he replied.

"Do you feel love for me?"

"I have found that I care deeply for you and, I think, it will grow into love when all is well and we return. I have not allowed myself to think about it."

"Will it cause a problem with Tapti?"

"Love is never a problem. She understands that. She believes and knows that."

Diana felt his hands massage her pubic area. She moaned as her passion intensified and her eyes closed so as not to compete with her sense of touch....

"I want you to make love to me, Tengri."

"Perhaps one day we will Diana ... But not now."

"Wouldn't that ruin your marriage to Tapti?"

"Not if she approved."

"I need to know, Tengri ... Am I desirable?"

"Very much."

"But you are not hard?"

"Diana, that does not mean you are not desirable," Tengri responded gently and with a compassion in his voice that soothed Diana, "it merely means I am preoccupied with what I must do. Perhaps, I will get hard if the balm touches me there ... or maybe because of my closeness with you while I carry you. It really isn't important ..." Then he thought, and then asked ... "Is it important to you Diana?"

"No, I suppose not. I understand." Diana was surprised ... and pleased with what he did next.

Tengri took her hand and placed it on himself. He continued to work.

Diana found enough strength in her fingers to lightly massage and hold his penis. She felt its hardness grow and, somehow, that soothed and comforted her. She didn't care if it was because of the balm or her touch. She only wanted to touch him. She asked no more questions.

She felt him sit her up so that their knees touched as they sat cross-legged on the grass. She watched as his hardness softened as he went about first marking himself and then her. She realised he was singing as he performed his task and she felt a change in the flow of energy. However, she was unable to determine how he did it.

Then, she felt strong arms lift her as she sat on his thighs while he rose to stand. For a brief moment, Diana felt his softness touch her between her legs and it excited her even more. Had it been hard, she knew it would have entered her very easily. She thought then that she would climax, but she didn't. Rather, as if in a dream, she slowly moved so that she stood behind him, seductively climbed onto his back and wrapped her legs around his waist and her arms around his neck. She felt her breasts against the strength of his back causing her to realise the hardness of her nipples. She held him, acutely aware of their closeness, of his body.

They moved ... they were going someplace ... the movement caused her pubic area to rub sensuously against him ... Just when she thought, again, she would release her arousal ... feel the intensity of her pleasure, she realised that she stood ... somehow stood alone.

Just when Diana was about to panic, his arms wrapped around her again and automatically, she climbed up his body, only this time, facing him ... Was it real? ... Was she only imagining it? ... Could she feel his erection? ... was it truly hard? She moved her pelvis and allowed her softness to find the tip of his hardness and then let it slide gently over it as she settled down and wrapped her legs around his waist. She *swore* that she felt his warmth enter deep into her rising up to her belly. She *swore* that she felt the pain of first penetration ... and she *swore* she felt his completion flow into her being ... because she did feel her own orgasmic thrusts as she moved against his body!

At that moment, her energies changed and she was vaguely aware of deep darkness pervading their unified consciousness ... their oneness ... which was only interrupted by a network of silver threads extending throughout the universe of stars and galaxies. No longer was she sexually aroused. Her arousal now surpassed ... transcended all that ever was or ever will be. She saw the hunter ... faces came to her and then melted away … she saw the glowing yellow eyes of a wolf ... and heard the gentle flapping of an owl's wings and the cool soothing touch of its feathers as it brushed against her face ... welcoming her to reality …

Diana never knew if their lovemaking was real or imagined and she never asked him because for her, it truly happened ... and that was all that was important. She had no way of knowing it then, but eventually she *would* make love to him, and her first child would be his ... but that wouldn't be for a long time yet. For now, she was satisfied.

It suddenly struck her that they were in the void and her

dimness became acute awareness. She remembered Tengri saying that something was wrong. That there was no song on the fibre ... Then she heard sobbing ... she felt anguish, but not her own ... and she thought she heard Tengri's name, but it wasn't a voice.

And then ... *Brilliant light and searing heat!* ... Diana's nostrils allowed air hotter than she had ever before breathed enter into her lungs ... She knew they had arrived!

37

Tengri completed the circle and turned to retrieve Diana who had somehow managed to remain standing. He paused to look at her and he recalled their earlier conversation. She had confessed love and invited sexual union. He wished that she had been able to start her training before reaching puberty so that the feelings she now had could be properly understood. It was *crucial* that they be understood because, as an initiate, if she *ever* confused the energies, she *would* travel the path of the Nameless!

For the uninitiated, it was common to link sexual power with the forces associated with spiritual ecstasy. That was a mistake. However, for the *initiated* to do the same, that was an evil! Not that sexual power was evil, because it certainly wasn't. However, that energy could be used to control or manipulate others by those types of people who worked their own ulterior motives. One's emotions were a very serious thing that needed to be understood completely.

Diana's inherent weave was one that was based upon love -- material, emotional, and spiritual. She ran no risk of becoming, by her own actions, a practitioner of the dark arts. However, by starting the severity of the training at her advanced age of seventeen, she would be susceptible to falling victim to those slaves of the nameless who sought out those of pure motive but who have not yet sufficiently strengthened their spirit.

Tengri knew she had already been targeted to become such a

victim because when he read the cast of the stones, he saw the intentions of an evil brotherhood -- the enemies of his cell. It was intended that Diana become, what they called, an *altar virgin*. In their ceremonies, she would be repeatedly raped and forced to perform a variety of depraved acts which included sexual relations with animals and even murder. Their intent would be to capture her spirit by degrading her body and emotions. If they were successful, they would have a new convert. If not, a sacrificial victim. In either instance, her life would become a tortured and tormented hell. He knew that in her case, the nature of her weave would necessitate that she *must* be killed.

But that was no longer an issue, at least for the moment. She would be trained to protect herself before any situation like that could ever again present itself. Besides, Tengri thought, they would have to go through me first.

Diana's training posed a unique problem. Normally, as was in Tengri's case, training started before the sexual energies awoke from dormancy. Also, spiritual experiences and the forces that they released were *contained* by the teacher until their awakening was proper. When the proper moment arrived, and the initiate understood what was to occur, he would be sent on a solo spirit journey which would culminate in meeting the smith and having his fibres rewoven. Just prior to that happening and depending upon the individual, he would meet his celestial wives who would teach him about other manifestations of energy as they existed in other realms ... including sexual energy. That individual would acquire from one to three celestial wives who would stay with him in the spirit world until they were impregnated. After which, the spirit wives would take him to the fire mountain in the spirit world to be reforged by the smith.

In Tengri's case, he acquired three celestial wives and the smith reworked his fibres for three summers before he was reborn as a baqca. His final training was a five year solitary hermitage in the world of the hunter. Normally, such spirit walks would never last more than a portion of a moon cycle. For Tapti, it took twelve moon cycles. He anticipated that for Diana, it would be about three or four of those.

And then, there was another problem! He had absolutely no idea what went on in women's training and their own mystery traditions. When Tengri married Tapti, she had to be introduced to and accepted by his celestial wives. She had to accept he was married to them and that they would be his consorts in other worlds. His celestial wives had to permit the marriage and they took Tapti for three days of, Tengri supposed, interrogation. That was women's business and he had no right to know what transpired. To inquire would be a violation of Law. The only thing he knew was that when Tapti returned to him, his other wives permitted the marriage. Had he married her without their permission, his life, and Tapti's, would be miserable. Every child she bore would be stolen ... never to be seen or heard from again.

However, there was irony. When Tapti married him, she never mentioned having celestial husbands nor did he ever meet any. In fact, Tengri didn't even know if male spirits even existed on that realm. They did on others, but on that one, he didn't think so. It was nature's realm ... the goddess ... the earth mother ... and subsequently, purely feminine. He knew that in women's training the sexual principle was worked, but he didn't know how.

These matters were sacred and the primary reason why Tengri was mad at Kaltak for spying on him while *he* learned of sexual energy was because it was men's business. Why she was able to seemingly violate Law was a mystery. Certainly, his celestial wives knew of her presence ...

Diana was indeed a problem. Her training was starting at the age of seventeen ... not nine, ten, or eleven as it usually did. Her sexual awareness was already in full force and her spiritual awakening was not. For her to fully appreciate either, she had to learn to separate them. She had already demonstrated confusion in her ecstasy. Tengri had no doubts that her love for him was real. He could feel its force emanating from her not unlike waves emanating from the ocean.

Were it not for a number of reasons, Tengri would simply make love to her. That would simply appease and balance the confusion in her ... at least temporarily and until the women's rites ... whatever they were ... balanced the forces with finality. However, Diana's sexuality originated from deep love and not merely physical attraction. It would be unfair to play with her emotions. Tengri would not leave Tapti nor would he ever prefer Diana over her. At best, Diana would remain second to his wife and, because of that, he would not do anything to Diana which could cause her turmoil.

Tengri had hoped that satisfying her curiosity by allowing her to explore his body and to feel his hardness would cause a partial balance in her energies. Perhaps it would have if the balm was responsible for his erection. But it wasn't. It was her touch, her love, and her beauty which caused his hardness. It was as much his feelings for her as it was hers for him. Soon, they would have to enter into the void and, simply, her fibres needed to be rewoven so her energies would adjust. There were too many chances of something happening to her unless that was done.

Tengri looked at Diana as she stood with her body aroused and her spirit soaring. They were both in other worlds and appeared as ghosts in the world in which they stood. But to him, she was real ... he was real ... and it was the trees ... the earth ... and the rain which were the ghosts.

He paused to look at her beauty ... at her excitement. She was indeed beautiful and he truly noticed that beauty for the first time. Her breasts were larger than Tapti's, but otherwise, their beauty was similar. Physically, they were different ... but their beauty was the same. He thought he could love Diana, but it was *Tapti* he longed for ... and missed. He would chance the void with Diana as she was. He was confident in his power to protect her....

"*Tengri ... my husband ... you have chosen rightly.*"

Tengri looked to his left from where he had heard the voice and saw Kaltak. But it was not she who spoke. The voice came from his first celestial wife ... the spirit nymph. She stood with Kaltak and his other two spirit wives. He hadn't seen his celestial wives for many years.

It was Kaltak who spoke next, "it is not expected that a man be confronted with the dilemmas of women's traditions, dear brother, and it was a wise decision on your part that you chose not to interfere in Diana's awakening."

As his sister spoke, Tengri's wives came to him and began to caress him seductively. He ignored them. That in itself delighted the nymphs and gave them greater reason to continue.

Kaltak continued, "it is good that you considered and weighed the dangers of taking her into the void while in such a state ..."

"*Yes, husband,*" sang one of the nymphs, "*we are here to prepare her.*" They left Tengri and went to Diana and began to speak to her in hushed voices that Tengri couldn't hear.

" ... Diana will not remember what will happen," continued Kaltak. "This will be the first phase of her training and will not be completed until much later." Kaltak said those last words with a hint of sadness in her voice. She then continued by saying, "she will only remember what is in her consciousness now, but intuitively, she will know that what she thought, is not really what happened. That is the first lesson in women's training."

"If I understand what you're saying, sister, the women must realise and work their intuitive energies in a manner that is unique to womankind...."

"That is correct, but you need not know more...."

"But why tell me this much? Is it not a violation of Law?"

"You have been told what you needed to know ... no more. And Law, dear brother, is governed by need, and as her teacher, you have that need and *right*. There is no violation. You must be a part of her training now, as you will be required in the future when her womanhood is firmly admitted into the mysteries. But for now,

I must teach you a song of possession. A song that you already know for your purposes, but one that is varied by tonal qualities for our immediate needs."

Kaltak taught Tengri the different variances of the song and told him what he must do. As they finished, his celestial wives returned to them. He did not see what they did to Diana.

"She is prepared, husband, and she has responded correctly. We accept her on behalf of the goddess and the goddess will initiate her herself when the time comes."

Kaltak and his celestial wives vanished in a mist and cool breeze. However, Tengri suspected his sister would continue to watch.

Tengri again looked at Diana. She didn't look any different than before the visitation. She was still aroused, betrayed by the hardness of her nipples and the flush of her skin. He was surprised that she still stood, because it had been some time since he placed her there while he made the circle. He was surprised that her body hadn't collapsed and retained the strength to remain standing. Clearly, however, her consciousness soared elsewhere ... Tengri began.

He walked over to her and rubbed his hand in her hair gathering the excess balm onto his fingers. He placed his hand between her legs and gently stroked her, arousing her even more. He heard a slight moan and he could feel her wetness. He then touched his tongue to her nipples and then took them into his mouth and gently bit them. When he looked up, Diana's eyes were open and she looked at him with complete awareness of the love she felt. But Tengri also saw that her eyes would have no memory. Memory would come with a later experience -- an initiation, not of love making, but rather, of the initiation of memory itself. But for the moment, her eyes revealed her awareness of the present reality.

She touched him and gently fondled his private parts. Her touch was exciting and he felt himself starting to stiffen. Again, he looked into her eyes ... Diana's were looking deeply into his own. Her eyes spoke to him as if to say that he was in her world, her mystery, and she knew what had to be done. Her eyes said that she would not interfere with his love for Tapti and that Tapti understood that need. Her eyes comforted him. Tengri knew that timing was critical. He would sing a song that allowed the fire spirit to possess his body and complete the act of love. He allowed such possession before, but for different reasons. His own spirit would leave and take his soul with it, but his body would remain in union with Diana. He would not know the pleasure that his body would feel. It would only tell him its memory when he returned. It would be the fire spirit, Mirança, who would make love to Diana. It would be *its* semen which would flow freely into her warmth after their mutual climatic release. But contained in that semen would be the fire that would begin the change of the weave of her fibres ... of her energy that would be burned, cleansed, purified, and separated, allowing an equilibrium to be realised.

This would be a severe test for Diana for she had to intuit the truth. Her body and mind would have a vague recollection of her lovemaking with Tengri. She would be uncertain if it *truly* happened and would doubt. Her *test,* however, would be to understand intuitively that not only was their union real, but that it was *only* with his body and not with him. She would not know that it was a fire spirit with whom she made love.

Diana allowed herself to slowly sink to her knees while kissing his body. Slowly ... finally ... her instincts taught her what her experience didn't. She took him into her mouth and teased him with her tongue.

Tengri closed his eyes as he looked to the sky allowing the cold and ghostly drizzle of the physical world, the *unreal* world soak his spirit. He grasped Diana's upper arms and raised her to her feet. Again, he looked into her eyes and saw in them the glimmer of light which told him that this is what she would remember ... *this* is what she would doubt.

He kissed her ... and while he kissed her, he grasped her thighs and lifted her up. Instinctively, she wrapped her legs around his waist ... held him tightly so that her breasts pressed against him. She held him so tightly that Tengri couldn't tell where his body stopped and hers began. As his hands held her buttocks, it was only the strength of his arms that held her high enough so he would not enter into her. Even so, hardness and softness still touched, albeit barely, and that touch, however slight, was felt with an unsurpassed intensity.

Tengri knew she would also remember, and doubt, that touch. He knew because he felt the change in her body.

She broke from their kiss allowing lips and tongues to part. She moved his hair aside with her hand and buried her face in his neck. He could feel her breath ... her intensified breathing as her hips began to move rhythmically ... harmoniously ... erotically against his abdomen.

At times, her movements caused her to touch his hardness and he was tempted to forego the song and allow her to slip down upon him. Instead, he chose to deny his desire and he began to sing as Kaltak taught him:

"Aya! Fire-King Mirança,
You who will last as a thought of eternity and who spins,
  The eight spoked wheel of Law arisen from the breath of One!
Manifested through the hermit's magic power,
You who knows pure, clean power;
  Sear your fires through that which is hard, dense, and confused!
You, who bring us the Light!
  Balance the fires of soul, spirit, and body,
  So that their purity is correctly used!"

With a shudder, Tengri was immediately separated from himself and he stood a few paces away watching the fire spirit within his body making love to Diana. His spirit self and soul was now even more ghostly. It was a bluish light floating in a mist of a ghostly reality.

Tengri watched as his arms moved from holding Diana's buttocks and as her weight caused her body to slowly settle downward ... as he entered her ... as their lovemaking intensified ... and as they experienced eternity together.

When he saw their bodies relax and their satisfaction complete, he vanquished the fire-king with a single command and suddenly found himself back in his own body. His hardness had not yet started to soften and he felt the last subtle contractions of Diana's dying climax ... of her warmth as it encased him ... of the softness that was not his. His own release was denied to him but his body told him of its satisfaction.

Diana's body told him it had changed. Tengri could feel that her weave was no longer confused. He lifted her so they were no longer united and he began to sing the song that would take him home, that would take him to Tapti. He held Diana tight so she could not fly away as her spirit soared along the threads on which they would dance. By the time he entered the void, his hardness had softened.

He leaped! ... They were in the void ... His toe told him they were on the correct thread ... but something was wrong ... there was no song ... Tapti did not sing ... Tengri said so out loud.

38

It only took a few moments for Diana to acquire her full capacities of the earth reality and to become acutely and clearly aware of her surroundings. It was extremely bright and that brightness caused her to squint. It was also very hot and the sun was beyond intense, but the balm protected her.

She realised she lay upon the hot earth and remembered that Tengri had gently laid her down just a few brief moments before. Now, she pushed herself up onto her elbow so that she partially sat, and partially lay. She looked, and saw Tengri with his back to her and she could feel his frantic concern ... worry. And then she remembered ...

At first, she doubted it as being a dream ... but no ... her body was not lying to her. It *was* satisfied in a way it had never felt before ... And then it dawned upon her ... *I have just made love! I have just made love to Tengri!* I can still feel him inside me ... I can still smell him ... taste him!

She looked at Tengri and smiled. She thought, I *am* pleasing to a man! At that moment, something else took over her thoughts as if someone else spoke inside her head. She knew it was her voice that she silently heard and she knew that it was her intuition ... but it was different ... stronger ... and more confident.

She looked again at Tengri and somehow realised that she knew his body but did not know him as she should after such intimacy. No, Diana thought to herself, I have yet to make love with the man I love. She subdued her confusion and sat it aside, deciding to contemplate upon the contradiction when she had time alone ... but right now she intuited Tengri's anguish and tears began to well in her eyes. Right now, at this moment, her only concern was for him!

She bit her lower lip and asked, "Tengri ... what's wrong?"

He didn't answer. Rather, he remained preoccupied with his task of examining the ground.

Diana struggled to her feet and as she stood, she had to fight to keep her knees from buckling. She managed to stay upright, although, for the moment, she knew that her best attempt at a walk would be a wobble. The heat was becoming almost unbearable and she realised the wisdom of forcing herself to drink as much water as she did.

She no longer felt the effects of the kymyz, at least in so far as being tipsy was concerned. Love making and the void probably took care of that. Again, her thoughts returned to their love making, her lower muscles were a bit sore, but pleasantly satisfied. Diana assumed it was the thoughts of love that caused her strength to slowly return.

The heat felt as if a god of great strength was pushing it down upon her and that it was the pressure as much as the temperature which caused her body to bake. She suddenly thought of the young man from Nicomedia and her excuse of sunburn. By tomorrow, she thought, that excuse would give way to truth.

Diana surveyed her surroundings. The sky was a beautiful deep blue without even a single wisp of a cloud daring to show itself. The sun ... the unbearable sun ... demonstrated its superiority over the sky and earth by its majestic dance through the heavens. Its present position revealed it was mid afternoon. The land of this region was a sight that she had never before seen. It was flat, dry, and treeless. She wondered if it was desert. The sandy soil was patched with areas of tall, yellow grass that was pointed at the tip. It looked sharp and extremely dangerous. There was ample scrub bush but no sign of water nor any hint it had ever rained in this desolate place. The most remarkable feature was the flatness. Blue sky and yellow earth met at the horizon far in the distance. Nothing lay in between to break one's view -- except to the Southeast where a gigantic rock trying to be a mountain but barely succeeding in being a hill established its earthly supremacy over an otherwise desolate land. Diana loved it! She *loved* this strange and harsh place she now called, without any equivocation, home.

Her attention once again turned to Tengri when she suddenly felt a wave of anguish emanating from his soul. His body, which looked out of place in Byzantium, was perfectly at home here. It was obvious that he *belonged* in this environment. Diana realised that her feet were indeed tender and they felt like they were already beginning to blister. She chose to ignore her discomfort.

She repeated, "Tengri, what's wrong?"

Nothing.

"Tengri!"

He turned and Diana noticed a concerned, almost wild look of confusion and anger in his eyes.

"It's Tapti," he said at long last. "She's supposed to be here."

"I remember you saying her song was not on the thread. What do you suppose happened?"

"She left no tracks showing that she left. But there are signs of seven riders, their horses, and their camp. They stayed here last night and left this morning."

"Could they have carried her off?" As soon as she said it, Diana wished she hadn't asked that question because it obviously agitated Tengri to hear or think about it.

"It's possible, but it doesn't appear that way. The tracks do not indicate a change of weight in the riders ..."

Diana didn't have the faintest idea of what he was talking about.

"... But, then again, there appears to have been a wind, maybe two days ago and ..."

Then Diana saw the change. A look of dangerous and uncontrolled anger appeared in his eyes ... but *only* in his eyes ... and only momentarily ... for when he next spoke, there wasn't a hint that anything was different. It scared her.

"When we started the ritual, a Buryat warrior watched. We did nothing about him because he appeared to respect our sacred journey. He *must* have violated Law and taken Tapti ... the wind would have concealed any signs of a struggle. The seven riders, they must have returned thinking that I was here ..." He turned and began to jog to the West. "They die!"

"Tengri."

No response.

"Tengri! ... Listen to me!"

He ignored her.

Diana vaguely remembered, as if in a dream, that she was told this would happen and at all costs, she must stop it ... *But she couldn't remember the dream!* She only remembered something about avoiding a war ...

"Tengri! ... Look at me!"

Tengri stopped ... he turned and looked at Diana and didn't try to conceal his impatience.

"Look at me!" Diana shouted. "I don't know where I am ... I'm in the middle of nowhere ... I don't have any water ... I'm naked ... and you're scaring me! *You're leaving me alone and I don't know what to do or where to go!*" She couldn't help herself. She started to cry and it embarrassed her.

Tengri looked at Diana and immediately calmed down. If they had taken Tapti, she would either be dead or enslaved. If dead, he could do nothing about it until later. If enslaved, she could wait a few more days. His first priority was Diana. He walked to her and held her. She returned the embrace but couldn't control the tears.

"Tengri," she said with a sob, "I'm sorry. I know how you must feel."

"Don't worry ... you're right. I must make sure that you are safe first."

"Tengri ... I have to, uh ... relieve myself."

Her comment was so out of place that it made Tengri start to laugh as soon as he realised what she said. Soon, Diana started laughing too.

"Well I do!"

"If you can hold it, it is better that you do ... at least until we can find water. The more water you can retain, the better."

"I suppose I can wait," she responded ... "Do you really think they took her? ... Could she have left and gone back home?" Her intuition told her she wasn't home and neither was she taken by the Buryat. She only suggested it to give him hope ... After all, it was possible.

Apparently, her words helped because his spirits rose. "That is very possible, Diana. She may well have done that! It is even hotter than normal and she may have sensed my perfection of the art of travelling the fibres and realised she wasn't needed ... Or even, she may have been called to go on her own spirit journey ... Her kobuz is gone and that could be a sign that her leaving was peaceful ..."

Then ... silently ... Tengri struggled with a thought. It was almost as if forces were attempting to keep it from him ... it was vague, but he briefly considered that perhaps ... somehow ... Tapti had become lost in the void. As difficult as it was for that thought to be brought into his consciousness, it was as easy for it to be swiftly deleted from his memory. There were other powers at work ... powers far stronger than Tengri's. He never had that thought again.

It never occurred to Diana that the voice she heard in the void calling Tengri's name might have been Tapti's -- at least until much, much later.

"What do we do now?" Asked Diana.

"If we leave now, we can reach that rock to the Southeast well before sunset." Tengri picked up Diana and carried her piggyback. "It is a sacred mountain the Buryat call Bordj. Only their shamans are allowed to go there so we'll be safe from the Buryat warriors. There is also, I hear, a large pool of water. We can rest there until nightfall and then start home."

"Tengri, did you say that the Buryat called that mountain ... *Bordj?*"

"Yes. They have a strange god of which none of the other clans have ever heard. Only the Buryat seem to know about him. He is said to be a rock born god and is the son of Bordj. Their songs say that when he was born, the mountain flashed forth a radiant ray of light."

Diana was *astounded* with what Tengri was saying and for a few moments, she was speechless.

"Tengri ... what is that god's name?"

"Mithras."

"Mithras! I can't believe it!"

"Why? ... Is that important?"

"Important! ... Tengri ... Mithras is a god that has been worshipped in my land for a very long time. The powers behind Christianity are now in the process of attempting to eradicate it.

That religion, the religion of Mithras is two, maybe three *thousand* years old. It is possibly the *first* religion! How in the world did it get *here?*"

"I don't know, but the Buryat have worshipped Bordj as a sacred place far longer than the ancient songs they sing can remember. Their mountain is called a fire mountain and is the home of a smith. Our songs say the Buryat did not understand the work of the smith as they could not understand the nature of fibres, so they perverted the original songs and arrived at new gods and new interpretations to universal Law. For instance, a baqca must climb a ladder of knives if he is to attain Truth. The Buryat have, also, a ladder, but not of knives. Their ladder has only seven rungs leading to the eighth and last rung. Their rungs represent metals -- lead, tin, bronze, iron, an alloy, silver, and gold. The only agreement between Buryat and Kazak-Kirghiz songs is that the last rung represents a sphere of the *fixed stars.* The Buryat call their ladder *klimax.* Ours, is simply a ladder of knives ... of which knives must always be stone."

"The Buryat songs," said Diana, "are exactly as the Mithraic religion teaches in the empire. Even the names. I wonder, did the religion spread throughout the world from Persia where it was thought to originate ... even to here? Or did it *originate* with the Buryat and it was they who spread it to Persia?"

"If it started here, Diana, it would not have originated with the Buryat. Their god Mithras is a new name for an older god ... a god whom you will probably meet. You can ask him yourself."

Their discussion placed Tengri in a seriously pensive mood. He realised something very crucial to the plan and for the rest of their journey to the mountain, they did not speak.

They arrived while the sun was still high and did, indeed, find a large, deep pool of water. They both swam and enjoyed the soothing water until the sun set. Diana then welcomed sleep but later awoke to Tengri's touch applying a soothing ointment to her chafed skin. He had hunted and prepared the plant while she dreamt. When she first woke, she thought they were back in the void but soon discovered it was merely the night and its starry sky -- so breathtakingly beautiful. He had allowed her to sleep well into the night and subsequently their departure was late. It meant they wouldn't arrive at his yurt until about noon the day after next.

The nights were still hot, but they were bearable. The night breeze helped tremendously. At sunrise, they found another outcropping of rock and they slept there during the day. Tengri told her they were now in his land and that she could wear her dress. After their swim, the markings and balm had come off, but Tengri decided, however, that neither needed to be put back on. Since they travelled only at night, there was little chance they would be seen by the Buryat ... and no chance of her exposure to the sun. He had said that her dress would protect her from the sun during their morning travel to their final destination. However, she doubted it. Tengri did not know what dress she brought ... Anyway, she preferred to remain naked.

When they arrived at his yurt, there was no sign of Tapti. The next day, he left her alone and went to retrieve his daughter. He returned by nightfall and told Diana that she could wear Tapti's clothes. When she returned, he had said, she would make some for her.

39

Diana's days were filled with learning both the shamanic arts as well as the Kazak-Kirghiz tongue -- and, true to her nature, turned out to be an excellent student. Within six months she had not only effectively mastered the language, she had also become so sufficiently conversant with shamanic healing and demonstrated such a profound innate talent, that Tengri allowed her to take over that aspect for the people.

Tengri had been right. His people had accepted her very readily

-- especially the children. Diana had always made it a point to carve wooden toys and take them to the camp on those rare occasions when a shaman was needed and the children truly loved them! And, Tengri had kept his word. He had made her a carving knife out of stone that was amazingly efficient.

Although his people moved several times during those first few months, Tengri and Diana never did. He waited patiently for Tapti to return.

Several days after they first arrived, Tengri had decided he was, regardless of contrary arguments, going to investigate the Buryat village. Diana was awed by how he did it. She watched a sacred ceremony ... she actually *helped* in that ceremony ... and saw Tengri shapechange into his totem, the owl. She watched in amazement as he flew ... as free as his spirit ... high and far away. He was gone for three days and when he returned he said there was no sign of her. He had even sought out and found the Buryat warrior, whom he discovered, was blinded that night, and entered into his dreams. He had no idea of the fate of Tapti either. Tengri told her that the only possibility was that Tapti had been called to make a spirit journey, and it probably had something to do with women's business because Kaltak never said a word about it. He had decided that if Tapti was in danger, Kaltak would know. She always seemed to have her nose in places where it didn't belong ... but after all, wasn't that the nature of a wolf? It was that night that he told Diana *everything* about his sisters. She now understood why her uncle had blushed.

When Diana asked how long Tapti would be on her spirit journey, Tengri merely shrugged and said she could return at any time ... or even after several seasons or a little longer. It was a woman's tradition and he didn't know of such things ... but one day, Diana would find out when she took her own journey.

Still, Diana noticed Tengri had his ups and downs. When he became *really* depressed, Diana would find some way to cheer him up. It was easier to cheer his daughter up, she could always give her carving lessons. But with Tengri, it was much harder. After about nine months when he became particularly and unreasonably depressed, Diana took out the red cloth Tengri had brought back and started to sew. When Tengri asked what she was doing, she merely replied if it was going to be a gift, it might as well be one that Tapti didn't have to make when she returned. Diana's tactic worked amazingly well.

They were very comfortable together and Diana was content and happy. She and Tengri never spoke about their lovemaking ... and they never made love. Also, Diana never wore her nightgown. In the summers, she slept as Tengri did ... in the nude. And in the winters ... the bitterly cold winters, they both slept in the nude but with each other for warmth. That was one of the reasons why winter was her favourite time of the year. Still, they never made love.

After twenty-one, or maybe twenty-two months, Tengri came to her and said that Tapti must be dead. He had to travel to the realm of the dead ... the domain of Erlik Khan and there perform certain ceremonies so her soul wouldn't be eaten by the eaters of souls. And that she, Diana, had advanced sufficiently in her training that she should go with him. She needed to experience this new aspect of shamaning ... and besides, he wanted her to meet, at least, Tapti's spirit.

Something in his voice ... the desolate sadness and solitude he had felt when he told her made her start to cry uncontrollably. Tengri tried to comfort her and held her tightly ... but to no avail. Even though it was spring, they, nevertheless, slept together that night. She sobbed, they both held onto one another very tightly, as neither wanted to be alone....

40

Just before dawn, three days later, Diana was awakened by Tengri's movements. Sleepily, she started to rise. When she threw off the covers, she desperately wished she could snuggle back down into her cosy bed and sleep. Instead, she forced herself to rise and valiantly faced the cold night air of spring. Although the sun warmed the day considerably, the night still belonged to the winter's cold. Spring was an awkward time of year.

She stood ... stretched ... and shivered. Not enough sleep, she thought, it was well past midnight when they returned to their yurt after depositing Tengri's daughter with Tapti's sister. She hugged herself, by pressing her arms against her breasts thereby hiding them from view ... not because of modesty or shyness, modesty didn't exist in this household. She hugged herself because she was cold. She felt the goose bumps on her flesh.

Diana smiled to herself ... she remembered a time when she would blush at the slightest hint of embarrassment. Since she had been here ... never once had she blushed.

Hearing Diana rise, Tengri turned to look at her. He was going to light a warming fire in the yurt before forcing her to get up ... but now, she had already risen. The fire cast a glow in the room and he motioned for her to stand by it for awhile.

While she silently stood there and did her little ... *dance of warming* ... as she good naturedly called it, Tengri watched absently in thought.

He examined her skin and debated as to whether it had toughened enough to protect her during the several days it would take to make the spirit walk to the Mountain of Iron. They would walk day and night, excepting the short rest they were permitted each evening at sunset. It was against Law to travel to the underworld from the time the sun first touched the horizon until it was clearly dark. As normal, they would only wear the marks made of sacred ash.

Diana's skin had indeed toughened, he noted. Over the seasons he had regularly prepared the ointments her body needed to assist the sun, heat, cold, and wind to adapt her for survival. Her natural complexion was fair, but the salves and a regular routine of exposure to the elements each day for short periods of time had sufficiently completed the needed process. Yes, Tengri decided, she would survive the ordeal without too much additional difficulty.

Her skin had changed colour from white to golden brown. Her muscles had become even *more* toned and the soles of her feet were now as strong as leather. But the most interesting change that had occurred to the young woman was in the colour of her hair and eyes. Her long, thick hair had become *fiery* red. No longer was it blond. It was her pubic hairs that first began to change colour and now, they were as red as the hair on her head. They were nowhere near as thick and because of that, it emphasised the thin dark brownish red line of hair between her legs. Tengri didn't know what had caused the change in her hair colour but suspected it was more than likely the result of her lovemaking with the fire-spirit.

Tengri *did* know why her eye colour had changed. It was the result of her seeing into the void. Before, her eyes were a beautiful blue. Now, they were still blue, but much deeper. Mostly, they were indigo, and at times, while in the proper light and mood, almost black in colour. That told Tengri Diana had a remarkable innate talent for dream work. An ability to traverse the indigo fibres through the void....

Diana noticed Tengri looking at her body and wondered what he was thinking. She realised that in her dance, her breasts were bouncing ... perhaps erotically ... and decided to tease him even though her intuition told her he had no erotic thoughts.

"Do they bounce too much ... or are they still firm enough for you?"

For a moment, Tengri had the eerie sensation it was Tapti who spoke those words because he remembered a similar question asked all those long years ago....

"No, they bounce just right."

His response almost embarrassed her and would otherwise have stopped her warming dance if it were not for the cold ... her only reason for dancing to begin with.

"Tengri ... you know I still do not think Tapti dead," she said changing the subject.

"If not, Erlik Khan will tell us. Diana, do you recall what was said about Mithras two summers ago?"

Diana was a little surprised because the subject had never come up since then. "Yes, why?"

"The song I will sing to take us into the second realm when we start our walk will refer to him. Not the one known as Mithras, but the *ancient* god ... the original god who the Persians, or Buryats, later renamed Mithras. He is the all knowing god and I will ask for his blessing to protect us in our descent."

"By what name is he known?"

"Mergen. The god resides on the seventh knife of the ladder of knives which is the realm of the sun."

Tengri rose and picked up his small pouch containing the sacred ash and a two foot long strip of hide he had recently tanned. He started to leave the yurt when Diana stopped him.

"Tengri, it is odd that you bring up the subject. I was thinking about it last week when you sacrificed the bull ... why a bull?"

"The bull is what gives us life. But my purpose was not related to its life-giving properties, rather, because of its great strength and power. This strip of hide is from the bull and it will be used to bind us together throughout our journey. It will be tied to our wrists by a special knot so we can never be separated. This will be your first journey into the realm of the dead. You are not known there and you would not know that Erlik Khan has bound *all* souls to himself by virtue of a variety of magical knots. Each knot has a significance and will determine each person's afterlife. The knot by which we will bind ourselves will tell him we are not yet dead and will, therefore, allow us to leave his sphere. For otherwise, we could not. The strip is for your protection for there is sometimes a great wind that blows through the underworld. I do not want you to be blown from me. The strength of the bull will keep us together."

Moments later, Diana joined Tengri outside the yurt. She sat on the ground cross-legged so that her knees touched his.

"Diana, we will walk this earth almost as ghosts. Of this, you are familiar. But our journey will last several days. We will travel day and night through the steppes first, and then a desert before reaching the Iron Mountain we call Temir Taixa. When there, we will climb until we find the jaws of the earth known as Yer Mesi. We will then descend into the underworld and seek out Erlik Khan."

Tengri then sang the song which caused them both to enter into the second state. They marked each other and then Tengri tied her left wrist to his right wrist with a magical knot. He then sang:

> *"Ayak! Gods of the East;*
> *in eternal strife and conflict,*
> *With your equals in the West!*
> *Benevolent gods, bless our souls!*
> *Evil gods, send not körmös!*
> *Mergen! ...*
> *You who live in the seventh realm!*
> *Mergen! ...*
> *You, God of the sun;*
> *All knowing god,*
> *Servant of Bai Ülgän!*
> *Bless our souls with wisdom!*
> *For we seek Erlik Khan, in our descent;*
> *Guide our way into the chaos of the abyss!*
> *Guide our descent into hell!"*

41

Never once for five days were Tengri and Diana separated. The binding of bull hide never loosened its hold upon them. It seemed to Diana that she had stumbled and fallen on *hundreds* of occasions and each time she thought the seemingly loosely tied knot would come undone. It never did.

They carried nothing with them. There was no sacred pouch containing dried horse meat nor a skin of water. When they first started, Diana had wondered what they were to eat and drink ... or even if they would. She never asked but chose to wait to see what Tengri did. She discovered that the land upon which they walked ... even though it appeared barren and desolate ... was rich in nourishment. A variety of seemingly unobtrusive plants and insects she would never have given a second glance, she soon discovered, were edible. Tengri taught her well and by the second day, Diana felt that if she were to become lost in this harsh environment, she would know how to survive.

Finding water was more difficult and Diana couldn't figure out how Tengri always seemed to locate -- and on one occasion, just before she thought she would *die* of dehydration -- that quenching necessity of life. She had finally asked him and he had explained that since this was a land he knew well, he knew where all the watering holes were. But also, he explained that the earth would *always* reveal its resources if needed, if one simply knew how to listen to the songs of nature. He showed her, each time they approached a watering hole, the various signs that always announced its existence. There were certain kinds of large flying insects which never flew more than an arrow's flight from water ... there were certain types of small birds ... there were many signs....

Diana's last vestige of modesty and privacy disappeared on this journey. She always enjoyed privacy when relieving herself. But no more. She ... and Tengri ... only went at night. Not out of shyness ... but to preserve their bodily fluids.

Late morning on the third day, they saw a rider heading in the same direction that they travelled. Tengri said he was a Buryat shaman who was also going to the realm of Erlik Khan. Diana asked why he was so elaborately dressed, on horseback, and apparently carried a wide array of items. He responded by saying that was custom when visiting the Lord of the Underworld. For safety, Erlik had to be bribed and made drunk before he would bless a shaman or allow him to leave. When Diana asked why they weren't doing the same, she wished she hadn't. Tengri's response caused her to worry. He had said he wasn't there to *appease* the god. He was there to *challenge* him! To arrive with nothing was a sign of strength ... of confidence ... and aggression. Even though Tengri knew he had no chance to defeat a god, he was nevertheless confident the act would earn him respect. As a result, Erlik might allow him to perform the proper ceremonies to release Tapti's soul from torment ... and there was even a chance that Erlik would *release* Tapti if she were not truly dead!

Now it was late afternoon of the fifth day. Early, the morning before, the *Spirit Walkers* entered the desert. Only once, the previous afternoon, had they found water. Food was unavailable. Now, life was *truly* miserable! Diana's tongue was swollen ... her lips cracked ... her feet bloodied from the heat and rocks ... and her body stinging from blowing sand. She could barely walk ... her strength and life ebbing away at each painful step. Tengri could not carry her as she, too, must appear before Erlik Khan with strength and confidence.

The wind had appeared from nowhere hours before and, with malicious intent, assaulted them with its vicious fury. Erlik *knew* that they approached and the god toyed with them for his own perverted amusement ... *and he was one of the good gods!* Fortunately, Tengri had found a desert plant that had a long, stringy leaf. He made, from that plant, a protective covering for their eyes. It was tied around their heads and thin slits were made so they could see. It kept the sand out, but Diana wondered what good it did because they couldn't see through the storm anyway.

At sunset ... Diana *assumed* it was sunset ... they came upon an outcropping of rock. If Diana had led the journey, she would have walked into it. She followed as Tengri felt his way around its surface and suddenly, as if there had never been a wind, all was still. They had entered into a cool cave ... and to Diana's delight ... *a large pool of clear water!*

Tengri did not allow her to swim or wash herself, but by the time they had to leave, both were refreshed. They had also eaten as the pool was *living* water and fish were plentiful. Was it luck, Diana thought? Or was it Mergen? When they left, there was no storm. It had spent its fury and could not defeat them ... Erlik must now know that she and Tengri were proficient in their art and that they *had* to be dealt with ... not as humans, but as shamans! The night sky was beautiful as usual and its cool air felt wonderful. For the first time in her life, Diana understood what it *truly* meant to be alive ...

Tengri saw and knew he had succeeded in training a shamaness born from a disbelieving culture. He now understood that their art was for ... *must* be for ... all peoples of the earth.

As the sun ... the *Light* ... purified the darkness in their eternal battle once more, Diana saw, for the first time the looming and majestic Temir Taixa. That evening, they would arrive and commence their descent. Never before had Diana been more confident. She could, and would if necessary, confront Erlik ... or any god for that matter as earned confidence released all fear of failure ... There was no fear of death ... There was no *fear!*

Tengri allowed himself to smile. Their journey was for Diana ... *not* Tapti!

42

Tengri had found Yer Mesi ... the gaping jaws of the earth ... around midnight. He sang a song causing both to enter into higher and higher states ... and then they jumped into the mouth of the abyss itself. They did not fall ... they floated ... floated through the endless chasms of the underworld ... a different plane ... a different reality.

Diana heard whispers of words she could not understand ... moans of anguish she could not feel ... she saw wisps of ghostly manifestations that caused her skin to crawl as they passed through her. She felt their emptiness. She saw the whitened bones of shamans who sang the wrong songs or mispronounced their words. She knew she was protected.

There was no passage of time and the only sense of measurement was the deepening sense of torment as they descended endlessly into the chasm of chaos. They could feel the endless deaths of wretched souls. They watched in horror as the körmös devoured the impure spirits and defecated writhing maggots in an endless cycle of nameless torture....

They landed and walked for eternity along the never ending steppe of the infernal abyss. They passed the Buryat shaman they had seen several days before. His tongue ... unbelievingly as long as his arm ... had been pulled from his mouth and staked to the ground. His eyes bulged in terror and he *screamed* in unintelligible agony as defecated maggots crawled and burned his flesh where his sacred marks had been. His clothing, horse, and bribes for Erlik were gone. Two hideously indescribable monsters ... demons ... attended to him. One had stretched his penis exceedingly far ... at least three feet ... and had hardened and shredded it with its stroking claws. The shaman was *continuously* ejaculating his seed and as its drops landed, they turned into tiny little creatures which scurried away. The other monstrosity was gnawing upon the pitiful man's testicles....

"Ignorant Buryat!" Exclaimed Tengri. "He mispronounced the words of his song, he improperly marked himself, and he stupidly came to this world for his own greed and lust."

"Can't we help him?" Diana said as she looked into his pleading eyes that betrayed his terror and hope.

"I'm afraid we cannot. Only his teacher has any chance of saving him ... if he is still alive. The shaman is young, so there *is* a good chance. When we return, I will seek him out. That is all I can do."

"But won't he *die?*"

"Unfortunately ... no. He is not of the dead and will not be killed. He is too valuable alive. Those two monsters are daughters of the nameless entity and they have discovered his life force and use it to create half breed spirits that grow to become körmös. See them scurry away in their foulness. As his semen touches this hellish earth, his life force ... his ability to create ... causes new evil. That is the *only* way evil can reproduce itself ... by the stupidity and selfishness that some of god's creatures choose. Soon, those daughters will mount him and his *true* agony will begin. His semen will give them strength and will cause the birth of demons. When they are born, they will be capable of entering both physical and dream reality. Fortunately, only the most powerful shamans who get caught in this trap can father demons capable of entering the material world ... but dream demons are bad enough."

"But if Erlik is a *good* god, how can he allow this horror to happen?"

"This is not Erlik's doing. Erlik has chosen to watch over this realm to *protect* the dead from this happening to them. He is here to do eternal battle with the true evil of this realm ... the Nameless One ... who possesses this realm as his domain. By Erlik's presence, he *checks* the spread of the expansion of the nameless hordes. But he cannot defeat them ... nor can they defeat him. Nor can Erlik save this poor shaman from the path he chose for it was indeed his own choice. We, as living creatures, *always* have choice. That is the truth the Law ... brought forth by the breathing word of the Supreme Deity. That Deity, Bai Ülgän, is unknowable to us and the conflict of good and evil is a lesser state overseen by his servants. Your Christians do not understand this and the god they worship is not the Supreme Deity ... the One God ... but rather, one of his servants ..."

"*Aaarrraaaggghhh*"

Diana turned and looked at the poor shaman who screamed and who interrupted Tengri's words. She looked in horror as she saw both daughters split his penis lengthwise down the middle and each mounted him simultaneously and moaned in their perverse pleasure. She shuddered at the thought of what would happen to a shamaness ...

"Let us hope that more daughters do not arrive," Tengri commented in disgust.

They walked on ... endlessly onward.

They came to a huge sea ... a sea of hell ... and neither allowed themselves to think of the horrors they saw ... the horrible things that people could do to themselves by their irresponsible acts ... the unspeakable things ... Diana vomited at the sight of what lay in store for those wretched souls in the underworld who betrayed a friend or a loved one in their earthly life. She closed her eyes and refused to look at the torment of those who *caused* others to betray by their intentional deceit and twisting of truth. Those who *professed* to be spiritual leaders with the intent to manipulate the naive for their own self glory thereby causing the desecration of the sacred, had the worst hell in store for them ... a hell that waited patiently for its many victims. When Diana saw their self imposed destiny, she would have passed out had not Tengri held her lovingly and with the tenderness of heavenly peace.

"Only love has *true* power ... Only love, Diana. Be certain that in your life ... you only love."

Across the vast and endless sea was a bridge ... a bridge that was the width of a thread and the sharpness of a knife. Tengri told her that only the pure of heart could safely cross. They both crossed. They walked for eternity in their crossing, but they both crossed without any fear of falling.

On the other side was another endless plain that finally became a shore to a river. On the other side was a mountain. On top of the mountain was a castle.

"We wait here," said Tengri, "for the boatman to ferry us across to the sane world of Erlik Khan's abode. We will climb seven heavens to stand before him. There, we will meet Tapti's spirit and soul."

They both sat and rested while they waited.

43

Diana did not sleep. She was wide awake and acutely alert. She saw an indigo fibre form and her intuition told her to allow her spirit to travel its weave ... to *leave* the underworld and enter into the void. She did. She followed her dream vision.

She saw;

She understood;

She felt love;

She was joyous;

She flew back to the underworld with her memory!

She remembered Kaltak and Tengri's celestial wives. She remembered what they told her:

"*Tengri* ... Tapti is alive! She is not here ... she is in the void! ... *I ... saw ... her ... Tengri. I saw her!*"

Diana was back in the underworld ... back with Tengri ... they were still bound by the strip of hide.

At her words, Tengri's mind exploded! He remembered what he had forgotten ... what he was *forced* to forget for the reasons of his existence ... for the purpose of their objective ...

"*Of course!*" He exclaimed. "She was drawn into the void by my power! I *had* to forget of that possibility. *It was absolutely necessary!* Erlik has blessed us by weaving the fibre for you to see, Diana ... See! ... Now ... a silver thread crosses the indigo."

Diana saw and jumped as Tengri jumped ... She danced as Tengri danced ... She had no choice because they were tied ... She was thankful they were tied ... Her intuition told her what to do. She never once allowed herself to interfere by thinking.

It was all an unintelligible blur ... and then ... crystal clarity.

Both Diana and Tengri understood with that clarity.

Standing before them, on the silver thread, stood Tapti with her back to them. She watched what they watched ... *a beautiful golden thread forming itself into a wonderful sight.*

The thread became a glorious and magnificent creature ... astoundingly beautiful to behold!

It was golden ... it had the body, head, and wings of a mythical dragon ... two legs with the feet of an eagle ... and a long, serpent-like, barbed tail. It was an exact replica of the carving taken from Diana's mirror ... only far more beautiful. It's grace, as it flew into future times, was indescribable.

It held a baby ... an infant ... who looked at his mother. But then, an owl flew to the little boy and with a gentle flutter of its wing, turned Mergen's head so that his beautiful eyes saw Tengri. There was recognition in those eyes ... there was a thread of love that was formed which connected father and son for a brief moment.

The owl looked at the three of them and in a distinctly human voice uttered one word:

"Wyvern!" The reality vision disappeared far into the future. Mergen, the owl, and the creature. Diana *never* forgot that word.

Diana realised that she was crying and when she turned to look at Tengri, she saw that he was crying as well. They were tears of joy and sadness unified into oneness.

"Tapti," said Tengri, ever so softly and gently.

She slowly turned thinking she was hallucinating in her grief. And then with astonished recognition, joy, and indefinable love ... Tapti embraced her husband. Tengri returned that eternal embrace. So, too, did Diana. She had no choice because she was tied to the baqca ...

44

Constantinople, 337 C.E.

Diana and her six year old son stood quietly in the hilly forests outside of the magnificent city where she had spent fourteen years of her life. From their vantage point, she could see through the trees and gaze at her tower rising high above the city walls. She longed once again, for one last time, to climb the three hundred steps to her room. But she knew she could not ... must not ... take that chance.

It had taken her and her son more than a year to travel from their home in the steppes to the city. They travelled with one of the baqcas who was a member of the secret cell and who was *assigned* to establish a branch in Babylon. The three of them had travelled along the trade routes by buying passage with a caravan and journeyed the long distance without incident.

After arriving in Babylon and saying farewell to their shaman friend, Diana and her son found passage with another caravan bound for Constantinople. That was when she found out her uncle had changed the name of his city.

She also realised the truth of Tengri's wisdom while she travelled with that caravan. It had been decided that when Diana arrived at Constantinople, she would contact only one person--the only person who Tengri felt could be trusted. A man whom he met twelve years before and whom he knew as Alexis. Tengri had always taught her that one should *never* believe in coincidence. Subsequently, Diana was not surprised to discover that the caravan on which she found passage in the ancient city of Babylon belonged to Alexis! And ... Alexis had happened to *personally* travel this particular route. She had brought several clay bowls and a skin of kymyz as a gift from Tengri. When Alexis found out, those gifts were the only payment he would accept. For the rest of that journey, Diana and her son travelled in comfort. Never once did Alexis inquire into her business. He only wished that she was returning to Tengri so that she would take his gifts to him.

The caravan arrived yesterday. Tomorrow, Diana would leave by ship that would take her to her intended destination. Not surprisingly, the ship upon which she would travel belonged to Alexis' trading concern and, again, he refused any payment. But today, she had work to do.

She looked at her son. He would be big and strong like his father, and like his father, he would be wise and determined. Her son knew his half sister ... but Diana was saddened that he would never meet his half brother. His hair was reddish brown ... he inherited that from herself. But his eyes ... his eyes were blue and even though hers were once blue as well, it could never be doubted that his eyes were acquired from his father ... Tengri.

Diana allowed herself to remember that day ten years ago when they retrieved Tapti from the void. Erlik Khan had truly blessed them for he had also woven the thread that would return them to their yurt. As soon as Tapti was safely in Tengri's arms, they returned home. From the time they entered Yer Mesi until they stood outside the yurt, only half a day passed. The three of them spent the day together ... talking ... eating ... and bathing, swimming, and playing in the water at Köso' Gol.

Diana had immediately fallen in love with Tapti. Even though it was obvious her experience had caused her considerable strain, Tapti never once questioned why Diana was present. It wasn't until three summers later she found out why. Tapti had always been kind and loving toward Diana and easily accepted her as an equal in their family. They took an immediate liking to each other and, indeed, had become as sisters.

She remembered that evening, as darkness began to encase the earth causing the temperature to dip considerably, the three of them entered the yurt and Tengri built a fire indicating there was still much that was needed to be discussed. They were like three adolescents ... speaking excitedly and out of sequence ... forgetting something and then bringing it up when it was remembered. Somehow, they each managed to follow and digest *everything* that was said. At times they laughed and later cried. At times they were seriously philosophical and later, completely frivolous. It must have been after midnight when exhaustion overcame their exuberance. Tengri didn't get up to put another log on the fire and allowed it to die to a soft glow. The conversation surrendered to sparse words and heavy eyelids. Sitting positions gave way to prone ones and finally, Diana had risen, collected her blankets, and made her bed.

The fire had heated the inside of the yurt considerably and the blankets would make it too hot to sleep. Still, they were very comfortable and would undoubtedly be needed when the last glow of the fire died and allowed darkness and cold to seep into their home.

Diana, ten years later, clearly remembered staring into the fire at its soft lighting glow gently illuminating the yurt with soothing flame. She remembered her thoughts of joy that she was a part of that family. She had worried that Tapti might have made it awkward, but her fears were unfounded. She was indeed home.

She remembered rising to go outside to relieve herself and debating whether she should first get dressed. No one had bothered to dress themselves that day so she decided not to bother and that the cold would only be experienced briefly. She darted out ... and dashed back in. She lay down and propped herself up to say good night to Tengri and Tapti. However, she noticed that they were gently touching and looking quietly into each other's eyes. She decided not to interrupt.

Diana, although choosing not to interrupt, did continue to quietly watch. The two of them were very beautiful together ... and it was that beauty, that love, which fascinated her.

Their gentle touches soon turned to passionate embraces ... kisses ... and fondling. They made love ... and still, Diana watched. She felt neither jealousy nor alienation. She did not feel as if she were left out. They did not exclude her. They were being themselves with her and that meant that she *was* included ... she *was* a part of them ... they *did* accept her! Although her body did not participate in their excitement, her spirit did. She fell asleep as they continued their intense lovemaking and even though her eyes no longer watched, her mind did. She dreamed that *she* was making love with Tengri ... and then she *became* Tapti. Diana felt as Tapti felt and in her dream, she couldn't tell if it was her that felt the climatic relief ... or if it was *her* experiencing *Tapti's* pleasure. It really made no difference.

The next morning, Diana awoke to find herself lying between Tengri and Tapti. She remembered Tapti telling her that their lovemaking lasted long after the fire died and both she and Tengri heard Diana moan in pleasure the same time Tapti did. They thought it amusing and when they looked, she was still asleep ... but uncovered and shivering uncontrollably. They then brought her to bed with them to keep her warm.

But ... the most memorable thing that Tapti told her was that she, indeed, had a true gift of dreaming. Tapti had felt her trying to enter into her dream consciousness and allowed her to do so. Soon, Tapti said all those long years ago, you will be taught a secret....

"Mother ... I'm going to explore for awhile."

"Speak Latin dear ... and be back shortly." Diana was not concerned about her son going off in the woods alone. After all, he understood nature.

She allowed her memories to once again go back in time.

A year later, Tengri decided that Diana was ready for the smith. Tengri had returned to his solitary ways and Diana and Tapti made their regular visits to their people. It was after Tengri's announcement, and on one such visit to the village that Tapti had told her she had known that a red haired woman would share her and her husband's life. It was Tengri's celestial wives that told her she must accept that fact if they were to allow their marriage. She was happy it was Diana and not someone she didn't love.

A month later, Tapti took her on her journey. Women never travelled alone on a dream walk as did the men, and it was usually a nature spirit that served as a guide. Even though it was intended that Kaltak escort Diana, Tapti insisted she be allowed and it was permitted. And so they went.

They were gone four months and together they experienced women's traditions. When they returned, they also shared Tengri. The three of them made love and shared their lives for years ... up until Diana left a little over a year ago. The day before she left, Tengri bonded the three of them together....

Diana absently rubbed the scar on her breast as she recalled the ceremony.

... That last night together ...

Diana did not want to leave, but it was necessary if the plan was to work. Tengri had taken Diana to his world in the hunter's belt and there she learned of the cell and the plan taught by the twenty-two stones.

Sadly ... *very* sadly Diana left her only true family. She had a son with Tengri and that was sacred to her. It was sacred to all three of them. Tapti never again conceived a child. The pain of losing her own son had made her barren.

Still ... even though separated, their bonding would allow them to feel each other's hearts beating as one. They would always know the welfare of each other. In many ways, that was more important to Diana than seeing them. She never learned to travel the fibres alone ... at least the silver ones ... but many times ... frequently ... they met in each other's dreams. After all, that was more real than reality itself!

Now, Diana prepared to keep a promise. She wove an indigo fibre and appeared to her uncle in his dreams. He lay in his bed and Diana knew he was dying ... he was a seriously troubled man and she discovered the horrors that caused his anguish. Her heart was heavy, but she chose not to judge him ...

"Father ... *Father!* ... I am here."

"Diana?" Constantine said in his mind.

"I'm in your dream, father. I am merely here to tell you that I am fine and all is well. I kept a diary as you asked ... although most of it is written on skins ..."

"Oh, Diana, my life ... the evil ..."

"Hush father ... I have a son ..."

"I wish I could see him ... I'm so sorry daughter ... I've missed you ... Had you been here, none of this would have happened ... I fear I've betrayed Tengri ..."

"No father, you have not betrayed Tengri. He understood a long time ago the necessities of your anguish. You need to know he still thinks of you as one of his closest friends. He has prayed to Erlik Khan to protect your soul. You have nothing to fear."

As if a great burden was lifted from him, Constantine sighed, smiled, and died peacefully.

Bishop Eusebius, who happened to be present and was baptising the dying Emperor, noticed the great relief and smile on the monarch as he died. He thought it was because of his conversion and that he had met God. He would never know the truth. If he did, he would have been disgusted that Constantine remained a *pagan* despite all that he mistakenly did for the Church.

****

The next day, Diana and her son set sail. They settled in a land that would soon become known as France. The village where she settled would later be known as Albi -- the site of a horrible massacre in the name of God almost one thousand years later.

When her son was seven, Diana married a blacksmith. He was a good man and accepted her son as his own. He taught Tengri's son his trade, and much later, the son became renowned in his abilities. He was also famous for his ability to flake stone. He never told anyone where he learned that art, nor did he teach it except to his own sons. They, and *only* they knew the secret of his real father. That secret tradition was passed on, father to son, for many generations. There are rumours that it still exists today.

When Diana's husband died shortly after her seventy-first birthday, she buried a box containing her diary, a wood carving of a creature she called a wyvern, and a thin white nightgown that had never been worn since she ran through her uncle's palace when she was only seventeen. Only Kaltak ... who later told Pouie ... ever knew of its existence.

Incidentally, the baqca who was a member of Tengri's cell and who settled in Babylon, became known as a very wise man. He was popularly known as a Mage. But the members of his *own* cell knew him as the Master of Moonlight. He brought with him twenty-two stones which he read and understood perfectly. The stones he brought with him were made by himself. It was *his* blood that marked the sacred symbols on the shiny black surfaces.

45

Deception -- Orion's Belt, 337 C.E.

Diana had already settled in the region around Tolosa and the 'Babylonian' Mage had already firmly established himself and his work before Tengri called the session. When called, nine baqcas travelled the silver fibre to that mysterious green and black world and sat in the small ancient hut.

The baqca who now resided in Babylon was present as he was still a member of the cell. However, Diana, who knew of the cell but was never made a member, was purposely excluded. In fact, the thread that *connected* her to this world had been severed so that she could never travel there again. Also, a memory thread was blocked so she would never even *think* to journey to that remote realm. The only references to her experiences during her visits were in her diary ... but the many times that she read and reread her journal entries throughout her life, never once did it occur to her that she had once known how to reach that strange world.

Tengri explained to Tapti and the other members that Diana had other work to perform and she would be more effective in that work if she allowed her *intuition* to guide her and was not burdened with arranged objectives.

Far into the future, he explained, the proper weave formed

from her influence would make one of her descendants receptive to initiation into the cell. If that weave turned out to be strong enough and the descendant was of sufficient character, it would be *highly* probable the cell will succeed in recruiting him or her. It would be necessary that they do if they are to have any chance of defeating the evil spirits infiltrating the West and the evil gods residing in the East.

At this point, one of the baqcas had brought up the probability factor and the unlikeliness of being able to affect situations far into the future. Tengri explained that all *effects* were the result of *causes* that did not concern themselves with the illusions of time. However, it was agreed that the work would be difficult and special care and understanding had to be maintained at all times. Besides, he had said, there was little doubt his sisters would decide to *meddle* in this affair!

For three days, seven members of the cell sat in absolute silence ... never moving or stirring while Tengri cast the stones over and over again. He read ... and reread them ... cast and recast ... Occasionally, he conferred ... in hushed and whispered tones ... with the Master of Moonlight. Finally, after three days and endless castings, Tengri spoke:

"The Ö' Trät stones, the deathwalker stones, have clearly spoken their message. They have revealed they do not belong to our people *or* our time and that their true nature is *not* to be unveiled until the distant future in an era the Christians and peoples of the West call the twentieth century. That will be the time when our descendants can *reveal* the secrets contained within the weave of the stones so that all peoples can prepare for the last stone's objectives. Whether or not they prepare properly will be determined by *our* actions and resolve to work in harmony with Law. The stones *demand* that a death oath be taken and perpetuated to future generations."

Everyone freely took the oath of death and swore to do what was needed.

"The stones have revealed that it is the nature of truth to be suppressed and perverted by those who desire to control and manipulate. That is the true evil. But, they also reveal that it is the innate nature of truth to be free ... that is its goodness and *our* work ...

"... The castings have said that since the stones do not belong to our people or time, never are we to use them again. Rather, the stones as they now rest on this floor are to remain as such, undisturbed until one arrives who has earned the right to possess them. I have made my last casting. However, the *Master of Moonlight* will perpetuate the tradition of the stones and his cell will henceforth be known as the protectors of their knowledge. It will be his responsibility to perpetuate the teachings of the stones within his cell until such time as a man from the West arrives and is initiated into our work. That man will carry the message of the Ö' Trät stones to his land and will establish his own cell. It will not be until then that the *true* work commences ...

"... Diana, in her own way, is crucial to our work. The stones reveal it is highly probable that her influence will cause *truth* to thrive in the hearts of a people living in the midst of oppression. The fourteenth stone reveals their final agony, but that will not occur until the West's thirteenth century. It is fortunate that later stones say there is a high probability that their work will survive that century regardless of a mass slaughter of their beliefs ...

"... The stones predominate their influence in Western lands ... the lands which are *now* being adversely influenced by the evil gods. They speak of a religion ... and then many religions forming from their one faith. They speak of that faith's inability to agree on truth ... and they speak of the subsequent subversion of that truth into deceit and lies for the sole purpose of greed and power ...

"... The prevailing attitude, as a result, is extreme fanaticism and intolerance. As you all know, we have experienced that here in our own culture. That is why our secret cell was formed ... to fight such perversion ... and that is why a cell *must* be formed in

Western lands at the appropriate time ...

"... The first, third, ninth, and tenth stones reveal a course of action to temper the onslaught of the insanity of religious intolerance. Another religion must be supported and allowed to thrive amidst the prevailing chaos. That religion already exists in their lands ... but is presently under a vicious attack because of betrayal as well as its own stagnation from within. It is known as Mithras but they have forgotten the truth of the true name of their god and his true role *under* the Supreme Deity. It is our task to correct that situation by reintroducing its truth, preserving, and protecting it. We must quietly and secretly encourage that faith's continued development ... always bearing in mind that any *true* religion must always maintain an attitude of adapting to the progression of society ... *indeed, it must ensure that its own nature causes such natural progression!* ...

"... A possible methodology we can utilise is to adjust our tradition so that we perpetuate a greater and lesser school. The greater school will be limited to the cells ... but the lesser school will admit carefully tested initiates and will be more expansive thereby ensuring that wisdom teachings will perpetuate alongside the growth of theological and philosophical teachings. By such additions, a *balance* will cause sane advancement. This, too, is also depicted in the fourteenth stone ... the thirteenth century ...

"... However, we must be absolutely certain our motives and attitudes remain pure and our methods do not stagnate or cause the careless and lethargic perpetuation of our purpose brought about by our *apparent* success in maintaining an equilibrium with opposing forces during some centuries. This is extremely important because events depicted by the fifteenth stone representing the fourteenth century reveals that our enemies will manifest their full power and glory. The stones sing the story that there will be a high probability that their scheming will cause us severe setbacks and that never again will the balance of forces enjoy a harmonious coexistence in the same fashion as before. Indeed, the level of life will drastically start to change ... it will become more complicated ... more sophisticated ... and *so* must we! We must survive that era and be strong enough to adjust. No casting of the stones indicate a guarantee of our survival ...

"... The events of the fourteenth century indicate a major victory of a battle won by our enemies. Though they will not have won the war, they will have suppressed and destroyed our strongest force. For five hundred years they will maintain the appearance of dominance and we must work secretly to cause subtle changes in their world. We must take humanity into a remarkable and new direction. We *may* succeed ... and indeed, we must ... but *not* at the great cost of a possible compromising of our position which will, at that time, *seem* to be the only possible solution. It is expected that many of our lesser schools will fail and become lost in the pit of ignorance. This is why the greater schools must remain pure and strong ...

"... The fourteenth century will indeed see the power and strength of the Nameless. It will manifest in the various outer names of an evil brotherhood that even exists today with great and secret influence ... but their power today will be nothing compared to what they will attain then ..."

"It is apparent," interjected one of the baqcas, "that we have sufficient knowledge *now* to more actively institute changes in the course of future events. Why must we work in such secrecy ... why cannot we be more aggressive now ... and *strike* while they are weak?"

"For two reasons," answered Tengri without pausing, "first, actions have already been set into motion that have caused the future weave. If we were to change the course of that weave and not allow natural events to occur as they have already flowed, or if we interfere with those energies outside of their natural rhythm, then we will run the risk of so *drastically* changing the natural order of things, that we will succeed in creating chaos. We would ultimately be responsible for causing our own failure. Remember, we must *always* work within Law. We are not gods. We are men and women who have merely learned to understand Law. At all times, must we maintain an equilibrium with that Law and flow its path ...

"... Second, by Law it is forbidden to destroy or *attempt* to destroy evil. To do so would cause an imbalance in nature which would give one or the other force predominate superiority unnaturally. Remember clearly, only the *lesser* gods are in eternal conflict and *because* they are gods, they understand how the Law works. We are men and it is not our place to attempt to determine Law nor to judge its methods. It is easy for us to forget this because we live in realms where the Law manifests in that way. Never forget that the unknowable Supreme Deity ... the source of Law ... is *not* in conflict. It behaves in a manner of pure Law and it is not understood by anything lesser. It is not our purpose to destroy evil because we know that if we, for example, kill an evil man, he will be *reborn* as an evil man. It is obvious that we would not achieve our objective if we were to kill him as to do so would serve no purpose. Rather, it *is* our purpose to *convert* him to good, because goodness is reborn as goodness, and that, dear brothers and sisters, is what we are to achieve ...

"... But all that I have said," continued Tengri, "is merely the song that the stones sing. The greater task lies in the future for our sons and daughters, living in another time and another place, to achieve. They will bear a great responsibility. They will experience untold horrors ... and they *must* endure in spite of any hardships that will be directed toward them. Indeed, they *will* be sought out for destruction for no other reason except that they speak truth and only seek to allow all peoples to choose their own beliefs and their own truths. In comparison, our task today is simple and peaceful, but let us choose to work in a manner so as to help alleviate their pain and suffering. Let us ensure that our wisdom enters into their souls ...

"...The stones reveal a plan that is intended to be instigated and set into motion by our cell. Only one stone reveals the participation and interaction of our peoples -- the thirteenth stone of the twelfth century. It is our task to see that events occur that will cause our peoples to influence the Western lands ...

"... As we all well know, our people are divided. Our clans feud with one another thereby making us weak and insignificant. *Now,* we must begin to plan so that by the thirteenth century we are united and strong. By then, we must, as a people, spread into the Western lands and take control of a segment that is controlled by the Christian Church. Specifically, we must remove Christian domination from an area that is now called Nicaea. The reason being that outside that town is a monastery which is the centre of an evil brotherhood ... our enemies. To take their centre from them will cause them a grave setback in their activities. It will not defeat them, but it will potentially cause them extreme concern in the twentieth century ...

"... You," Tengri pointed to one of the baqcas, "will form a secret society of the lesser mysteries which is to be *exclusively* for the training of blacksmiths. It is crucial that a relative of the *eagle* be the unifying force of our people. It will be from your secret school of blacksmiths there will arise a great warrior of the calibre to achieve our objectives ... *Teach your Initiates well!* ...

"... Tapti, you are to form a lesser *and* greater school of women's traditions so that nature, wisdom, and intuitive insight are preserved for all peoples ...

"... By the time of the fourteenth stone shall our work *fully* manifest. We shall have caused to exist, by that time, nine greater schools consisting of eighty one people, one school for each branch of the Great World Tree, and innumerable lesser schools in the hopes that some will survive the onslaught of terrible persecution and internal greed ...

"... I, Tengri, Son of the eagle, Tengere Kaira Kahn and a Kazak-Kirghiz Baqca, have spoken! I have cast the Ö' Trät stones for the last time and I have sung to you their final song. Henceforth, only the Master of Moonlight has the right to enter into their weave."

Tengri flaked eight additional blades from the stone of that eerie and ghostly place and fashioned them into knives. Those knives were given to each member of the cell who would pass them on to their successors in a sacred ceremony that sang the story of the beginning time when the first baqca was born and had ascended the ladder of knives so that wisdom could be attained and made available for all peoples. Those knives, as they would be passed from generation to generation, would identify lineage and purpose ...

****

Indeed, the members of the cell worked diligently to fulfil their mission. By the seventh century, the Kirghiz people united to form an empire. However, that empire was short lived and did not succeed in uniting all Mongol tribes.

However, in the sign of the thirteenth stone, the twelfth century, in the year 1167, a Mongol nomad, whose name would be known throughout the world, was born. He was a cousin of the eagle and was trained in a lesser school of blacksmiths. In fact, his name, Temujin, *meant* blacksmith. It was by his talents and efforts that he united all Mongolian tribes under one banner. When he accomplished that deed, he became known as Genghis Khan. That was in the year 1196. It is not surprising that his army was known as the *Golden Horde!* Perhaps it referenced his intent as perceived by the golden fibre of time ...

It was Genghis Khan and the advance of the Mongols which caused the Evil Brotherhood to *indirectly* experience their greatest and most devastating loss at a time when they were enjoying the pleasures of their greatest victory -- during the time ruled by the fifteenth stone.

The advance of the Mongols caused the Moslem nomads to migrate West from Turkistan. In the fourteenth century, in the year 1301, Osman I, who was an Emir of a community of Ghazid warriors, proclaimed himself Sultan and established the Ottoman Empire.

In the year 1326, he seized the town of Nicaea and the surrounding countryside. He renamed the town Iznik and captured the monastery belonging to a community of monks who wore greenish brown robes. He was so swift in the capture of the monastery, that the secret documents and journals, particularly the journal of Ossius, that were confiscated by the monks, could not be retrieved before they fled. They remained buried and undiscovered deep beneath the ground in a secret crypt for centuries.

The brotherhood never forgot their existence, but all hope was lost of ever regaining them -- at least until much, much later -- because in the following year, Osman's son, Orkhan, captured Nicomedia and renamed it Izmid. The brotherhood's closest base was now in Constantinople. It might as well have been on the moon.

In the year 1204, Constantinople was plundered by Christians during the fourth Crusade. That Crusade was supposed to go to Egypt but was redirected to Constantinople because Alexis III, the Byzantine Emperor, didn't carry through with an alleged agreement with Rome to reunite the Eastern and Western Churches. Unknown to anyone except the brotherhood, the French King, Philip II, and a number of his nobles, deceitful negotiations were entertained by the brotherhood to redirect the Crusade so that their lost monastery could be regained. However, that proved unsuccessful and really only resulted in pitting Christian against Christian. At least it was unsuccessful insofar as a Crusade went because it did manage to produce, for the French, an *extremely* lucrative trade agreement with the Venetians.

Finally, as people's actions determine the weave of the fibres, Constantinople finally fell to the Ottoman Empire on the 29th of May, 1453. It would be over five hundred years before *any* chance of recovering the contents of the secret crypt could occur.

But, the brotherhood of monks who wore greenish brown robes were not always frustrated in their endeavours. In the year 1232 the Inquisition was formed for the purpose of eradicating heresy. But under the sign of the fifteenth stone, the fourteenth century, the brotherhood acquired control and that was when the *real* perverted acts were sanctioned and enforced to the horror and terror of all people.

As for Diana, she was still alive when the Empire embraced Christianity as the state religion in 391. She was old and had great-great-grandchildren. She cried when she heard the news because she remembered a time long in her past when she fully believed in the miracle of ideals. But now, as an old woman, she realised she would not live to see that miracle manifest ... if it ever did.

Instead, she reflected upon other memories. Upon her training, upon the pain and sorrow that Tengri had felt, of shared hardships. But she also thought of happiness and the thrill of discovery, and most of all, of love. It had been fifty-four years since she last saw Tengri. She knew he was still alive. She could feel him!

She remembered him ...

She smiled ...

And then she died.

She was buried where she lived, in the land of the Franks, and the few people who attended the funeral, the pagan funeral, were not overly concerned that a black wolf with yellow eyes watched from a distance.

As to the lives of Tengri and Tapti, their daughter died a horrible death in a Buryat raid two years after Diana left. Shortly after that raid, peace came to the Buryat and Kazak-Kirghiz peoples. There was no real choice left to the Buryat, as most of their warriors, the lucky ones, were left incapacitated by insanity as the result of a mysterious ghost wind of considerable power.

Tapti was over ninety years of age when she died. Tengri took her body, spirit, and soul to his home world in the hunter's belt. No one ever saw him again and it is assumed that he remained there in his simple hut and lived out his remaining year of life. It was known he would die at one hundred and four years of age as was the custom of his kind ... as was the reality of his elder eight brothers.

Despite the loss of two children, Tengri and Tapti otherwise lived a peaceful, meaningful, and harmonious life together. Even today, a small Mongolian clan still lives in a remote and extremely harsh area of the People's Republic of Mongolia and maintain a loyal, traditional life. That clan was never touched by Buddhism, Islam, Christianity, or communism. That clan, today, still sing songs of the depth of love shared between Tapti and Tengri. They also still sing songs of a fiery red haired woman, a son who was mysteriously taken from his mother by the weave of a golden wyvern, and songs about an owl and a wolf.